I NEVER PLANNED on You

BOOK 1
I Never Series

STEFANIE JENKINS

I Never Planned On You
Copyright © 2019 by Stefanie Jenkins

Editing by One Love Editing at https://www.facebook.com/OneLoveEditing/
Proofread by Angel Nyx at https://www.
facebook.com/ProfreadingBayouQueen/
Cover Design by Net Hook & Line Design at https://www.facebook.com/
groups/nethooklinedesignsales/
Interior Book Formatting by Clara Stone at https://www.
facebook.com/readercentral

To those that have carried us through the darkness to find the light.

"You will survive and you will find purpose in the chaos. Moving on doesn't mean letting go." — Mary VanHaute

PROLOGUE

*I*t had been a blast skating around the rink with my friends, though my feet were killing me, so I decided to sit on the sidelines for a quick breather. A slow song came over the speaker, "I'll Never Break Your Heart" by the Backstreet Boys. I watched the skaters pair up to skate to the song. The hairs on the back of my neck stood up, and I felt a chill come up my spine as Emmett, my older brother's best friend, took the place next to me.

"You didn't want to skate with anyone on your birthday?"

"I needed a break." I shrugged, never taking my eyes off the skaters. "That, and umm...no one asked me."

Emmett tilted my chin to his face with his forefinger and thumb and looked at me in a way he never had before, or maybe I just hadn't noticed. It was strangely comforting. "Danielle Kathryn Jacobs, will you skate with me?"

I felt the breath rush out of my lungs as I tried to find the words to answer him. A simple yes, and I couldn't even find that. My brain wasn't working, so all I could do was nod. Did Emmett really just ask me to skate? Maybe he just felt sorry for me. He reached his hand out in front of me and threaded his fingers with mine as he escorted me from the wall to the ice.

As the song continued to play, we skated around the rink. His hand remained in mine, and the smile never left his face. When the song came to an end and his hand hadn't moved from mine, I looked at him nervously and began to pull away from him. "Well, thanks for the skate. I'm sure there were plenty of other girls to skate with than me, so I appreciate you humoring the birthday girl so ugh...I didn't look super pathetic."

As I went to turn to skate in the other direction, he tightened his grip on my hand. "Woah, Dani, I didn't ask you to skate because I felt sorry for you. I asked you to skate with me because I wanted to. If I wanted to skate with someone else I would have, but I only wanted to skate with you. I just wanted you. Don't you see that?"

I could feel my cheeks instantly flush. "I...I..." Again I couldn't find the words to say anything, so I just kept looking into those baby blues. I'd had a crush on Emmett since before I even knew what crushes were, but could he, in fact, have a crush back? People continued to skate around us, but all I saw was him. "I don't understand. Really?" I asked him when I finally found the words.

He inched even closer to me and brushed a stray piece of hair that had fallen out of my beanie, behind my ears. "Yes, you really didn't know?" he asked with a confused look.

I shook my head.

"I thought it was pretty obvious, but if you don't like me like that, then I get it. I'm just your brother's best friend—or your best friend's brother." Emmett took his bottom lip between his teeth; he wasn't the usual confident Emmett I had always known. It was my turn to surprise him.

My own confused look turned to a smile as I took my other hand to his cheek. "Em, you have never been just my brother's best friend or best friend's brother."

He covered my hand with his own as his dimple appeared

with his wide grin. *God, I loved that dimple. I had tried for years to do things to always make him smile so it would appear.* "Good, because I wanted to know if..."

He looked down at his feet nervously.

"If what, Em?"

His baby blues met mine again. "If you would be my girlfriend."

My eyes grew big. Oh my God! Pinch me. I quickly felt a pinch and realized that I had actually said that aloud. I began to flush again but then giggled. "I didn't mean to say that aloud."

Forgetting we were in the middle of the ice rink, we were quickly brought back to reality when we heard my brother, Zach, skate up to us. "Will you just give him an answer already? Mom said we had to wait for you to get off the ice to eat cake!"

I quickly turned to my brother and gave him the death stare. "If you would leave, dummy, then yes, I would." *I turned back to Emmett as Zach skated off, rolling his eyes at us and flipping me the finger.*

With both of my hands now in Emmett's, I smiled at him and nodded. "Yes, Emmett Adam Hanks, I would love to be your girlfriend, although, I don't really know what that means. I think this may have just become the best birthday ever."

There it was—that dimple again. There was something in the way he was looking at me, as if I had just made him the happiest boy on the planet, maybe even the galaxy. That look ignited something in me that I didn't know what it was just yet, but I couldn't wait to find out.

"Well, for starters, I get to do this." *He put his hand behind my neck, pulled me closer to him, and kissed me gently on the lips.*

"Wow! Yep, this is definitely the best birthday ever," *I*

managed to say as we broke apart. His grin went all the way to his eyes.

"Yeah, no kidding. I never thought my first kiss would be that...perfect."

Wait, did he just say that I was his first kiss? I had dreamed of my first kiss for like, forever, and I had hoped one day it would be with Emmett Hanks, but I figured that was about as likely as getting kissed by Justin Timberlake. Hey, can't a girl dream? But, he just admitted that I was his first kiss too.

Emmett looked up and began laughing. As I turned to see what was so funny, I saw my brother making kissy faces at us just before he lost his footing on his skates and fell on the ice. That made me laugh hard.

Emmett turned to me as he began to take the lead, skating me toward the exit. "Well, I guess we better get over there so you can make a birthday wish and he can feel better by shoving cake in his mouth."

As everyone sang Happy Birthday to me, I tried to imagine a wish that was better than the reality that happened today. Emmett Hanks had asked me to be his girlfriend. Was I sure I wasn't dreaming? Emmett leaned in to my ear and whispered, "Make a wish, beautiful."

I looked over at him, smiled, and knew my wish was that we could have our happily ever after just like Cinderella and her Prince Charming. Closing my eyes, I made my wish and blew out my candle.

CHAPTER 1

Danielle

*E*mmett and I sit on the swing on my parents' front porch with my feet in his lap, rocking back and forth. End of summer in Maryland is my favorite time of year. Yes, the weather can sometimes be temperamental, perfect one day, like today, the next super hot. But the leaves are getting ready to change, and there is a smell in the air that lets me know fall is just around the corner.

There is a light breeze passing by as Em runs his fingers over the dolphin anklet he gave me for my thirteenth birthday. It has a turquoise gemstone, my birthstone, in the center of the dolphin. It was that birthday that Emmett had given me my first kiss and changed my world.

I find myself lost in the memory of that day—the way my hand fit in his, the way his lips brushed against mine, and the look on his face as I opened his present. I'd started to cry because it was so beautiful, and knowing he had bought that prior to even asking me to be his girlfriend and admitting his feelings made my heart swell with emotion.

"Hey, beautiful, where were you just now?" Emmett runs his thumb over my anklet again and smiles at me. I'm not sure if the goosebumps covering my body are from his touch or from the breeze.

"I was just remembering when you gave me that anklet. That was the best day of my life."

Em leans over to me just inches from my mouth and whispers, "Oh really? I thought the first time we..." He waggles his eyebrows at me. "...was the best night of your life."

My cheeks heat at the thought of our first time together. Of course, my mind then goes to thinking of the last time we were together too. I love that after all this time, he can still make me blush.

I roll my eyes at him. "Yeah, that was all right," I whisper back at him while closing the distance and placing a sweet kiss on his lips. Well, what started out as sweet soon turns passionate. I will never tire of Emmett Hanks' kisses. I want to spend the rest of my life getting those kisses.

Pulling back breathless, Emmett laces his fingers with mine. "I'm gonna miss those."

Emmett and Zach are headed off to college at the University of Pennsylvania. Our parents had gotten them a two-bedroom apartment outside of campus. I still have to finish my senior year of high school, and then I'll join them. Zach and I are what are called Irish twins, born within the same year. People often confuse us for regular twins since we turn the same age each year, but people never understood why we were in different grades. I don't think my parents planned to get pregnant with me so soon, but, hey, if you're going to have sex, you might as well be prepared for anything, right?

It's only a two-hour drive from Annapolis to Philadelphia, so Emmett and I can easily make the drive to each other, but I hate the thought that I'll have to go days without being with him.

Fighting back my tears, I cup his cheeks. "There will be no shortage of those, Em, not now, not ever. I will just have to save them up in a jar, and every time we see each other, we can open the jar and make up for lost time." I kiss his cheek on each side, then his forehead before placing my lips against his. I'm not sure how much longer I can hold back my tears, because I'll miss those kisses too. I just want to be strong and not show how much his leaving is breaking my heart.

"I love you, Cupcake. Forever and always," he breathes as his lips touch mine.

He started calling me Cupcake when we discovered how good of a baker I am. If it wasn't for lacrosse and the gym, I think Emmett and Zach would weigh five hundred pounds because they're always eating the sweet treats I bake.

Our kiss is quickly interrupted by a throat clearing. We both turn toward the noise to see Zach walking out onto the porch, carrying the last two duffle bags.

"You about ready, man? I think you've had enough time sucking face with my sister," he says while making a gagging face.

I stick my tongue out at him.

"I'll never have enough time for that. You're just jealous after Melissa broke up with your sorry ass," Emmett responds. Rising from the porch swing, Em grabs my hand and pulls me up, then walks down the steps toward his Jeep.

"Nope, not even in the slightest, dude. I'm single and ready to mingle with all those college girls away from their families and ready to throw themselves at anything with a dick. And I just so happen to have a dick ready and waiting for them."

I roll my eyes at my brother. "Real classy, Jacobs," I mutter under my breath. Emmett laughs while Zach pulls me into a hug.

"You might not want to admit it, but you're going to miss me, sis."

He's right—I will miss him terribly. I wrap my arms around him and squeeze tightly, tucking my face into his chest. This is becoming too real. They're leaving me. We'd agreed we would say our goodbyes here instead of at the apartment in Philly. We were there just last weekend setting most of it up. All they have left is the rest of their clothes.

"I'll take good care of him, Dani, I promise," Zach whispers in my ear before kissing my forehead.

"All right, let my girl go so I can get in there or we're never gonna hit the road," Emmett interrupts, tugging on my hand to pull me away from my brother and back into his arms.

Waving him off, Zach finishes loading the bags in the back of Emmett's Jeep. Zach's Jeep was left at the apartment when we drove back the other day. I can feel the tears starting to fall as Emmett pulls me to his chest. This is harder than I thought it would be.

He cups my cheeks with his hands, and his thumb brushes away my runaway tears. "No tears, Cupcake. I'll see you next weekend when you come visit. Okay? We got this. You are going to kick ass during your senior year, and then this time next year, you will be coming with me. Zach will have to find a new place to live, because I don't think he wants to be living with us when we have free rein to have sex anywhere, at any time."

A giggle bursts through my tears as I remember the one time we thought we were home alone and Zach walked in on us on the couch. He was absolutely mortified and couldn't look me or Emmett in the eye for a week.

Wanting to avoid him seeing my tears, I turn my head and look at the ground.

"Look at me, baby girl." So I do. "We can get through this. Having you as my girl for the past four years has been the greatest gift ever. We're not going to let these silly two hours tear us down. It's only preparing us for forever."

The tears falling down my cheeks go from sad to happy, but the smile on Emmett's face turns to a frown when I start to shake my head. Smiling back at him, I put my forehead against his and whisper, "See, that's where you're wrong. I haven't been your girl for four years...I've been yours my whole life."

Emmett lets out a breath and kisses me as if I'm his air. Holding on to him tighter, I can hear footsteps approach, belonging to our parents and Haylee, Emmett's younger sister and my best friend. Reluctantly pulling away from him, I know it's time for them to leave. There are hugs, kisses, and tears by all, and I walk with Emmett to the driver's side with his hand still in mine.

"I love you, Emmett Adam Hanks," I profess, wiping the last of my tears away.

"Good, I was hoping you did," Em jokes. "Forever and always, Danielle Kathryn Jacobs."

After one last kiss and hug, Emmett hops into the Jeep and gives me his famous wink once he closes the door, mouthing "I love you" as he starts it up.

Haylee wraps her arms around me in a big bear hug as they drive off. "We've got this! They won't be too far away, and plus, you and my brother are grossly cute and have the rest of your lives to make us want to gag with your cuteness. Now, what do you say we head inside and binge scary movies and eat our weight in junk food."

I laugh at her and turn around once the Jeep is out of sight. "Why, Hails, I thought you'd never ask."

CHAPTER 2
Danielle

*M*y first day of senior year is strange without my brother and Emmett. I've never attended high school without them. At least Haylee will be there with me. And, of course, Emmett is with me even if he isn't physically here. I'll miss sneaking kisses at my locker and Emmett taking fries off my tray after he finishes his entire lunch but before I could eat half of mine. I'm thankful that soon enough we'll be back together.

As I pull up in front of Haylee's house to pick her up, I can't help but smile thinking of our conversation this morning.

EMMETT: *Happy first day of school, baby! Kick ass.*
ME: *You know what I did this morning while thinking of you?*
EMMETT: *Whoa, baby, is it the same thing I did?*
ME: *Perv. I watched the sunrise and remembered sitting out here with you last year.*
EMMETT: *Yep, that's exactly what I did too. Not anything else –*
God I love your dirty mind though.
ME: *And for the record, I did that too.*
EMMETT: *And you're now just telling me?! What a tease!!*
ME: *Need to get ready and then pick up Hails.*

EMMETT: *Love you, Cupcake! xo*
ME: *Forever and always. XOXO*

ONE YEAR EARLIER...

Emmett and Haylee had spent the night at our place before the first day of school. It was the boys' first day of senior year and Haylee's and my junior year. I woke up that morning to Emmett leaning down next to my side of the bed, rubbing my cheek with the back of his hand. "Good morning, beautiful," he whispered, kissing my forehead.

As I slowly woke, realizing this wasn't a dream, he put his forefinger to his lips to tell me to be quiet before pointing over to his sleeping sister. "Shhh, I want to take you somewhere."

Climbing out of bed, I grabbed a hoodie off the chair and took his hand in mine. Emmett led me downstairs quietly to the front door.

"Where are we going, crazy? We have to get ready for school," I tried to protest.

Emmett smirked, grabbing the blanket off the umbrella stand, and escorted me out the front door to the porch swing. Emmett took a seat, then pulled me into his arms. It was easily my favorite spot in the entire world. There was no other place I would rather be than with him. He covered us with the blanket as I leaned my back to his front, even though once the sun rose, it would be too hot for anything covering us.

"What are we doing out here?"

Em smiled before leaning closer to me and confessed, "I want to watch the sunrise with you. Today starts another chapter in our lives. I can't wait till we are both out of this town starting our future. I've got big plans for us, Cupcake. One day..." He paused. "I'm gonna put a ring on this finger." He laced his fingers with mine, then brushed his lips against where a diamond would be.

"We're both going to get to UPenn, graduate, get married, and have two kids and a dog. You can bake all you want at your own little bakery you're going to have, but I might need to buy stock in a gym to keep off the weight from eating your treats. Although, I love eating your treats." He gave me a playful wink, making me giggle and slap his chest.

"I know all that will happen—we just have to get through these next two years and we are on our way."

Looking up at him, I was no longer sleepy. I felt all of his love, and I couldn't help but smile. I turned my body toward his and placed my palm to his cheek. "How did I get so lucky to have you in my life?"

He leaned his forehead against mine. "I'm the lucky one, Cupcake, and I hope I never have to go a day without you in my life."

I responded before placing a kiss on those beautiful lips of his. "Forever and always."

Then I had to pull away, knowing that if I didn't, we would potentially not only miss the sunrise, but get caught by my parents in a position I didn't want them to catch us in. I spun back around to snuggle up to Emmett, and we watched the beautiful sunrise. I couldn't wait to spend the rest of my life watching all of the sunrises with this man.

Lost in memories, I don't even notice Haylee walking toward my car and opening the door. She makes me jump when she slams the door shut, yelling, "Happy first day of senior year, bestie!"

She then pulls a single rose out from behind her back and rolls her eyes. "Em told me to give this to you." She pauses and giggles. "He also told me to give you a big smooch, but, well, that's not happening."

I break out into giggles too before leaning over the center console to smack a big loud kiss on her cheek. We both end up with tears in our eyes from laughing. "Shall we?" Haylee holds up Katy Perry's latest album, *Teenage Dream*. We've seriously been obsessed with every song since its release. I'm pretty sure everyone in both our houses knows all the lyrics.

I take the CD out of its case, place it in the player, and crank up the volume as we head down the road to school. Another step closer to the rest of my life.

LATER THAT EVENING I SIT AT THE DINNER TABLE WITH MY parents discussing our days as we eat the traditional first-day-of-school meal, crab cakes and corn on the cob.

"So how was your last first day, Dani?"

I finish chewing the bite in my mouth and wipe my mouth with my napkin. "It was good. Weird without them there, but Hails and I survived. It's the final countdown." I sing the last part to the tune of the classic 80s song.

"I just can't believe you girls are seniors already. When did my babies grow up?" Oh Lord, here we go—my mom is getting choked up again. "I mean, you guys were just out back learning to swim, and now you'll be going off to Pennsylvania and Haylee all the way to California."

"Mom, we'll be fine. Were you this emotional last year with Zach?"

"No, but you're my..."

My phone begins to vibrate and I reach for it, seeing Em's name appear on the screen. I go to get up from the table.

"Umm, excuse me, young lady, where do you think you're going? You need to finish eating first." My dad's voice is stern.

"But..."

"No buts—you can call Emmett back."

"How did you know it was him?"

He tilts his head and laughs. "Really, Danielle Jacobs? You think I don't know that Emmett calls you every night for you to talk about your day even on days that you spent with each other."

"Oh, Adam, relax. Don't you remember what it was like back then, to be young and in love? That boy is her whole world."

Dad sighs, knowing she is right. I have heard plenty of stories of both my parents and Haylee's from their younger days.

My mom turns to me. "Just finish up your dinner and then you can go."

I quickly finish off the last few bites of crab cake on my plate, shoving them all into my mouth at the same time. With a mouth full of food, I push my chair back. "Thanks for dinner, guys. It was delicious."

My dad laughs at my lack of manners, and my mom just shakes her head. "You are more like your brother each day. Lord help us!"

I let out a loud laugh and hit Send on my phone as I walk out of the dining room toward the stairs. I drown out the rest of the conversation once I hear his voice. My day just got that much better.

"Hey, Cupcake, how was your day?"

CHAPTER 3
Danielle

The only sound I can hear is the sound of our heavy breathing from our post-frat-party lovemaking session. I slowly climb off Emmett and lie next to him, naked and wrapped in his arms, only covered by the sheet. Em brushes the hair off my face. I can only imagine how attractive I look all sweaty and with my hair a mess right now, but, oh my God it was worth it.

"You are amazing, Cupcake. If I could just live inside you, I would move there tomorrow." He kisses my temple before pulling me closer to him. Our bodies are sweaty, but I don't care. We can shower later since we have the apartment to ourselves. We left Zach at the party flirting all over some random girl. I swear, every time I come here to visit, there's a new girl. Maybe one day, he will meet the right one who gets him to settle down and change his manwhoreish ways. I'm sure hell would freeze over before that actually happens.

I go to ask Em if he wants to shower now or later when we hear a loud noise on the other side of the door followed by a giggle. My brother has returned home, and he is not alone. We hear a few loud bangs—mostly Zach walking into furniture, followed by some curse words, and giggles by his female counterpart. We are both trying to hold back our laughter at their sad attempt at making it to Zach's bedroom. We then hear his door slam followed quickly by "Oh God! Yes! Fuck yes!" I try to cover my ears.

Oh my God, gross! I am so not going to listen to my brother bang some random chick he will probably have me or Emmett kick out in the morning. Her moaning gets louder and louder, and Emmett can't hold back his laughter. I slap his arm. "This isn't funny, babe. This is gross. I'm going to have to go through so much therapy for this."

Em removes my hands from my ears. "Oh babe, please, this is nothing compared to the time Zach walked in on us, with you mid O-face. Plus, how many times has he had to hear us?" He continues laughing. I shake my head at the memory. Clearly this is payback.

"Oh my God, *yes*! Oh Ethan, right there!"

I instantly sit up and look at Emmett, both of us confused. "Did she just call him Ethan?"

He nods his head yes because he is now laughing with tears in his eyes. Wow! Where does my brother find these girls? At least make sure she knows your name. Well, I can't even guarantee my brother knows her name, so there's that.

I fall back on the mattress and sigh. "Ugh, I can't unhear this shit."

I feel the bed shift as Emmett rolls over toward me. "Oh no? I can think of a way to drown them out."

Leaning on his bent elbow, he slowly comes down and sucks on the sensitive spot right behind my ear that makes me instantly ready and panting for him.

I squirm as he continues sucking and licking. "Mmmmm, I'm in, well..."

He shifts his weight so he is on top of me and settles himself between my thighs.. "If you can't beat 'em, join 'em."

He begins to tease me, grinding his hard cock against me. Emmett kisses me with such passion and fury, as if I am the air he breathes. His lips move down from my mouth, to my neck, to my chest where he licks, bites, and feasts on my nipples, causing moans to spill from my throat. His hands travel down to my sex where he begins to rub and apply pressure to my clit. He can feel how wet he makes me. This man is insatiable. I will never be able to get enough of him. I grab his shoulders as if needing him to steady me as an orgasm begins to build and rip through me.

The moans from the next room have quickly died down—whether Zach passed out or maybe had a case of whiskey dick and couldn't deliver, whatever it is, I don't care. Emmett and I are in our own world, and he makes sure I forget those noises—twice in fact. Now extra sweaty, a shower would be the smart thing to do, but there's no way I'm getting out of these arms. Falling asleep in my man's arms is exactly how I want to end every day.

The next morning Emmett and I are sitting at the counter eating breakfast when my brother's door quietly opens. His figure appears, and by the way he closes the door, I can tell he hopes to not wake his overnight guest. Here we go again. Emmett and I both give knowing looks to each other. Zach has not noticed us as he creeps toward the front door.

"Good morning, dear brother," I say rather loudly as I bring a forkful of scrambled eggs to my mouth.

Zach jumps, clutching his chest. "Jesus Christ! What the fuck, guys! I thought you were still in bed."

"Oh no, your welcome home last night was plenty to make sure we didn't sleep well." He doesn't have to know that we weren't bothered by the sounds that were or were not coming from his room while we were busy making our own, but I am having way too much fun messing with him.

Zach shrugs nonchalantly. "What can I say, the ladies love me." He brushes past us and grabs a water bottle from the fridge, his back toward us.

Emmett chimes in. "Whatever you say...*Ethan*."

We both break into a fit of giggles as my brother turns around. I wonder if he has any recollection of his guest calling him the wrong name. "What was that, man?"

"Oh nothing. Where you headed this early?" Emmett finishes off the food on his plate and begins to pick at what's left on mine. I swat at him with my fork.

"The gym."

I roll my eyes, knowing exactly where this is going. "The gym, huh? That couldn't wait until *after* your little friend woke up?"

Walking over to me, Zach places a quick kiss to the top of my head. "Nah, little sis. The early bird catches the worm."

"As long as that's the only thing you catch."

Emmett spits his coffee back into his mug at my comment and lets out a roaring laugh.

Zach places his hand over his heart as if my words had hurt him. "Shhh! You're gonna wake up...wake up..." He bites his lip as if he is trying to recall her name. The longer he takes, I realize he actually doesn't know her name.

"Oh my God, Zach! You seriously have no idea what her name is, do you?"

"I don't need to know it. Not like I'm gonna call her and see her again."

I shake my head at him. Gathering up our dishes, I walk them over and place them in the sink. I walk toward my brother and slap his shoulder. "One day, Zach, we won't be here to help you out of this situation. Now go so we can get rid of your skank."

I stalk to the bathroom to take a shower as I hear my brother grab his gym bag from the door and shout, "You're the best! See ya," before shutting the door.

An hour later, Emmett and I have both showered and are enjoying a movie on the couch. Shocker, my brother is nowhere to be found. I wonder how long he is going to avoid the apartment this morning. We finally hear movement from Zach's room, and my hand on Em's thigh tightens to pull his attention to the door without making it too obvious.

Appearing in the doorway is a skinny redhead with big boobs and legs for days. Ahh, so that's Miss Fake Moans from last night. She is wearing one of my brother's favorite Hopkins lacrosse T-shirts and a pair of his shorts, which makes me laugh a little. Well, payback is a bitch, big bro—maybe if he had been here, then he would have been able to save his clothes.

"Hi." Miss Fake Moans looks confused while searching around the apartment, no doubt looking for my brother.

"Hey." I reply.

"Is Zach around?" Oh, so she does know his name. I bite my lip in an attempt to hold back my laughter and feel Em's elbow in my side trying to get me to knock it off. When I don't answer, he does.

"Umm, no, he's out."

Her face falls. "Oh, okay. I guess I should probably go, then." Em nods and reverts his gaze back to the TV. She, who shall remain nameless since we have no clue what her name is, stands there for a few moments as if she's expecting us to ask her to stay, but nope, not happening, sweetheart.

Finally, she turns around and heads back into his room and moments later returns with her clothes, I assume, and purse in hand—still wearing Zach's clothes. She heads toward the front door and pauses.

Very quietly, only loud enough for me to hear, Em whispers, "Oh shit." I swat at his chest.

"Hey, can you tell him to call me?"

I don't even turn around and throw my hand up. "Yep, you got it."

"Don't you need my name?"

Fuck. This girl actually has a brain, sort of. I get up and look to find a piece of paper on the coffee table and walk toward her.

"Sorry, I don't have a pen."

"That's okay, I have one."

Of course she does—she pulls a pen out of her purse. Oh my, my brother really knows how to pick them. She writes something on the paper and hands it back to me. I look down and see the note she wrote as she exits the apartment.

I had a great time last night. Call me! Xo Whitney 215-218-8359

As soon as I heard the door click I crumple up the piece of paper and throw it. Yeah, sorry, Whitney, there's no way in hell my brother is calling you.

Em's phone vibrates and I see my Zach's name appear, as if he had some sixth sense that she had finally left. I quickly reach for it before Em can and answer it.

"Hello, my darling brother. For the record, *Whitney* is gone and she left a lovely note for you."

"Great. I'll be home shortly. Just leaving the gym."

"Take your time. Oh, by the way, she took your favorite lax T-shirt and gym shorts." I hear my brother curse but interrupt him by ending the call. I toss the phone on the table, satisfied with myself.

"You're evil, you know that, right?"

I snuggle farther into Emmett and look up at him. "Would you have me any other way though?"

He smiles and leans down, bringing his lips to mine. Just before they touch, he whispers, "I love you just the way you are."

We lose ourselves in each other on the couch, not even caring that my brother will arrive home soon. That's what he gets for making us do his dirty work for what seems to be the millionth time.

CHAPTER 4

Danielle

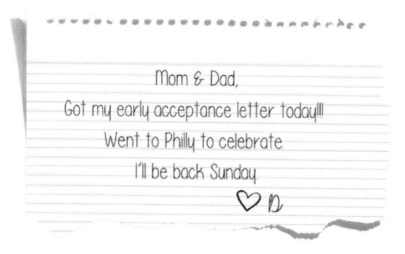

Mom & Dad,

Got my early acceptance letter today!!!

Went to Philly to celebrate.

I'll be back Sunday.

♡ D

I had left that note on the kitchen counter for my parents earlier today after getting my early acceptance letter in the mail from University of Pennsylvania. My phone rings shortly after I am on the road and I answer. My mother's voice chimes throughout my speakers.

"Hey, Mom."

"Hi, sweetheart. I just got home and got your note! Your dad and I are so proud of you!"

"Thanks! I am so excited. I just couldn't wait to tell Em."

"I know, just do me a favor and be careful. The roads are slick out there, okay? I heard there was going to be some ice tonight in Philly."

"Yes, Mom, I'll be careful."

"I know you will, Dani. Doesn't mean as your mom I don't worry."

"Well, I see some traffic ahead, so I'm going to be a *safe* driver and get off the phone now."

"Yeah, yeah, yeah. You get your smart ass from your father."

I let out a loud laugh. "You know it."

"I love you, Dani. See you Sunday. Tell the boys I say hi."

"Love you too. Will do!"

"Bye."

Happy songs play loud out of the speakers on the drive. I'm flying high knowing that I'm one step closer to being back with Em and my brother. Just like he had said, I did miss him—of course I do. Yes, I see him often, but it's different when it's just visiting and not him actually living down the hall from me.

I hadn't planned on being in Philly this weekend since Emmett would be studying for finals, but I couldn't wait to tell him the good news. The drive flies by even though I hit some Friday traffic on the way, and the next thing I know I'm pulling into the parking garage at the apartment complex. I don't see either Jeep in their spots, so I park in the guest parking space, where I typically park, and pull my phone out to call Emmett, but he doesn't answer. That's strange, but I'll just head up to the apartment and wait for him.

I grab my purse and the letter before exiting the car. I don't usually bring an overnight bag with me anymore since I have quite a few things here already. Using my key to open the apartment door, I can't help but imagine what our life will be like in the fall when I officially live here. A time when we will no longer need to say goodbye on Sundays, no more determining whose weekend it is to travel, no more nightly good-night calls, or going days without feeling the warmth of his embrace.

My phone buzzes as I set my purse and keys down on the desk in Em's room.

EMMETT: *Sorry I missed your call, babe. At the library for study group. Can't wait for these fucking exams to be over.*

EMMETT: *My brain is ready to explode.*

ME: *It's okay, I have a surprise for you!*

EMMETT: *Oh yeah???*

ME: *Yep!*

EMMETT: *What is it? Is it a naked surprise?*

ME: *Nope, but it could be when you get home...*

EMMETT: *Wait, where are you?*

ME: *At the apartment. I got something in the mail today and I couldn't wait to tell you!*

EMMETT: *Shit, Dani! You should've called when you were on your way and I would've blown this off. And is it what I think it is?*

EMMETT: *P.S. You're gonna make me hard thinking about you naked rather than English Lit.*

ME: *You're crazy! You need to study for finals and YES....*

I send him a photo of the letter.

EMMETT: *Fuck yeah, baby, I'm so proud of you! Holy shit, we need to celebrate. This is amazing.*

EMMETT: *I will be here about another hour or so and come pick you up, then we will go out and celebrate. Zach is out at some party tonight and I'm sure he will find someone to go home with, so we can come home and have naked celebrations all over the apartment without him bothering us!*

ME: *Okay, take your time. I'm going to shower the drive off and get ready.*

EMMETT: *Fuck me...how the hell am I supposed to concentrate knowing you're naked in my shower?! Yep, def rockin' a boner in the library. Thanks, sweetheart.*

ME: *You're welcome! Anytime (Kissy face)*

ME: *Now hurry your sexy ass up studying so you can head home to me and we can be naked together.*

EMMETT: *I love it when you're bossy!*

ME: *Be careful driving home.*

EMMETT: *Always am. I love you, Cupcake. See you soon.*

ME: *Love you too XOXO*

I fight back and forth on whether to wait for Emmett to take a shower, but after a full day at school and the drive here, I decide it's better for both of us if I shower now. We can always take another shower later.

I head to the bathroom and shower quickly. Once done, I hurry back to the bedroom and grab a pair of leggings from the drawer and an over-sized sweater tunic from the closet. I'm not sure what we will do to celebrate when he gets back, so I go with cute and comfortable. Worst case, I need to change if he wants to do something fancier.

Reaching over to the book on the nightstand that I had been reading the last time I was here, I scoot back up against the headboard and lean back, opening the book to where I left off.

Before I know it, my eyes feel heavy. I look over at my phone and see Em still isn't due home for at least twenty more minutes. A quick power nap can't hurt. If his texts are any indication as to what's to come this evening, then a nap is definitely in my favor. Emmett can always wake me up when he gets home. I love when he wakes me up kissing me in all places, not just on my mouth.

I fall asleep in his bed peacefully and happy, unaware that our lives would be forever changed in just a few short hours.

CHAPTER 5

Danielle

I am jolted awake when I hear the front door to the apartment crash open and slam shut followed by Zach yelling my name. "Dani? Danielle! Are you here? Fuck! Please, God, Dani, be here!"

Zach barges through the bedroom door and it slams against the wall as it swings open. "Oh thank fuck, Dani, you're here," he exclaims while pulling me into his arms. He's sweaty as fuck, as if he's run here. Did he run here? I thought Emmett said he was out at a party tonight.

"What's wrong? What time is it? Why the hell are you so sweaty?"

Zach tries to catch his breath. "I ran here, like literally left my Jeep and ran here to find you."

"You ran? And why were you looking for me? How did you know I was here? Did Em tell you I was here?"

Wait, where is he? I look around for Emmett, for any sign of him. He should've been back from the library by now. Maybe he's in the kitchen.

"Em?" I call out but get no response. When I look back to Zach, the color has left his face. "Zach, where's Emmett?"

I start to feel a tightness in my chest. Zach opens his mouth to say something but closes it quickly. I go to reach for my phone and see I have fifty-three missed calls. What the hell is going on? Fifty-three missed calls—a mix of calls from my parents, Zach, and Haylee, but only one from Em and that was two hours ago.

Where the hell is he? I begin to panic. What the fuck.

"Zach, what the fuck is going on? Where's Emmett?" Before he can respond, my phone rings again. I sigh in relief, thinking that it's Em, but it's not. It's Mom.

I answer it, but I don't even get to say hello before my mom speaks. "Danielle? Are you there? Baby girl, are you there?" She sounds upset and clearly has been crying.

"Mom, I'm here, I'm at the apartment. What's going on?"

"Oh, thank goodness. We couldn't get ahold of you and knew you had gone to see Emmett and feared..." Mom doesn't finish her statement, but I can hear a commotion in the background of the call—a bunch of crying and wailing. Is that Ms. Natalie crying? And is that my dad yelling, "We will be there soon—I don't give a shit if a cop wants to pull me over, I'm not stopping"?

"Mommy, you're all scaring me. Zach just flew in here like a bat out of hell and won't tell me what's going on. I have a ton of missed calls from you all, and Emmett isn't back from the library."

My voice begins to catch in my throat. I can feel my hands begin to shake. I get a feeling that whatever it is they have to say I'm not going to like and my world is about to fall apart. Zach scoots closer to me on the bed as if to comfort me, but I quickly jump up to my feet.

"Will someone tell me what the fuck is going on?" I scream into the phone. My whole body is visibly shaking.

Mom continues to cry. "Sweetheart, I need you to sit down and be calm, okay?"

Tears have begun to fall down my cheeks. "No! Tell me what the fuck is going on? Why are you acting so strange, why do I hear crying in the background?"

My legs feel weak as I hear her say, "Honey, we are headed to Philly now." She pauses to catch her breath. "Emmett... Emmett was in an accident."

"He's okay though, right? Why are you headed here since he's okay? He's gotta be. We're celebrating my early acceptance tonight." The world starts to go black around me.

"Danielle, I need you to listen to me." I shake my head as if she can see me right now. "I need you and Zach to meet us at the hospital, okay? We're about forty-five minutes away. I'm pretty sure your father has broken every driving law tonight."

I hear Dad say in the background, "I don't give a shit!"

I realize I haven't said anything. I am focusing on Em's sweatshirt that's currently draped over the desk chair.

"Dani? Are you still there? Dani?"

Somehow, I find the strength and voice to say, "Yes."

Mom responds by saying, "Is your brother still there? Please put him on for me, sweetheart?"

I reach for my brother to hand him the phone, and he talks to Mom softly. Or maybe it's regular-voice volume, but I have begun to tune it all out. I am trying to process what she said. Let's see if I got it all... Emmett was in an accident. They are all headed here to the hospital. Zach and I need to meet them there. Emmett was in an accident.

Em. Was. In. An. Accident.

I happen to look up at my brother the same time I see him close his eyes as he processes what Mom is saying to him. I feel the air leave my chest, and my legs give out beneath me. The next thing I know, I am on the floor shaking and screaming and feel my brother's arms wrap around me. "Dani, we don't know anything, okay? We should head there. Can you walk?"

I don't even acknowledge him. I continue to stare at nothing. He cups my face, forcefully pulling my attention to him, but I stare through him. "Dani, I need you to get up so that we can go, okay? I'm sure he's fine and we'll walk into the room and he'll be wondering what the big fuss was all about."

I manage a nod but make no attempt to move. Suddenly, I feel myself lifting off the ground. Zach is now carrying me. I reach out and grab the hoodie that was on the chair and pull it close to my chest, inhaling Emmett's scent—he must have worn it recently—as Zach carries me out of the apartment and to my car. A sense of calmness quickly overcomes me as if he were here holding my hand.

Zach opens the passenger door and sets me down in the seat before kneeling down to look me in the eye. "D, Em is a fighter. You can't think like that. We don't know anything. Don't let your thoughts go there."

He rises to his feet and shuts the door before walking around to the driver's-side door. I close my eyes and begin to pray that it isn't what I'm thinking.

Why is my brain even going there?

Why hasn't he called if he's just fine?

Why are our parents and the Hanks family rushing to get here if it's minor?

I beg my brain to stop thinking, but I can't. I am so lost in my thoughts that I don't even realize we have arrived at the hospital already.

Zach grabs my hand, and I turn to face him; his eyes are red and rimmed with tears as are mine. My heart races even more after seeing the emotion on my brother's face. He squeezes my hand three times to signal "I love you." Ever since we were kids, when we needed to channel each other's strength, we always did that. I nod and open the door. I freeze and take a deep breath, trying to compose myself. Zach exits the car first, walking around to my side. He helps me out of the car and puts his arm around my shoulders keeping me close to him as we walk toward the entrance.

CHAPTER 6
Danielle

*T*hrowing the hospital room door open in a frenzy, I can finally breathe when I look up to find Emmett sitting up in the hospital bed, a few cuts on his face and his left arm in a cast. I release the breath I've been holding since Zach came running into the apartment when his eyes meet mine.

"Hey, Cupcake," he says with a smile.

I run over to the hospital bed and fling my arms around him in a force that knocks him back, and he lets out a gasp and winces a bit. "Ow, careful, baby. I'm fine, just a little sore."

I pull back and look into those baby blues of his before I slam my mouth on his and kiss the hell out of him. After a few moments, the heart rate monitor starts getting louder, and Emmett pulls back breathless. "Wow, what a hello." His smile takes over his face, and it instantly brings me peace of mind. He's okay is all I keep telling myself.

I can feel the tears spilling from my eyes. Emmett places his palm on my cheek, and I lean into his touch while he uses his thumb to catch the falling tears. "I...I'm sorry. I...I...was so...so... scared. You said you would be home soon, and then I fell asleep and...and woke up when Zach came racing into the apartment screaming my name like a madman. Then Mom called and said *you were in an accident, and I felt like I couldn't breathe. Baby, it was awful. Zach had to carry me to the car. All I could think was what if..."*

Emmett cuts off my words by pulling me by the back of my neck into another kiss. He begins stroking my hair as we come up for air. The softness in his eyes tells me all I need to know: I need to calm down and stop thinking what if.

"I'm sorry you were so worried, baby. I'm fine. I'm okay, just some bumps, bruises, and a broken wrist. Can't say the same for the Jeepster though." He shrugs with a smirk. "Guess we'll just need to start shopping for our family vehicle." He follows this with a wink. Emmett has been saying that as soon as we get married, we will start popping out kids. He jokes that he wants three kids, two boys and a girl. I always joke back saying, "Well, you better let your balls know that because I'm pretty sure it's your body that decides that."

"You're really okay?" I ask as he leans back in the bed, pulling me with him. I wrap my arms around his body, being careful not to squeeze too hard knowing he's sore everywhere. I lay my head on his chest and listen to his heart beating. My head rises up and down in time with his breathing.

He kisses the top of my head. "I'm sorry I ruined our big cele-bratory night. I am so proud of you, baby girl. I'll make it up to you, I promise."

"Shhh! I don't care about that. We have the rest of our lives to celebrate. I'm just so happy you're okay. I don't know what I'd do if you weren't. I love you, baby."

"I love you too, Cupcake. Forever and always," he says so softly that I almost don't hear him.

"Dani? Dani?"

Emmett's voice sounds so far away at this point. Where did he go? Why does his voice sound so far away when he's right here with me?

"Dani! Dani!"

I'm jolted awake for the second time tonight. I didn't even realize that I had closed my eyes when I open them and see my parents rushing toward me and Zach in the waiting room. My mother throws her arms around me, and I collapse into them.

"Natalie and Brian are at the desk trying to get information. We should head that way, and hopefully they have something on what's going on."

In between my tears, I respond, "They wouldn't tell us anything, not where he is, not how he's doing—nothing."

Mom tries to calm me down by stroking the back of my head. "Shh, it'll be okay, sweetheart. Just have faith," Mom reassures me in that soothing tone. I shake my head, and she gives me a weak smile. My dad places his hand on my mom's shoulder, and I watch her lip quiver slightly before she straightens up. It's as if she needed my father's reassurance and strength to get her through this. That is what Em is to me—my strength.

We walk the few feet over to join Natalie, Brian, and Haylee, who are standing at the desk talking to the nurse who wouldn't give us any information earlier. Haylee wraps her arms around me and squeezes for dear life.

"My brother is going to be okay. He's going to be okay."

I don't know if Haylee keeps repeating that for me or herself. I'm not sure how she is in one piece at the moment; if the roles were reversed and this was Zach I had no information on, I would be crawling over the counter demanding information. In fact, that sounds like a pretty good idea. I look over at the desk, and as I go to make a scene, the nurse says, "Ah. Emmett Hanks, here we are."

The nurse stands and walks around the front desk to escort

us through a set of wooden doors and into a small private room. She lets us know the doctor will be in in just a moment. I am sick of waiting. My dad suggests I sit down because my pacing back and forth might wear a hole into the carpet. I don't really care. It seems like we've been here for hours. Looking around, I see the walls in this room are white and there is no decoration. Why do I feel like we're about to be sentenced, potentially for a lifetime of pain?

"Why can't we just go see him," Haylee shouts.

Her father places his hand over hers in an attempt to calm her down, but it doesn't do much. They've been in the car for two hours or, well, under, thanks to my dad's lack of respect for the speed limit. We know nothing—why can't they just tell us what room he's in so I can run and throw my arms around him?

I continue to pace, and I quickly feel a pull on my hand and instantly drop into the chair. I look up to see my brother holding my hand with a sad smile on his face. I guess my pacing was making him anxious. Zach and I stare at each other in an attempt to draw strength to get through whatever is about to happen. I can tell he is as anxious as I am as to why it's taking them so long to talk to us. *I won't cry, I won't cry.*

I break our staring contest to pull my legs up to my chest. I'm wearing the hoodie that I had taken from the back of Em's desk chair while racing out of the apartment to get here...only just to wait and wait and wait some more. I place my head on my knees and take a deep breath of his scent. He's worn the same cologne since he was younger, a scent that makes me feel safe and at home. It's a comforting scent that I can't wait to inhale while actually lying with him, trapped in his arms.

From the corner of my eye, I see a figure enter in a white doctor's coat. Oh look, something else white in this room. Jesus, they need some color here; it's so depressing. I quickly rise to my feet, and there's some feeling deep down that instinctually tells me to take my brother's hand and not let go. I can't figure out what that feeling is, but at this moment in time, I refuse to not listen to it. Haylee walks over and takes my other hand. I guess she had the same feeling.

Surrounded by my best friend and my brother, I'm ready for them to tell me we can go see him now, that it was all a misunderstanding and that Em is just fine, like he was in my dream. I'm ready for him to heal so we can begin planning the changes to the apartment for once I move in there in the fall.

"Mr. and Mrs. Hanks," the doctor says. "I'm Dr. Foster. I was the doctor that was on call when your son, Emmett, was brought in. As the nurse had informed you, Emmett was in an automobile accident earlier this evening..."

All of a sudden all of the air is ripped from my lungs and I am gasping for air. My vision blurs and I want to wake up from this nightmare.

"...We did everything we could..."

No, no, no, no, this isn't happening. They clearly didn't do all they could or they would still be working on him. My ears are filled with devastating wails. I begin to shake, and my brother's arms are around me, keeping me upright as I rock back and forth.

"No!" I hear Ms. Natalie scream through her tears as Mr. Brian tries to console her. My parents currently have Haylee in an embrace while her body shakes uncontrollably. This can't be real—this can't be happening. I turn and grip Zach's shirt and place my head into his chest. I hit his chest with my fists, not in anger at him but anger at the world. He allows me to release my feelings on him. I can feel liquid running down my forehead and realize they are not my tears but the tears of my brother, who just lost his best friend.

I start to whisper to no one in particular, "No! He's not gone —we have plans, he told me we did. He said, 'I've got big plans for us, Cupcake.' We're supposed to be celebrating my early acceptance right now."

He is supposed to be holding me in bed and finding ways to celebrate me getting into the same college. The doctor continues to talk, although I'm unsure if anyone is actually listening to him. I hear, "... injuries too extensive ... say goodbye ... I'm sorry." The tears I had fought back earlier start to fall as if a dam just broke. How can he be gone? We spoke only a few hours ago.

Haylee has since gone to the comfort of her parents' arms, and my dad has pulled Zach into a hug while my mom joins me sitting on the floor. She strokes my hair as I rock back and forth. "I am so sorry, Danielle," she keeps saying over and over.

Zach's sobs overtake my mother's soothing words, not that her soothing tone will make me feel any better. He has always been the rock between us, so to watch him fall apart and crumble to pieces breaks my heart even more. I'm so thankful for my dad holding him right now because when one holds everyone together all the time as the rock, it makes you wonder who's there to hold them together?

I'm not sure how much time passes from the time the doctor left the room till now. Time stopped for me the instant I heard "He's gone." How can he be gone? My mother stands and brings me to my feet although I need to lean fully on her. If she releases me, I may just fall back to the ground. I can't make eye contact with anyone, but in my searching for something else to look at, I sadly lock eyes with Ms. Natalie and she instantly begins to sob louder. I pull from my mother's arms and fall to the ground in front of where Ms. Natalie is sitting and sob uncontrollably in her lap.

"Oh Dani, I'm sorry. I can't believe this. It's a nightmare I'm ready to wake up from. My baby boy can't be gone."

All I can do is shake my head. There are no words to speak. If I were to open my mouth right now, I might just scream. I can feel the pain building in my chest ready to burst. My heart has been torn from my chest and smashed into a million pieces. Reality hits me in the face with the words the doctor said I had tuned out. They keep replaying on repeat in my mind: "There was not much we could do by the time he arrived here, but we did everything we could."

He was suffering as I was sleeping in his bed...our bed. We were just a few short months from me graduating and moving to Philly to the apartment where we would share that bed full-time, and it was all taken away in a blink of an eye.

Mr. Brian tries to compose himself. "Dr. Foster said we are able to go back two at a time to...to..." But he doesn't need to continue for us all to know what he was going to say. There is a deadly silence throughout the room where no one wants to admit what is about to happen nor anyone wanting to volunteer to go first. Mr. Brian stands up and offers his hand to his wife. I rise to my feet as well when I feel my mother's arms on my shoulders.

Mr. Brian extends his other hand to Haylee. "I don't want to do this, but we should go first." My father nods at him while holding my brother, who is still breaking down in his arms. The Hankses leave the room to do the unthinkable. The doctor said two at a time, but that's such a stupid rule. What are they going to do, tell a grieving family one person can't go in to say good-bye? Yeah, I don't think so. The hospital can go fuck themselves on that rule.

Turning in my mother's arms, I let out a cry and shake my head. "I don't think I can do this, Mommy. Don't make me say goodbye to him. I'm not ready to do this. We're supposed to be old and gray and have a bunch of grandchildren when I am forced to do this, not now. Not...not when we have our whole lives ahead of us. It's not fair!"

My tone went from soft to angry, but my mom doesn't falter as I yell at her as to how unfair this situation is; she knows I'm not yelling at her. Her arms wrap around me so tightly I feel like I can't breathe, although I'm not really sure if I have been breathing at all since the doctor came in earlier. Maybe my breath stopped at the same moment and this is all a nightmare now.

Mom leads us to the double chair and pulls me to her chest and allows me to cry against her. Time doesn't seem to exist in this moment, so I'm not sure as to how long we've been in that room.

Haylee is the first to return, her eyes all red and puffy, tears overflowing from them. She grabs her bag and mutters something before walking out of the room. Mr. Brian calls out after her, but she yells that she can't be in here anymore and she needs air.

Air...I need air too. I'm suffocating at the thought of having to go in that room. Maybe I won't. I make no move to get up. Ms. Natalie collapses in her husband's arms and hits his chest, crying out for her loss. I can feel my mother nod against the top of my head, and out of the corner of my eye I see Zach and my dad leave the room. My turn will be next. How do I prepare for this? My mind races through the last time I saw him, what he looked like, felt like, smelled like, sounded like, tasted like. These are all things I will never feel or know again—a distant memory.

I'm not sure how we get to the point, standing in front of room 209. The door is currently closed, but I know what awaits me on the other side. My mom opens the door slightly, but my feet don't move. Reaching for my hand, she gives it a gentle squeeze. "Come on, sweetheart, it's time."

I take a deep breath and count *one, two, three* and then follow her into the room. The curtain is partially pulled, but I can see the end of the bed. His feet have a sheet draped over them. The tears flow down my cheek at a rapid pace, and I'm having a hard time catching my breath. My mother goes first since I refuse to move any farther, drawing this out. Through her tears I can make out only some words: "Oh honey, I'm so sorry ... a life cut too short ... watch over us ... I love you."

It's time. My feet slowly move forward around the curtain, and my breath catches as I watch my mom lean over and kiss the top of his head. My mother moves back to give me some space but not going too far, knowing I need her strength to do this.

I move to the side of the bed and take a seat, grabbing Emmett's hand in mine. I lace our fingers together. His skin is cold, no longer full of life. This person lying here is not my Emmett. I don't recognize this person. Emmett was so full of life and warm. This version is cold, still, and lifeless. I want to my touch to warm him up. I bring our hands to my lips just as he had so many times before. I close my eyes as my lips touch his skin, trying to memorize everything. I bring our clasped hands down to my lap and stroke his blond hair with the other. He is... was...fuck, I'm not sure if I can refer to him in the past tense. Em *was* the best-looking guy I have ever seen.

"Oh baby, it wasn't supposed to be this way. Why did this happen to us? Please...please wake up. I'm not strong enough to do this. I don't know...how to do this without you. I don't want to do this without you."

My tears overpower me, and I throw my arms around Emmett's cold, lifeless body, praying my warmth will wake him up and he'll put his strong arms around me. But that's not reality —that won't happen. I will never feel the warmth and safety of his embrace again. My mother comes up behind me and rubs my back. "It's time, sweetheart."

"No! No! No! I'm not ready to say goodbye."

"I know, baby girl, I know." She doesn't need to say anything else.

Leaning over, I kiss his forehead before placing mine against his, a natural move between the two of us that will happen no more. "You're it for me, Emmett Adam Hanks. I will love you forever and always," I whisper before placing one last kiss upon his lips. Why can't this be like in the fairy tales where true loves kiss wakes up the sleeping princess, or in our case the sleeping prince?

I bring my head back and trace his face with my fingers, trying to memorize it all: the scar above his left eyebrow from the time Dad and Mr. Brian were teaching us kids how to skip rocks and Zach threw a rock and it ricocheted off a stump and hit Emmett in the forehead; the cluster of freckles that would appear across his nose after being in the sun; and that dimple... fuck I loved making that dimple appear when he smiled.

Kissing his hand one last time, I rise to my feet and somehow end up out of the room walking back to the waiting area where everyone is congregated, our lives irrevocably changed—a life without Emmett in it.

I look back to the hospital room door one last time as it closes behind us. The weight of the world at the very moment makes my chest feel as though it's going to collapse. I struggle to catch my breath, and my vision is filled with unshed tears. My mother presses the button to open the double doors. My feet move forward, and I look up to see Zach standing there. Before I know what's happening, his arms are around me. I'm unsure if he is holding me up or the other way around. I collapse in his arms and allow the pain to overtake me, letting the tears flow freely from my eyes. It hurts to breathe, it hurts all over, it hurts to live.

Why did he have to leave me here all alone?

CHAPTER 7

Danielle

I can still smell him as I hug the pillow tight to my chest. There's nothing that can be done to alleviate the giant ache now residing in place of my heart. I squeeze the pillow tighter as the tears continue to fall down my cheek. I thought by now there wouldn't be any left to cry, but I was wrong. My body has decided to betray me and keep a solid flow of tears coming. It's been two days since my heart was shattered into a million pieces. In the blink of an eye, the happily ever after I had dreamed of my entire life was gone.

The police report told us that the Jeep slid on ice when attempting to stop at an intersection, causing Em to run a red light, and an oncoming vehicle T-boned the side of Emmett's, killing him almost instantly. The thought rips me apart in a way that I know will never be able to be put back together. He will never graduate college, become a husband, become a father, or achieve all the dreams he had set out to accomplish since he was younger. I'm past the point of sadness, past the point of exhaustion. I can't even try to sleep because every time I close my eyes, I see him lying there, smiling at me. Emmett Hanks had been the love of my life for as long as I can remember. To be honest, I don't feel anything at all. I'm numb, and I don't want to feel anything anymore...because the honest truth is, who am I without him?

Mom, Dad, and the Hankses headed back home along with Emmett's body, which was released to the funeral home that would take care of arrangements. I begged Zach not to make me go home just yet, but I'm not sure honestly how much longer I can stay here. Why am I torturing myself being this close to Emmett knowing that I'll never see him again? Is this my punishment for having to live the rest of my life without him?

Clinging to the pillow while wrapped in one of his flannel shirts that still smells of him, I imagine he is lying here with me and we're discussing what we would do first upon graduation. A talk that will never occur. The thought makes my body feel as though my chest is caving all over again.

I pick my phone up and see the photo of Emmett and me from prom last year as the backdrop. I quickly unlock it only to be greeted with a photo of Em shirtless at the pool from this summer. I pull up my voicemails and hit Play to hear the message that I have listened to over and over again. It took about twelve hours for me to actually gather the courage to hit Play the first time. Emmett had called as he left the library while I was napping. The what-ifs play through my mind—had I only answered his call, would we still be in this situation? I could have just met him somewhere so that he wasn't on that road at that moment, and it would be someone else's family mourning the loss of a loved one instead of us...

"Hey, baby, I'm just leaving the library now. Shit, I don't think my brain can handle any more information now. I should be at the apartment soon, but I just wanted to call and tell you that I am so proud of you, Dani. I know I told you earlier, but I'll keep saying it. I'm thinking dinner, so you think of where you

want to go. Another step closer to the rest of our lives. I'll see you soon. I love you!"

Click.

I hear the front door open, and I want so bad for this all to be a nightmare and I'm waking up from my nap on Friday waiting for Emmett to come home from the library just as his voicemail had stated. I'd see him walking up to the door, lean on the doorframe, and make a comment like, "That sweater is hideous, Dani. You should most definitely lose it. It would look better on the floor. Fuck going to dinner—we'll just go straight for dessert."

Realizing that conversation never happened nor will any further conversations happen, the tears threaten to drown me. My wails overtake the silence of the room, and a sliver of light from the hallway lights up the dark room. The bed dips and my brother wraps his arms around me, cradling me to his chest. Emmett was always my protector, but who is supposed to protect me from this pain? Zach's arms tighten around me as he tries the best he can to protect me and support me, but he along with everyone else, myself included, isn't sure as to how to go about doing that. I squeeze the pillow so tight I might burst it. That's how my grief feels—ready to burst like a volcano waiting to erupt. I pull the pillow to my mouth as if to stop the air I am breathing and scream. I'm not sure how long I scream into it, but I just let it out. I can feel my brother's body vibrate against me as his body trembles from his tears.

We just sit like that for I'm not sure how long; time no longer has a meaning. In between sniffles, I hear his voice, so low it's almost a whisper. "Dani, I know this is hard, but we need to get going soon." I shake my head no. I'm not ready to face that. At least staying here I can avoid the planning and the funeral and what comes next. "I know, sweetheart. I don't want to do it either, but we need to. We need to do it for Em, for Hails —she needs her best friend right now."

I am quiet, not wanting to admit he is right. I wanted Haylee to stay with me, but she refused. She couldn't stand being in the apartment just for the night before heading back home.

"Okay. I need a few minutes though."

He nods and slowly stands up and retreats to his room, I assume to finish packing his things for the next few days. I allow a few more tears to fall while lying on the bed before finding strength deep down to pull myself together. I grab Emmett's duffle bag out of the closet and throw some shirts and a few hoodies in there. I know these items won't always smell like him, but until they don't, I will have to savor his scent and pretend that it is him wrapped around me. Again, with the torturing of myself, by myself.

I look over to the desk where my early acceptance letter sits. I go to grab it and hesitate. If it weren't for that letter, Emmett might not have left the library when he did to come here to meet me. I crumple the letter and the envelope and throw them to the other side of the room. I gather the duffle bag and throw it over my shoulder along with my purse. I take a quick look around this room and remember all the good and bad times we had here —more good than bad, but hey, we weren't perfect. We still fought at times. But the makeup sex...the makeup sex always made the fight worth it. Whoever was at fault for the fight was usually the one worshiping the other's body. For the most part, he was usually in the wrong, but I didn't complain.

I take a deep breath knowing what awaits me when we arrive home. Scared of the unknown and the new life that awaits, I close the bedroom door behind me and meet Zach at the front door.

CHAPTER 8
Danielle

I wake up fully drenched in sweat, screaming out for Emmett, tears running down my cheeks. I want him to come barging through the door and wrap his arms around me, running his hands along my hair and telling me it was just a bad dream. But no, it's not a dream. I am living in a real-life nightmare—a world I'm not ready for. A world which Emmett is no longer in. How is that possible?

The past few days have been a blur. Zach basically dragged me out of the apartment to come back here to say goodbye. *Goodbye.* How do I say goodbye to him? I can't. I refuse to—then that means he is actually gone.

Today is his funeral. I would say it's the worst day of my life, but no, that winner was crowned four days ago when the love of my life was torn from this world forever. I pull my knees to my chest, wearing Emmett's UPenn hoodie that still smells of him. How long will his scent be able to stay with me? I don't hide the tears as they fall.

Looking around the room, I see Em everywhere. How can I not? We'd been together since we were thirteen and a part of each other's life since we were born. I see the mirror hanging next to my closet where I would be putting the finishing touches on my outfit when he would wrap his strong arms around me from behind and tell me how beautiful I looked. I see the window Em once broke while throwing rocks one night to get my attention—he had thought it would be romantic, however it turned out to be pretty expensive. I look at the bulletin board above my desk and see the photos of endless memories. I see the rug we would sit on attempting to do homework that nine out of ten times would lead to a heavy make-out session.

There is a light knock on the door, and I close my eyes imagining it's Emmett about to walk in, but instead I am pulled to reality when I hear my mother's soft voice as she opens it. "Sweetheart, we will need to go soon. I laid your dress out on the back of the chair. Do you want me to help you get ready?"

I shake my head but make no attempt at getting up. Looking at my mother, I see her eyes are red-rimmed and bloodshot—I am sure a mirrored image of my own—and her shoulders are tense. Not only has she been trying to manage her household falling apart these past few days, but her own best friend is burying her son today. Emmett was my mother's godson. I don't know how she can be strong for everyone right now. I just want to climb back under the covers and forget this whole thing today. However, I know that if I don't get up now, she won't leave me alone, and that's all I want...to be left alone, like I will be for the rest of my life.

I swing my legs over the bed and try to find strength to stand. Mom walks toward me and places a kiss on my temple. "It will be okay," she says into my hair.

I shrug her off and rise to my feet. "No it won't. It never will be. You can't make this better with words or anything—no one can." Walking over toward the dress, I see she picked a simple black dress I had worn once to my grandma's funeral two years ago. I thought I would never get through it, but Emmett had held my hand the entire time and was my rock. Who would be my rock today? I stare at the dress, hoping my eyes can make it disappear while I hear my mother's footsteps walk toward the door and she quietly shuts it behind her.

I'm not exactly sure how I get myself ready, but I am now looking in the mirror fully dressed in my black dress that lands just above my knee and black flats. Mom had set out a pair of black tights to put on since it's winter, but I didn't put them on. I'm sure I should have since it's cold, but the past few days I haven't felt anything. I am so completely numb that I thought maybe being freezing in the cold would force me to feel even the littlest something.

There is another knock on the door. "Come in," I say softly. My eyes rise from the floor up the mirror to meet Zach's. His eyes are full of pain and sadness like mine. I give him a mix of a forced smile and a pout; it has been kind of like my go-to expression when I am forced to be around people. It helps in an attempt to keep the tears at bay, but fuck, who are we kidding, the tears haven't really stopped lately. I don't have to hide in front of my brother though, of all people. He knows the pain I'm in.

Walking up behind me, he places his hands on my shoulders and stares at me in the mirror. "Dad said it's time to leave and pick up the Hankses before we head to the funeral."

I nod, but again I don't move. My shoulders begin to tremble. Zach spins me around so fast I think I might have gotten whiplash. "I don't know how to do this," I cry into his chest. His arms tighten around me. "I can't breathe, Zach. I don't know how to be without him—his laugh, his smile, his love."

Zach lets me break down in his arms for a few moments. The only sound in the room is my loud sobs. Zach pulls me away from him for a moment, and I can see tears streaming down his cheeks before he places his forehead on mine. "One day at a time, Dani. We're going to take it one day at a time. And we're going to do it together, okay?"

I have no words, so I just nod my head. He leans in to kiss my forehead and grabs one of my hands. "Come on, let's go get this over with."

My brother is hurting just as much. I hate this for him, I hate this for me, I hate this for the Hankses and my parents and for anyone who had met or would have met Emmett.

The ride over to the funeral home is silent. Dad and Mom are in the front of the minivan, Mr. Brian and Ms. Natalie are in the middle row staring out the window at nothing, and Zach, Haylee, and I are in the very back row. I sit in the middle, and they both hold my hands. We would be going from the funeral home to the church followed by the cemetery riding in the limo.

Once we arrive at the funeral home, we all exit the van and switch to the limo to be church-bound. The last time I was in a limo was prom last spring. It was one of the best nights of my life. I'd danced the night away with Emmett and our friends, and then we'd spent the night in a hotel room together, which included a smorgasbord of breakfast foods delivered to our room the next morning by room service. I smile sadly at the memory, and I don't even realize we've pulled up to St. Vincent's, the church that we grew up at.

I take a deep breath and squeeze Zach and Haylee's hands, trying to find the strength to get out of the limo and walk into the church knowing that Em awaits us to say goodbye. Haylee looks over at me with tears in her eyes and running down her cheeks and attempts a small smile at me. Her smile punches me in the gut. She looks so much like Emmett, I almost can't bear to look at her. They both had the most beautiful blue eyes—we're talking like Caribbean ocean blue; they were eyes anyone would have no problem getting lost in. In fact, I got lost looking into

Emmett's eyes many times. They also had the same smile, so when Haylee gave me even the weakest smile, I saw Em and my heart broke just a little bit more.

I feel the limo beginning to cave in, and I need to escape. I quickly release their hands and jump up and out the door to try to catch my breath. I wrap my arms around my waist in hopes no one will try to comfort me.

I am so sick of hearing "I'm sorry for your loss. He was a great guy. I will miss him. He's at peace now." What the fuck do all these people know? He was at peace here on earth too.

I stop in the vestibule of the church when I see the casket straight ahead. No, I can't do this. The only time I was supposed to be in a church walking toward Emmett was when we were to get married and promise to spend the rest of our lives loving each other. Not now, not like this, not until we were old and gray and had plenty of babies, grandbabies, and possibly great-grandbabies—definitely not at eighteen.

Zach puts his hand on my lower back to gently escort me into the church. As we walk up the aisle, all eyes are on me —"the one Emmett Hanks left behind." How am I going to make it through this? We take our seats in the first row along with Haylee and her parents. My fists are wound so tight, I almost think blood might start dripping from my palms from where my nails are digging into my skin as the funeral begins. Lisa Lois's version of "Hallelujah" plays on the speakers throughout the church as the minister, Father John Ryan, makes his way to the altar.

In death, the same as in life, I can't remove my eyes from Emmett, who is lying in the mahogany casket just feet away from me. Even with a closed casket, I can sense his presence. I want to run up to him and tell him, "Wake up, baby. Please just open your eyes, joke's over." I picture him opening his eyes and grabbing my arms yelling, "Gotcha!" followed by his laugh. Shit I loved his laugh—a laugh I will never hear again.

As the music gradually gets louder, I feel my strength quickly fading. This is real life. I am supposed to say goodbye, and I'm not ready. The trembling begins in my shoulders followed by my hands shaking. I can't do this. The tears begin to fall again, and I feel my brother's arm grip tightly around my shoulder and pull me to his chest. Haylee grabs my hand and squeezes so tight she could almost break my hand, but I would welcome that pain, just so that I can feel anything else besides this gut-wrenching ache.

I can hear sobbing throughout the church, but I try to block it out. I can only deal with my own grief at the moment. That may be selfish, but it's all I know how to do at the moment. It's my pain, my loss. Father John begins to talk, but I block him out.

I force my mind out of this horrible place and remember the good times we had. Closing my eyes, I leave the church filled with people behind and travel back to a time when Emmett was alive.

"Have you made a decision yet on what you want?" the man behind the counter at Daily Scoop whose name tag read "Eric" asked me as I browsed the different flavors of ice cream in the case in front of me. I tilted my head and thought of the four different flavors I'd just tasted: cotton candy, double fudge brownie, caramel swirl, and chocolate chip cookie dough.

"Yes, can I get two scoops of mint chocolate chip in a waffle cone?"

I felt arms wrap around me from behind, and Emmett laughed in my ear softly. "You always do that."

I turned my head to face him but kept our position with my back to his front. "Do what?" I said teasingly.

He kissed my temple. "You always taste a bunch of flavors

and spend all this time deciding what you want and literally every time you get the same thing. Every. Single. Time." He laughed at me again.

"What can I say? I know what I love, and that will always be mint chocolate chip ice cream. Our love affair goes way back."

Emmett ordered a scoop of chocolate and a scoop of peanut butter brownie in a bowl topped with Reese's Cups. He always joked it was the ultimate Reece's Cup lovers. Even though he gave me shit for my predictable order, he did the same thing, although he didn't try all the different flavors.

"While I appreciate your love affair with mint chocolate chip ice cream, do you want to know what I love?"

I leaned back into him while we waited for our ice cream and closed my eyes, taking in the moment. Nothing could top this amazing feeling right now. I nodded to him, wanting to know.

"I love you, Danielle Jacobs."

I slowly turned around to face him and placed my palm over his cheek. Was this really happening? Did he just say he loved me? "You love me?"

He nodded. "I've loved you my whole life, I'm pretty sure; it just took me a little while to say it aloud. You don't have to say it back if you don't want to."

I was so shocked that I didn't even hear Eric call that my ice cream was ready. I was still staring at the amazing guy in front of me who'd just admitted that he loved me.

Emmett stepped forward and took the ice creams from Eric and handed me mine. He went to walk toward the register, but I grabbed his arm and pulled him back toward me. "I love you. I always have and always will."

Emmett's eyes filled with so much love that he scooped me into his arms and spun me around. It startled me so much that I ended up dropping my ice cream on the floor.

"Oh no!" I shouted and giggled.

Emmett looked down and waved to Eric to ask for a new one and said that he would pay for the one that dropped. He turned to face me again and brushed his lips lightly across my mine.

"I love you, Cupcake. Forever and always."

I lifted my arms around his neck, and he wrapped his arms around my waist. He pulled me in for another kiss, and my heart felt so full, I didn't care that I was only fifteen. When you know, you know.

I've zoned out for most of the funeral, standing and sitting when necessary just because I see those around me doing so. Haylee somehow found the strength to get up there to give the eulogy. She talked about how Emmett was always there for her, looked out for her, what a great friend he was, and shared a few memories. But what I hated about her speech the most was the term *"was."* He *was* a big brother, *was* a best friend, *was* my love, *was* a strong athlete—none of those present tense, because this is now a world without Em in it. He *was* in this world but no longer is.

I had finally gotten control of my tears and refused to look at Haylee while she gave her speech because I wouldn't have been able to hold back. After Haylee spoke, Zach stood at the microphone and read a poem called "The Dash." It's a poem about the day you were born or the day you died not mattering, but it was how you lived your "dash," the life in between the dates. What a joke—the date you die does matter, especially if you are taken too soon. Emmett wasn't supposed to die at only eighteen. He had plans—he told me so.

I feel like I blink and the service is over. My father, Mr. Brian, Zach, two members of the lacrosse team, and Haylee and Emmett's cousin, Cooper, all rise and walk toward the casket to be the pallbearers to escort the casket out to the hearse. Father

John says one last prayer and how we will lead Emmett to his final resting place. "Bridge Over Troubled Water" begins to play; Ms. Natalie used to sing this song to Emmett when he was baby.

Throughout this whole time no more tears have fallen, but I also don't feel anything. As the funeral director leads the men and the casket down the aisle, Mom wraps her arms around Ms. Natalie and begins to follow them. Haylee and I join our hands and try to find strength in each other for this walk, but both of us are drained of strength at this point. We are just going through the motions. I take a deep breath and exit the pew, and Haylee and I slowly stride to the limo.

The drive to the cemetery is a bit of a blur. I stare out the window with my hand on my chin holding up my head. My other hand plays with the folded piece of paper for the poem I'm supposed to read graveside, "If Tomorrow Starts Without Me." Isn't it ironic that tomorrow will start without Em? It's not a matter of *if*—it's a fact.

Mom hands me a tissue, but I push it away. There are no more tears. A fog has rolled in over my mind. I'm not sure sunshine and blue skies are in the forecast of my life anytime soon.

CHAPTER 9

Danielle

My phone has been buzzing all night and day with phone calls, texts, and social media notifications. They all read the same: "Happy 18th Birthday, Dani!" Having a birthday four days before Christmas always sucked, but my parents had always made sure I felt special by making a big deal out of my special day. But there is nothing happy about today. I am officially an adult, and the saddest part of that is I can say at only eighteen I have not only found my once-in-a-lifetime love but also lost him. I'm not talking about high school romance bullshit where you grow apart or break up because of the distance of college. I mean full brokenhearted, world torn apart, grief-stricken loss. What a way to start off adulthood, huh?

I've managed to stay in bed all day avoiding the living as I have for the past two weeks. That's all I've been doing the past two weeks. I've replayed Emmett's last voicemail over and over; his voice has been instilled into my brain, but I fear one day it may fade. I refuse to let it.

There is a knock at my door, but I don't acknowledge it. Whoever is on the other side knows I won't tell them to come in which is why I hear the door begin to open, and I roll over onto my side and pretend to sleep. If I close my eyes long enough, maybe the darkness will just consume me completely. Whenever I manage to fall asleep, I see Emmett in my dreams. Some are memories from the past, others are wishes for what our future would have looked like.

The bottom of the bed dips as my brother sits down. I can tell it's him because it's not large enough of a dip to be my father, and my mom always makes such a commotion when she comes in here.

Zach has been gone the past the two days, back in Philly to take his exams. His professors let him push them back a week since there was a death in the family. I heard him come home earlier when he and my dad were talking just outside my room. I feel his hand on my ankle, but he doesn't say anything, just leaves his hand there. This is his way of letting me know he's here without saying anything since he thinks I'm sleeping. Actually no, he probably knows I'm not sleeping, just avoiding conversation. I don't open my eyes to look at him, but I can hear his heart breaking, as mine has. The only difference is that mine is fully shattered. The more days that pass without Emmett break it even more.

Moments pass before either of us say anything. Zach squeezes my leg and says, "I know you don't want to do anything, but Mom has been cooking downstairs all day, and the Hankses will be here soon. Mom would really like it if you came down for your birthday dinner."

I haven't had much of an appetite lately. My parents have forced me to eat but have at least been nice enough to not make me come downstairs to eat meals with them. It always amazes and confuses the hell out of me when people think food is what people want when someone dies. I overheard Mom say that there were nine lasagnas delivered to the Hanks house. If they feel anything like I do, then I imagine most of that food is going to waste.

I guess my luck has run out since they are forcing me to come join them to celebrate this stupid day. There was a time when my birthday was so special, my parents always made sure it was separated from Christmas, and then later Emmett made a huge deal out of it since our anniversary was just right before. December used to be my favorite month; it brought me such joy with my birthday, Christmas, *and* our anniversary. Now it is just a reminder of all I lost and will never have again.

Maybe if I continue to ignore Zach he will just leave me alone, but highly unlikely. I decide to just pull the cover my head so he'll get the hint. I think I've won when I feel him get up off the bed and expect him to leave. Instead he crouches down close to my face and pulls the cover back. My eyes are swollen and red still. I haven't showered in a few days, and I'm wearing one of Em's old T-shirts. I haven't worn this one yet, so it still smells of him faintly. His clothes are mainly what I wear now—anything to feel him close to me again. Zach places one hand on mine and strokes my hair back off my face with the other one.

"Hey, look at me." I don't want to open my eyes again to see him. "Please, Danielle, look at me."

Slowly, I open my eyes and meet his blue eyes. My brother and I look so much alike, I understand why people think we are twins.

"Please, just come down for dinner, and then you can come back up right after. But you've shut us all out, and this is one day that I am asking—no, I'm not asking, I'm begging you to not shut us out. We are all dealing with this as a family, getting through this together, and you are making it difficult."

I go to speak, but he cuts me off, cupping my cheek. "I know you're hurting—and trust me, I get it, Dani, I fucking get it—but shutting us out isn't going to fix this. Now I suggest you get your ass up in the shower and change your clothes and join us downstairs. Don't think about it being your birthday, just a dinner with us all together."

He rises and stalks out the door, closing it a little harder than even he possibly expected, causing me to jump from where I'm lying on the bed. Together...Zach said it would be us all together, but he lied. We will never *all* be together again. I throw the cover back over my head and lose myself in the hollow of the darkness.

"Why, baby, why did you leave? You are supposed to be here. It's my birthday...you used to tell me how important these were, and now it just doesn't matter because you're not here. *Please* come back." My tears overwhelm me into sleep.

I feel the bed dip and the chill of the air as the blanket is pulled from my face. Blinking my eyes open from my nap, I expect to see my mom or Zach, but I see my best friend's beautiful face. Her eyes are heavy with sadness like mine.

"Hey, birthday girl. I'm here to help."

Help? How can she help me? She can't bring back her brother. She crawls up the bed and snuggles in next to me wrapping her arm around me how Em used to.

"I know today sucks—fuck, every day sucks—but please come downstairs. I'm worried about you."

How can she be so selfless that she is worried about me? It has been only eight days since her brother was placed in the ground. "Your mom made chicken Parmesan, my mom's recipe. She knows you love it. And we picked up a triple-chocolate cake from Annette's. Come on, D, let me help you get a shower and dressed and then go down. I have a feeling our parents aren't opposed to coming up here and eating in bed with you. I sure as hell know Zach and I aren't. If you don't want to shower, that's fine too, but I think it might make you feel better."

Haylee wraps her arms tighter around me. "I miss him too. I miss him so much. I'm so angry still. I have a hard time getting out of bed. I walk past his door and expect to see him standing in the doorway smiling at me even though he hasn't even lived at home for months. I know it's crazy but…"

She doesn't continue, but I can feel the back of my neck getting wet with her tears.

"Okay." I say it as a soft whisper but loud enough for her to hear me. I can't sit here and listen to my best friend cry. I sit up and she follows. She throws her arm over my shoulders and leans her head against mine.

"We are somehow going to get through this. I haven't fucking figured out how, but maybe we can figure that out together. I'm not ready to get through tomorrow or the next day, but how 'bout we just start with dinner, birthday girl?"

I nod my head, and she smiles at me. "Come on, stinky. You're smellin' pretty ripe, like the guys' gym-bag-level stinky, and we know I can't handle that."

Her comment makes me laugh. I actually laugh for the first time since the accident. The memory of Haylee throwing up literally after I dared her to smell one of the guys' gym bag comes to mind, and I actually fall over laughing.

"Come on, it's not funny. That was so gross! I can't believe you actually made me do that."

"Hey, I didn't *make* you do anything, Hails. Not my fault you can't refuse a dare."

After a few more minutes of laughter, we both wipe our tears away. I instantly feel guilty for our laughter just now since Emmett will no longer laugh, no longer reminisce over memories, no longer sit on this bed with me or have his arm around his sister. My tears turn from happy to sad. I look back at my pillow, and Haylee can sense my hesitation.

Before I can go back under the covers, she hops up and grabs my hand. "Oh no you don't. Shower, missy—*now!*"

Haylee smacks my ass while pushing me into my bathroom. I close the door behind me, turn the shower on, and strip out of my clothes before stepping in. I let the warm water run down my hair and face, hoping it will drown me. At least in the shower I can't see my tears as they mix with the water. I hear the door hit the wall stopper, and I know that Haylee is sitting in the doorway. I don't need to look out the curtain to confirm; it was always our thing. No need to stop our conversation just because the other needed to shower, although there was one time I was not alone and she started talking to me, and it almost got very awkward. Lucky for me and Emmett, he remained quiet till she got a phone call and left. I am also glad she didn't reveal any crazy secrets that day. I'm pretty sure if she would've brought up boys, kissing, or sex, Emmett would have made it known he was in the shower with me.

This time, though, it's different. Neither of us say anything as I shower and clean the few days of filth off my skin. After I turn the shower off, Haylee hands me a towel, and I dry off before stepping out. I walk out into my room to see Haylee standing in front of my desk looking at all the photos on my bulletin board of me and Emmett. Some include her and Zach as well. I walk past her and grab underwear, a bra, black leggings, and Emmett's Washington Capitals hoodie. I turn around the same time Haylee does, and she takes in my choice of attire. Her breath catches, and she wipes away the stray tears.

"I'm sorry. I know I seemed big and tough earlier, but I just can't... I'm sorry."

Before she can run out of my room, I grab her into a hug. I hug the shit out of my best friend, who is now an only child. I hold her while she cries and somehow find the strength to not crumble myself. I pull back and place my forehead on hers, and we both take deep breaths.

"Come on, you forced me out of bed and to shower, and I'm sure Zach has already eaten all the chicken Parm, so maybe we can get downstairs for the dessert."

She gives me a weak smile before turning toward the door. I release her hand.

"I'll be right there. I'm just going to brush my hair real fast."

She nods and exits the room. I walk back into the bathroom and open the drawer where my brush is and find one of Emmett's shaving cream bottles. I reach into the drawer and pull it out, lifting the lid so I can smell his scent. I close my eyes and envision him standing in front of me just inches from my face. I inhale, trying to control my breathing to keep from having another meltdown. I quickly put the lid back on and throw it back in the drawer, slamming it shut. Fuck brushing my hair. I grab a hair tie off the counter and pull my brown waves into a messy bun on top of my head.

This is about as good as it's gonna get for me. They should just be happy that I'm out of bed. I don't have to eat; I can just shuffle around the food on my plate so it looks like I have, but to avoid anyone else coming into my room today, I will have to humor them and join them.

The first seventeen birthdays in my life got better each year. Now it has become a day I'll dread for the rest of my life.

CHAPTER 10

Danielle

$\mathcal{I}$t's been five weeks since Emmett passed, and Mr. Brian asked for my parents' help with clearing out Emmett's room from the apartment. Ms. Natalie didn't feel up to coming, so Mom went over to their house to hang back with her. I knew this day would eventually come. I guess I was hoping we could have put it off longer or maybe I could have gotten out of it completely.

The spring semester will be starting at UPenn soon. Zach doesn't plan on getting a new roommate; my parents can afford the rent, so no need for him to fill the empty room. He can set it up as a guest room. I'm surprised he doesn't move out of there completely. It's bad enough for me being at home without Em, I can't imagine how my brother lives at that apartment alone.

My father drives us all in the minivan, and sitting in the back, I am having flashbacks to driving toward the funeral home for Emmett's funeral. There is small talk throughout the car, otherwise it remains pretty quiet. It's all there ever seems to be anymore these days—*quiet*.

We arrive at Zach's building, and as we start walking to the main door, I look over and see my brother's Jeep and next to it an empty space where Emmett used to park his. I stop and stare at the empty space. Closing my eyes, I remember our first time visiting this place last summer. Emmett carried me over the threshold as if we were a married couple when he brought me here to see it.

I hear his voice in my head as if he were beside me. *"Welcome home, baby! Next year, when you join us here at school, this is your home. I already talked to Zach about it, but you'll move in for real and we can start our next chapter together."*

I am snapped out of my memory to see Haylee standing next to me, holding my hand. She gives me a brief smile, and although I return it, I turn my attention back to the empty parking space before following her lead back toward our family.

Walking into the apartment, we are greeted with an eerie silence. I notice the door to Emmett's room is closed. I guess Zach keeps it closed since there isn't a reason to go in there. Are we really about to do this? This can't be happening. Maybe he is still just on vacation, at lacrosse camp like he had gone to all those years. My brain still refuses to accept he's gone. No, it's not just my brain; it's my heart that refuses to believe it too.

Zach comes out of the kitchen area with Sharpies, scissors, and packing tape. My dad and Mr. Brian had carried boxes up for us to pack the stuff up. Mr. Brian said that most would be packed up and put into Emmett's room at their house and could be dealt with when ready, some taken to the church donation bin, and we could take whatever we wanted to take. I plan to take as much as possible. These are all I have left of him. Someone else doesn't need the memories; they wouldn't understand the importance of the suit he wore at special events, his favorite tie to wear on our fancy dates, his winter coat that he would wear when we would travel to Liberty Ski Resort for fun weekend getaways, the blankets that we would use to snuggle under after using our bodies to show how much we loved each other. Instead of assisting in packing everything, I want to get what I want and get out of there. I already feel like the apartment is shrinking in size.

We are all standing around when Mr. Brian announces, "Come on, guys, let's get this over with before I don't have the strength to anymore and change my mind."

We nod somberly, yet no one makes a move from where we are sitting and standing in the room. My dad chimes in, breaking the silence and placing his hand on Mr. Brian's shoulder. "Bri, you know we don't need to do this now. We don't need to clear out the room just yet. We can take our time, do this when you're ready."

Holding up his hand, Mr. Brian cuts my dad off. "I know there's no timetable for this, Adam, but we need to do this. All of the stuff that you all don't want to take—" He looks at Zach, Haylee, and me. "—we're just boxing up and taking back home to later sort through thoroughly."

We all again nod in silence, taking in what is about to happen, but yet again, no one makes a move. We are all consumed in the silence and somberness that encloses the small apartment where Emmett lived his last days.

It's Mr. Brian who eventually makes the first move toward the bedroom door that is still closed and stands there with his hand hovering over the handle. It's visibly shaking. Movement to my right brings my attention back this way to see Haylee wiping her eyes with her sleeve but doing it in a way she hopes no one will see. I pull my knees to my chest and take a deep breath. I need to be able to do this. Get this over with so that I can leave. It's too painful here.

Mr. Brian lets out a loud exhale, loud enough for us to hear from the other side of the room, before he turns the knob and walks inside. My dad follows, then Haylee rises from the couch.

Zach walks toward me and takes a seat on the table in front of me, grabbing my hands in his.

"You okay?"

I don't say anything, only nod, because my brother would know if I was lying. Nothing about this is okay. Five weeks and this is still not okay. He squeezes my hand, stands, and extends his hand to me. I stare at it before looking back at the door and trying to decide how easily I could jump over the couch and run out the door and away from here. In my mind, I keep running. In reality, though, I place my hand in my brother's and allow him to pull me to my feet.

Together, hand in hand, Zach and I walk toward Emmett's room, where for three months, we would discuss our hopes, dreams, and future, love each other, laugh with each other, and only occasionally yell at each other, followed by making up with each other. I could do this. I *had* to do this. My grip on my brother's hand tightens as we walk through the doorway and watch everyone else begin to fold and tape up boxes, pull things from drawers and the closet, and lay things on the bed.

Haylee goes to open the top drawer on the nightstand, and before I can tell her not to, she slams it shut and lets out a loud giggle. Her laughter breaks through the uncomfortable silence but for the tape gun and cardboard. She looks over at me as does everyone else. Realizing what was in that drawer, I blush. It was no secret that we were together in that way, but it's another to see your brother's collection of lubes and lotions.

"How about I take care of that drawer," I say, then bite my lip and walk in that direction.

She scrunches her nose up and nods. "Probably a good idea, D."

I reach for a trash bag from the dresser and begin to clean out the drawer. I don't plan to use these again, and there's nothing grosser than using someone else's private items like that. My face puckers at the thought. Once the drawer is empty and other nonsexual contents are on the top of the nightstand, I walk over to grab an empty box to start gathering up belongings. I place photos, books, and random memorabilia that we have collected over the years and fill that box up. I write my name on it and tape it up and gather a second box. I begin going through the rest of the dresser drawers and throw T-shirts, long-sleeved shirts, flannels, a few hoodies, and his favorite pair of gym shorts in the box. I go through the motions and don't concentrate too hard on what I'm doing, or else I'm going to break down. While I am in the process of taping up the second box, my brother is working on the desk drawers.

"What is this?" He pulls out a box, wrapped in beautiful paper—the paper is beautiful, not necessarily the wrap job on it, which means that Emmett wrapped that himself. There is also a card along with it with "Cupcake" written on the front in Emmett's sloppy handwriting. I stare at the present and card as my brother walks over to me. I am still staring when he touches my arm to grab my attention after apparently calling me over and over. Snapping out of my trance, I lift my eyes to meet Zach's.

"Well, I guess this was meant for you." He places it in my hands, and I don't know what to do with it. I can feel a bigger lump forming in my throat than earlier. He had bought me something and wrapped it? Am I supposed to open it now? Do I wait? I keep it in my hands and back up till I'm fully seated on the bed, unsure what to do next.

Haylee takes a seat next to me. "Do you want to open it?"

"I don't know. I mean yes...no...I don't know."

"You can go to my room, sis, if you want to do it now in private."

I nod, acknowledging him. I look around the room and think this is it. This isn't like in *P.S. I Love You* where the husband knew his time was coming to an end, so he wrote her letters to help move on. Emmett didn't know he was going to die that night. He planned to leave the library and come back to this apartment and see me. He didn't know that he wouldn't make it home.

This is my final gift from Emmett. I go to get up from the bed to move to Zach's room, but I'm scared. I somehow found enough strength to come here today, but this is just too much. I set the item on the top of my boxes and continue cleaning out the room so that we can go through this as quickly as possible and I can go back home to my bedroom to be alone in peace...or whatever form of silence my room provides. I look up from where I am standing to find everyone's eyes on me as if they were waiting for me to either open the gift or break down. I brush them all off and go back to the pile I'm currently working on.

Over the next three hours, we go through and pack everything up through tears, recalling memories brought up by some items and laughing at the ungodly number of empty orange Gatorade bottles. The man was seriously obsessed. The best part is that they weren't even out in the open; most were shoved in the back of the closet or behind the dresser. By the time we're done, we've found thirteen. Maybe that was Emmett's way of sending a message to us to lighten the mood. He was always so great at that. Making light of the hard things.

Walking out of the room for the last time seems harder this time than when I had to head home for the funeral since now the room is completely empty. It's as if Emmett never lived here, all things Emmett packed up and put away. I don't want to break down in front of everyone yet again, so I grab my bag and shove the card and box in there and walk out the door without another word. Once I am in the stairwell, I allow the silent tears to free fall.

After loading the boxes in the van and Zach's Jeep, who is coming home for the weekend, we head back to Annapolis. The ride home is quiet, everyone still wallowing in their memories. After dropping Mr. Brian and Haylee off, my dad tells him that we will come back with dinner and to help unload the boxes. Today has been another emotionally draining day, so when we get back home, Dad helps me bring the boxes into my room.

"Dad, is it cool if I just stay home instead?"

"Are you sure?"

"Yeah." I fake a yawn. "It's just been a long day, and I'm pretty tired. I just wanna lie down."

With sad eyes, he nods. He takes one last look at the stack of boxes, pulls me into a hug, and kisses the top of my head.

"I know it hurts still, Danielle, but we will get through this."

"I'm just tired, that's all."

Dad holds me a little longer. "Okay, well, you get some rest sweetheart. I'm going to go pick up some pizzas and take them over. We will be back later. I'll bring you some leftover slices."

"Thanks, Daddy."

He kisses the top of my head before pulling away. I shut the door behind him as he exits, and I flip back and forth between staring at the pile of boxes and the bag that contains Emmett's present. I walk over to my dresser and pull out a T-shirt, one of Emmett's lacrosse tees that says "Stop Staring at my Balls." I grab my bag and sit with my legs crossed on my bed. I pull the gift and card out and stare at them. One day I'll be able to open them; however, that day is not today. I place them on top of my nightstand and grab my headphones, turn the music on, and lie back, bringing the covers over my head.

CHAPTER 11

Danielle

*T*oday is February 17, 2012.

Today is Emmett's birthday.

Today *was* his birthday.

Today he *would* have been nineteen.

My Emmett will never celebrate another birthday.

He will forever be eighteen.

Today everyone is headed to the cemetery to take flowers to the grave site. I haven't been back to the cemetery since the funeral. What's the point? I just see it as a reminder of what's no longer here—*him.*

I walk into our kitchen and find Mom cleaning up from breakfast. No matter how many times she asked, I still refused to change my mind about going with them. I reach into the fridge for the bottle of orange juice with my back to my mother when she asks again, "Are you sure you won't come with us? Your brother is coming down to join us."

Zach had returned to school and started his semester in an attempt at getting back to normal. He keeps himself busy with his schoolwork. I haven't been to visit him since we packed up Emmett's things, nor do I plan to. I can't be in that place. I'm not sure how he can stay in that apartment himself. I went from visiting almost every other weekend to none at all. He has only been home once since he came back to visit the weekend Em's room was packed up, but he checks in daily via text and phone calls with me. I know him well enough that he is probably sharing any scrap of information I give him— not that there's much— with my parents since everyone is so worried about me.

I choose to ignore my mother's question. She steps closer to me and places her hand on my arm. "It might help going there and us all being together."

I shrug her off. Nothing is going to help. I take the glass that she placed on the island in front of me and fill it halfway with juice and take a sip in hopes she will drop the subject.

"Honey, please, come with us."

The emotions have been bottling up for weeks, waiting to burst into flames, and apparently her persistence is the just the gasoline I needed. "No," I say barely above a whisper.

"Please!"

I slam the glass down on the counter, causing juice to spill out. "No! Get that in your head—*no*! Do you need me to get a plane to write it in the sky? N-O! It hurts so fucking much, I don't want to go there. I don't need another reminder that he is not here. I hate him. I hate him for dying...for leaving me. He lied. He told me he would be careful driving home." The tears have been unleashed; there is no stopping them now. "I'm never going to be happy again, don't you see that? Don't you get that? Every day I wake up is another day that Emmett doesn't. I feel like I'm suffocating—fighting for air to breathe." I slam my hands on my chest. "What about me? What about my feelings? Didn't my feelings matter? He just up and died, left without saying goodbye. He left me here to pick up the pieces. I can't...I can't..."

I'm struggling to breathe in between my words. My father has since come into the room after hearing the commotion. I can see him standing in the doorway, not daring to say anything. "I don't know how to be without him—I don't want to be without him. I didn't want him to go."

Before I know it, my legs have given out and I'm sitting on the floor and my mother's arms are around me. My mother's tears freely flow down her face. I can feel them drop from her skin onto mine. She always tries to be strong, but she is giving in to my sadness.

"Oh honey, none of us did. That's not how this works though. Life is cruel and unfair, and the reality we face is we never know when our time is up. We wish it was only when we are old and have lived a full life, not at only eighteen. I hate this for you, for all of us. I'm forced to sit here and watch my best friend grieve the loss of her son. My own kids have to learn to live a life without their other half. Sometimes when Zach comes home I still expect to see Em behind him. There is no greater pain for a parent than to watch their child hurt, and there's not a damn thing I can do to make you feel better. I've spent these last few weeks watching you slip further and further away from us. I can't lose you too. I wish I could bring him back."

"Mommy, it hurts so much...make the pain stop."

Her arms tighten around me. "I know, Danielle. I wish I could." I allow myself to cry in her arms and seek comfort in her embrace. "This is why I don't think you should be alone today. Please just come with us, Danielle."

I push out of her arm and stand, then take the glass and throw it against the wall. "No!" I scream and storm past her and my father and run to the stairs to retreat to my room.

When I reach the bottom of the stairs, the front door opens and my brother walks in. "Dani? Are you okay?"

I ignore him; he should know the fucking answer to his question. Will I ever be okay again? I run up the stairs, slam the door, and crawl back into bed to forget about today. Pulling his photo off the nightstand and into my arms, I whisper, "Happy Birthday, baby."

CHAPTER 12
Danielle

They say the worst day of loving someone is the day you lose them, but I'm not sure I believe that. Yes, it's the worst feeling ever, but what about every day you wake up *after*? Those hurt worse. I'm only eighteen years old and already have enough heartache to last a lifetime. Each day that passes is just another day to wake up, exist, and go to bed. After 2.5 months of having work sent home, my parents forced me to return back to school, to try to return to normal and enjoy the last few months left before graduation. The school was understanding of the circumstances as long as I kept up the work, but my parents said I couldn't stay holed up in my room forever. I didn't see anything wrong with that plan though. There wasn't much left for me anymore; all the plans I'd made for my future had revolved around Em, and I wasn't sure what was next anymore.

Everyone is always staring at me. I know they talk about me behind my back, and I frankly don't give a damn. I'm the girl left behind, the broken one, the sad one, the freak, the one who has emotional breakdowns in class. The first few weeks back at school, everyone hovered, asking if I was okay, how I was holding up, telling me how much they missed Em, how great a guy he was. Now, everyone will just ask how I am doing in

74

passing and I just give a brief "I'm fine." I know I'm lying, and I know they know I'm lying, but they know not to push since I won't tell them the truth. I feel like they are all just waiting for me to break again, to lose it as if they just expect it from me. They don't get it—they don't get the emptiness I feel every day. Nothing they do or say will bring him back.

Each day is the same: I wake up, go to school, come home, push food around on my plate, then go to bed. I thank God I made it through the day, but I still end up crying myself to sleep. My usual wardrobe of jeans and bright-colored tops is replaced with yoga pants, T-shirts, and hoodies. Haylee will ride with me some days, but most days I prefer to be alone. On days that she does ride with me, we don't listen to music or laugh like we used to. She is getting through the days just like I am. We're not the same as we once were. I'm not sure we ever will be again.

While our friends are spending their senior year doing normal things—preparing for college, soaking up the last few months of high school, going to bonfires, parties, and games—I spend my time alone either in my room or on the swing on the front porch. I've pushed everyone who once mattered away, shutting them out. Spending time with old friends doesn't heal me; it hurts. Spending time at places we used to hang out such as the ice cream shop or the mall just remind me of the memories of the past. It all just reminds me of what is lost, seeing happy couples and remembering I'll never have that again. I don't have the answers I want, the answers to know why this had to happen to us. I find myself falling further and further into this black hole of darkness. I don't know how to describe it. I don't feel, I don't think. I'm just numb.

My parents tried to take me to see a therapist. In the beginning, they drove me and waited in the office, and then in the parking lot over time. There wasn't anything I wanted to share with her. Eventually I stopped going. My parents had plenty to say, but eventually they, with the help of my brother, came to the conclusion that I wasn't ready to talk.

But over time I did need to talk to someone. It didn't matter who as long l as I got it out. It wasn't healthy for me to keep it all bottled up inside is what they said. The therapist had suggested keeping a journal. I tried that too. For about two weeks I wrote in the journal as if I were writing letters to Emmett, talking about my day, asking questions, venting about everyone hovering. But during those two weeks, with no response from him, I continued to get angry. I'm not really sure what I expected since he was gone. How would he respond? It was the principle of the matter, I guess.

It's a typical Friday night here, with me alone in my room. Well, not totally alone, sometimes I hang out with Jack, Jim, or Jose. This time though, I was able to sneak a bottle of Mom's wine up here. Tonight is the senior prom, and even though Haylee and some other friends begged me to attend, even going as a group, I just couldn't do it. So, here I am sitting in my room, half a bottle of wine gone. I know it was probably a bad idea, but I'm not the best thinker these days. Mom had gone over to the Hankses' house to see Haylee off and ended up staying to hang out while my dad went to Philly to see some sports game with Zach. They had both protested leaving at first, but I promised them I was fine and that I had a night planned for one: movies and Chinese takeout.

While yes, I do have a movie on and ordered way too much food for just one person, I find myself sitting on the bed. To the left of me is a photo of me and Emmett from prom last year. It was one of the photos I had taken from his room at the apartment. I loved that dress—I had instantly fallen in love with it, but then I saw the price tag and thought it was better to move on. My mother had other ideas though; she convinced me to just try it on. As I walked out of the dressing room, the room went silent and the next thing I knew we were walking out of the store carrying a garment bag filled with that dress.

To my right is something a little more emotional—the card and box that Emmett had hidden in his desk drawer. I still haven't opened it. Every day I stare at it on the nightstand. It's like it's taunting and teasing me, knowing once I open this, that's it. I'm not sure if it's nerves of the emotions swirling around with what tonight should have been or the amount of liquid courage running through my veins, but I reach out for the card and slide my fingers along the top to slice the envelope open.

As I pull the card out, my breath catches, and I try to swallow the lump of Chinese food that's creeping up my throat. I flip the card open to see more of his chicken-scratch handwriting. I used to joke with him that he should be a doctor since his handwriting was so shitty. What I wouldn't give to see his shitty writing.

Blinking back the tears, I read his handwritten message:

Cupcake,

Happy anniversary, baby girl! Can you believe it – 5 years? I can't believe it because it seems like I loved you for a lifetime. I know these past few months apart have been rough. Having to always leave you tears me up inside, but we have the rest of our lives.

Shit, if only he knew the impact of his words now. Having him leave me in the way he did didn't just tear me up, it full-on gutted me.

Here is only a little something I have planned. Looking at all these cheesy cards I just couldn't decide which one to buy. But this spoke to me because the words couldn't be more true. You will forever be my always. I love you, Emmett.

I look over to the other side of the card and read the inscription. "I loved you yesterday. I love you still. I always have. I always will. Happy Anniversary." My eyes travel back to his note on the left, and my fingertips trace the writing. Placing the card on the bed, I allow myself a few moments to take it all in before I continue. There is no stopping the tears now. I could hear his voice reading these words, and I would give anything to still hear it outside of my own thoughts. I take a sip of the wine and tear at the wrapping paper. Once unwrapped, I find a long black velvet box. Fuck! I feel not only sadness filling me, but anger. To open it or not open it...of course I'm going to fucking open it.

Staring back at me is the most...shit, it hurts so much right now...the most stunning necklace I have ever seen. It is a silver-plated heart with a diamond in it and engraved in a beautiful cursive "Always." Dropping the box on my bed, I pull my knees in and try to control my breathing. I run my fingers through my hair and pull at the ends, feeling heartbroken all over again.

I'm not sure how long I sit here wanting time to move quicker, but in fact it feels slower, possibly even stopped. My head is spinning, and my heart hurts. I clutch the necklace box and bring it to my chest before setting my head on the pillow., I look around and see every memory this room holds. It's a prisoner for my broken life and fallen dreams. Emmett always talked about the big plans for us he had, but I doubt he ever thought my big plans would not include him.

I can't stay here. I can't do this. These people, every single one of them expect me to be something I'm not and to find the strength to move on. I can't. I won't. I don't want to. Instead of sleeping, I pull the notebook out that I keep in the drawer on my nightstand and begin my great escape. What I need to do, possible places to go, what to pack...I make notes on all of it before I finally succumb to the exhaustion that has overtaken my body tonight. The wine of course was not a help.

As I allow myself to drift off to sleep, I continue to think about my future plans, and only one thing is certain: no one can know, not even Zach. Although, he has been pretty busy lately with new friends he's making. Guess some of us can just forget.

This is the best for everyone. Everyone is so concerned on beginning to figure out how to move on that this is for the better. I'm not ready to move on from him, nor will I probably ever be. There is nothing left in this place for me, so it's time to just move on from here.

CHAPTER 13

Danielle

I walk across the stage as they announce, "Danielle Kathryn Jacobs." I look up to find our families cheering loudly. I scan the row and spot an empty seat next to them, and I'm reminded again that he isn't here. I haven't forgotten. Another moment we will never get to share.

To be perfectly honest, I wasn't sure this day was going to come after everything we went through this year. Hell, it hasn't even been a full year, just six months. In the past few weeks after deciding to leave after graduation, I spent a little bit of time with each of my family members including Haylee, knowing that my time with them was limited. I had hoped that in their mind I was finally coming out of it, whatever the darkness was that I fell into, and was ready to start dealing with reality.

By the time the last name is called and they announce that we have officially graduated, I am ready to get the hell out of here. In this place I have only had two identities: Zach Jacobs's sister and Emmett Hanks' girlfriend. It's a life I have only ever known, but tomorrow I put it all behind me. Tomorrow I start a new life—one where I am only known as me, Danielle Jacobs. Leaving for a place where no one knows my past, no one knows the hurt, no one knows Emmett.

"We did it! We actually did it!" Haylee and I shout at the same time as we exit the stadium and search for our families. I am taken by surprise and scream when arms wrap around me and I am lifted off the ground. For a moment I think that it's Emmett, but I know that is impossible. My brother's voice cuts the sadness.

"You did it! I'm so proud of you, sis!"

He continues to spin me around in circles. "Zach, put me down. You're gonna make me sick." Those are the magic words. I am put back on my feet so fast, I almost fall over. My parents are next to pull me into their arms followed by Natalie and Brian. I am pretty sure they take enough photos to fill our entire yearbook and then some. The irony of all these photographs is that as of tomorrow, this is all they will have left.

I look around at the smiling faces and take a mental photo of this.

"Reservations tomorrow at 5:30 at Boatyard," my dad shouts to everyone as we begin to make our way toward the parking lot.

As we reach the cars, I realize this will be the last time I see Natalie, Brian, and Haylee. I wrap my arms around Haylee's parents.

"Thank you for everything. I love you both so much."

"We love you too, Dani. And we are so proud of all you have accomplished."

I turn to my best friend and wrap my arms around her and think for a moment I might not let her go. I pretend that is this is a hug just like every other hug and not goodbye.

"You're going to squeeze the life out of me, D!"

I release her from my arms and laugh along with her.

"Sorry, I just can't believe this day is finally here and gone. It seems surreal."

"I know! No more high school! Woo! Now on to bigger and better things."

"Yep. Crazy!"

My brother shouts from where he's standing beside his Jeep, "Hey, D, are you riding back with Hails, or you wanna ride home with me?"

"Is it cool to ride back with you?"

"Yeah, hop in." Zach gets in the driver's side of the Jeep as I say goodbye to Haylee one last time.

"I'll see you guys tomorrow," Haylee shouts as she gets into her car and I walk toward my brother's car.

"Thanks." I get in and buckle my seat belt.

"Want to sit out back like old times? I figure that's as good a way as any to celebrate the end of this chapter of your life."

I nod. "I'd like that."

If only he knew the truth behind that statement.

My parents and Zach left for the restaurant twenty minutes ago. I stood in my bathroom with the shower running, telling them that I was running late and would meet them there. Little did they know that I would never make it there. Last night before going to bed, I sat out on the back deck with Zach just talking. We talked about the fall, and he tried to find out what was next for me after deferring college for the fall. I told him I wasn't sure but would be spending the summer trying to figure that out, and that wasn't a complete lie. I do plan to spend the summer figuring out what's coming next, just not here.

I don't know how much time I have before they'll start calling, so I have to be focused and get this done quickly. When the coast is clear, I run downstairs and pull my SUV into the garage so I can load it up without worrying about someone passing by and possibly tipping my family off to my impending departure. I quickly grab the boxes I put together late last night and stored in my closet and throw my belongings in there: my clothes, photos, important documents, the money I've been withdrawing from my bank account over the past few weeks so my parents wouldn't notice huge withdrawal amounts, mementos, and the rest of Emmett's belongings that I'd packed up from the apartment.

A rush of memories fills my mind, and I struggle to fight back the tears. I know that come end of summer I would have been packing this room up to head to college, but it wasn't final. I would still be able to come home when I wanted to and for holidays, but this is different. I need to start fresh and figure out what the new plan of my life will be without Emmett in it. Most eighteen-year-olds might not know their path either, but since I was thirteen, I had planned on only one path. It may have been naïve to think that I could have met my soul mate at birth and create our plans so young, but that was our life—there was nothing I wouldn't have done for him and vice versa.

Maybe that was the issue, that our lives were consumed by each other that there was no other foreseeable end but heart-break, but I just never expected this. That's the thing with death, I guess—no one expects it. I mean, we all know that it's inevitable, the only constant in life, but we are so caught up in our own worlds and problems that we have this thing where we think we're invincible and death only comes to us at old age, not when people are just starting their lives.

It takes eight trips to load everything up in my car—well, sixteen if you count going down *and* up the stairs. Wiping the sweat across my forehead, I am worn-out. Maybe I shouldn't have packed so much. I take one last look around my room and swallow the lump in my throat. This is going to crush my parents and Zach. I need to stop thinking about it before I change my mind. I wipe away the tears falling down my cheek as I take one last look at the room I grew up in—the one I had slumber parties with Haylee in and danced around to Katy Perry for hours, where I told my mom I was in love, where I used to get in popcorn fights with my brother and have heart-to-heart talks late at night. It was the place where I would share my deepest secrets with Em, watch movies, and laugh. I could sit at the window and watch him and Zach play basketball in the driveway even though they both sucked at it. This was my space to be me since I was a little girl. If only those walls could talk of the good times and bad, the heartache and the friendship, the love and the bonds. It would also speak of goodbye.

I at least had the decency to write a short note for my family. Too bad I'll be gone by the time they get back from the restaurant and see that I'm gone. "I'm sorry," I say aloud but not really to anyone. Maybe it's to myself, maybe it's to my parents in hopes that when they walk in here and find my note they would hear my voice, or maybe it's to Emmett, wherever he is now. I'm sorry that I'm not strong enough to face this all without him, that I have to leave.

By the time I close my bedroom door and walk down the stairs toward the garage, my phone buzzes.

ZACH: *Hey, are you on your way?*

I ignore the text and keep walking to my car. When I get in and start it up, I sit there, close my eyes, and take three deep breaths...

One.

Two.

Three.

I can do this. I have to do this. I have to be strong.

I pull out of the garage and down the driveway, refusing to look back on the life I'm leaving behind.

CHAPTER 14
Danielle

"Dani, where are you? We're all here waiting for you to get here so we can order. Can you call and let us know you're at least on your way?" – **Dad**

"Danielle Kathryn Jacobs, this isn't funny. What is this note? You left? When will you be back? This isn't funny. Call us." – **Mom**

Zach: *Where are you? Are you okay?*

"Danielle, it's mom. Where are you? Please call someone back. It's been two months. We...I need to know you're okay. Please, sweetheart, call us. I love you." – **Mom**

Mom: *Danielle, I need you to call me! Please!*
Mom: *Please just let us know you are safe.*

"Dani, for fuck's sake, you need to cut this shit out and come home. You're being a bitch making Mom worry about you. We're all worried about you. Just let someone know you're fucking alive!" – **Zach**

ZACH: *We need you. I need you.*
HAYLEE: *Just tell us where you are and we can come get you.*
HAYLEE: *I miss you!*

"Where are you? Please talk to me, D. I need you back here." –
Haylee

"Enough is enough, young lady. Get back here now. I know you are hurting—we all are—but this is not how you go about doing this. When we told you it was time to move on, we did not mean this shit." – **Dad**

"Getting ready to leave for college. I don't know where you are, but I wish you were here." – **Haylee**

"Dani... You know what? Fuck this shit." – **Zach**

"How can you be so selfish putting us—putting the Hankses through this. Mom and Dad need their daughter, I need my sister, and Haylee needs her best friend. I know you are in a dark place, but for the love of God, Danielle, come home." – **Zach**

CHAPTER 15

Danielle

I can't imagine the pain I continue to put my family through by staying away. It's been six months, and the calls and texts still come through. I finally texted Mom back, letting her know that I was alive, but that I needed to do this, that she shouldn't worry about me, and that I was fine. *Fine.* There is that word, a word that women have been using since the beginning of time to falsely describe how they are feeling. No one is ever fine; they can always be better if they choose to use the word fine. I know she will continue to worry, though, that I am okay and wondering where I have found myself these days. I told her I was alive, but most days I'm not sure that I really feel that way. I died the same night Emmett did if I'm being honest...one year ago today to be exact.

One year of pain.

One year of anger.

One year of what-ifs.

One year of replaying his last voicemail just to hear his voice.

One year of remembering what *was*, not what *is*.

One year of asking *why*.

One year of moments never getting to share.

I'm sitting on a swing in a small town in North Carolina

called Surf City. The sun is rising, which always makes me think of Emmett, not that every other part of the day he isn't on mind. I'm sure my family and the Hankses will be headed to the cemetery today. I thought about going back, but then the reality of today sets in. How have we survived a year already?

I look out over the ocean, happy that even though it's December, it is still fairly warm. I have only a light hoodie and a pair of capris. This weather is definitely not the weather I am used to. The ocean reminds me just how small we are in this world, yet the pain we deal with is so much greater. My world crumbled, and I'm just not ready to accept a life without Emmett Hanks in it. Will I ever be ready?

I feel like the number of tears I've cried could fill this ocean and still drown us all. That's how it feels—like I'm drowning. What I am feeling changes on a daily basis. Even if it is excruciating pain that overtakes my mind and body, it is still something which is more than I can say for how I've been living the past year. Sitting on this playground swing, it reminds me of the front porch swing we used to hang out on at my parents' house. I look over at the empty one next to me and wonder what life would be for us now had the accident not have happened. Emmett would be in his second year of college and I in my first, living together at the apartment, or maybe we would have ended up getting our own place. Would there finally be a ring on my finger with the promise of forever?

I reach over to the empty swing, wishing to the gods above that they would send Emmett back to me, just for five more minutes. Fuck, who am I kidding—if they could give me five more minutes, then why not ten? Fifteen? One day? Why stop there—why couldn't they give me forever back?

I think back to the conversation we had at my parents' house before he left for college, when I joked that we would have to bottle up his kisses in a jar for later. Oh how I would give anything and everything to have that jar now.

My phone vibrates and even though I know it's a bad idea, I look at the incoming text message.

ZACH: *I told myself I wasn't going to do this today, but here I am reaching out knowing you will ignore this. Dani, I know you are hurting today and every day for the past year, but come the fuck home.*

ZACH: *Whatever you are facing and battling, we can do it together. We are headed to the cemetery around 10, and then Mom is having lunch at the house. I don't know where you are, but please come home. If not for you, then for me, for Haylee, for mom and dad. We all need you for fuck's sake. I miss him too you know.*

ZACH: *Please just answer me. I'm going out of my mind that you are out there somewhere by yourself and you won't let me help you. I'm your big brother and I'm supposed to protect you from all things big and bad, and I couldn't protect you from this, so I feel as though I've failed you. D, I didn't want to do all of this over text, but I know that you wouldn't answer if I called you, and I would be limited on what I could say via voicemail.*

ZACH: *I have to have faith that you are actually reading these texts and not just ignoring them. I need you today and every day, Danielle. Please, I'm begging you. I love you, sis.*

I drop the phone in the sand as my tears continue to fall. My grief overtakes me the same way a Category 5 hurricane would wipe out this area. The pain tears through me as if it just happened. Will it always feel like this?

I open the reply message on my brother's text message and almost type a response. In my head I see it perfectly...

Me (DRAFT): *I'm sorry. I'm sorry I left the way I did. I'm sorry I let you all down. I'm sorry he's gone. I'm sorry for so many things out of my control. I knew that I would be alone the rest of my life, and everyone told me I needed to begin to move on with life, so that's what I attempted to do. I moved on from my old life, a life with daily reminders of what I had lost. I know you all meant for me to move on from Em, but I'm just not ready to let him go. No matter what I did, I still felt empty. The pain never went away no matter what I tried. I know you all think I'm crazy, and yes, maybe I am, but I needed to do this. Everything always was so easy with Emmett. Even if it was something I was doing without him, life was easy. I felt...I feel that I need to relearn how to do everything including how to breathe. I need you so bad, Zach, to help me. Every day I wake up feeling like I can't breathe, that I'm drowning. I want to wake up and this year was all a lie, a bad dream, and I wake up in Emmett's arms. Please help me. I don't want to feel like this anymore. I don't know how to live in a world without him? I want to come home. I am too far away to meet you there at 10, but I will be there...*

I read and reread my words over and over, and my thumb hovers over the Send button. I am so close to hitting it, but instead my thumb moves to the Delete button and I hold it until the entire response is gone. I want to come home...but I want Emmett back, and well, we don't always get what we want. I close my phone and place it back in my pocket.

After the sun has fully risen, I stand and walk down to the shore and breathe in and out, imagining Emmett's arms around me giving me the strength to make it through the day, through tomorrow, through the rest of my life.

"I'm so sorry, baby."

I pull my phone back out and grab the headphones from my

hoodie pocket and plug the cord in. Recently I discovered a new song by Michael Schulte, and it's been playing on repeat. I shuffle through the songs and press Play on "You Said You'd Grow Old With Me." I hit the Repeat button and put the earbuds in my ears. Blocking out the world, blocking out the reality, I sit down in the sand and pull my knees to my chest and play this song and cry. I cry for the past and the memories, I cry for everything we've been though and have yet to go through, I cry for all the plans that will never happen, a love cut short, a life ended too soon. I cry and I pray for strength to be able to get by. My silent tears continue to fall against the sounds of the ocean. I cry for the thoughts I want to turn off, and I cry for the life I hope one day that I will be able to have—one that includes being able to see my family again. I pray that that day happens, although prayers these days don't really go answered much, so I won't hold my breath.

I sit here for hours, and when I next look at my phone, it says it's 10:00 a.m. I picture my family and the Hankses at Emmett's grave, hovering and seeking comfort within each other. I imagine them telling stories of Emmett, maybe from when he was younger as a wild, rambunctious kid always getting into trouble with Zach, or maybe from when he was protecting me. Maybe a story from his lacrosse days when we thought he might want to continue professionally, but that wasn't where his heart lay—his heart was with me. I think of the funny and happy moments of Em's life, but with that brings the sad ones.

I think about calling Zach to tell him I'm okay, but I change my mind. It's better this way, better for them. They need to move on from not only Emmett, but me too.

CHAPTER 16

Danielle

Three years later...

*A*fter ignoring my family and friends' calls, texts, and requests to come home for the holidays, it was finally time to stop running away from my life. When I had left the day after graduation, I did not really have a destination in mind other than the fact I needed to get as far away from that town as possible. After spending time in Surf City, North Carolina, I needed a change. I randomly picked a town on the map and drove north to Manchester, New Hampshire. As I drove through Maryland, I felt as though I had held my breath the entire time, overwhelmed with memories of the past.

I wasn't even sure if my brother would answer the phone when I had called him three days ago. I sat there on the couch looking at my phone for hours before I had enough courage to press Send.

Ring. Ring. Ring. He's not going to answer. This was a mistake.

"He...hello?" Say something, Dani. *He sounded half-asleep. I pulled the phone back to see that it was only 9:30 p.m. He cleared his throat. "Hello?"*

"Zach?"

"Dani?" His breath caught on the other end of his phone. It was so good to hear my brother's voice. "Dani, are you there?"

There was no denying the emotions battling inside me now. My voice was brittle. "Yeah, I'm here." I allowed the tears that I was holding in to release. We both didn't speak for a few moments, and I pull my phone back to confirm he hadn't hung up. The call was still going. There was some shuffling in the background. I hoped I hadn't interrupted anything. Maybe I should just make up an excuse to hang up. No, I can do this. Just breathe.

"I didn't think you would answer."

"What?" His voice raised slightly. "Why wouldn't I answer? Dani, you're my sister. Of course I would fucking answer." I pulled my legs up under me on my couch. I felt like such an asshole that I'd ignored him for so long.

"Where are you? Are you okay? Shit, I've had this conversation in my head over and over again for years, and now that I finally have you on the phone, I don't even know what to say."

I laughed. I guess it wasn't just me feeling like this. "Well, that's funny because I've been sitting here for hours rehearsing what to say, and a few times I almost backed out from calling you altogether. But just hearing your voice, I know I made the right choice."

"I'm so happy you called."

"Me too. Zach?"

"Yeah, sis."

"I want to come home."

ZACH TEXTED ME HIS NEW ADDRESS, A HOUSE IN A SMALL town just outside Philadelphia. When I park in front of the house, I don't see my brother's Jeep, but for all I know he sold it. There is a black Toyota Tundra truck parked in the driveway, so he must be home.

I take a deep breath.

Knock. Knock.

I look back at my car and wonder if I could run back to it and drive off before my brother even opens the door. *No, Dani, you can do this. Breathe in and out.* I push those thoughts aside and decide to keep my feet planted where they are. I really want to see my brother. I remember how good it felt to hear his voice after all this time.

I raise my hand to knock again, and the door opens. Standing there is a man about six foot two inches, with brown messy hair, and he's shirtless—definitely not my brother. Wait, maybe I have the wrong house. I quickly check my brother's text and then look back at this man, who is looking me up and down. I feel my cheeks warm at his stare. It has been a very long time since a man looked at me like that, at least that I'm aware of. I've kept to myself the past four years, no men, hell, not even very many friends. I'm not sure how I feel about this man, a stranger, staring at me like that. I'm not sure if I should run or worse, reach out and touch his tight stomach muscles. What the hell is wrong with me?

The man raises his eyebrows at me, waiting for me to speak. Finally, the words come to me. "I'm sorry, I must have the wrong place. I was looking for my brother, Zach Jacobs."

He looks me up and down once more and then smiles. "You're Danielle?"

I shrug. "Dani, yes."

He puts his hand out to shake my hand. "I'm Kyler, Kyler Lawson, your brother's best friend."

His words almost knock me off my feet. Had he not been

holding my hand at the moment, I would have fallen over. *Umm no, you're not his best friend. That job is Emmett's.*

"Zach should be home any minute. He got held up at work. Why don't you come in?" He opens the door wider and steps to the side to allow me to enter the house.

"So, you just hang out at my brother's house when he's not here?" I ask, confused. I have no knowledge of who this stranger is and why he's in my brother's house.

"Oh no, I live here too." My brother failed to mention that part to me on the phone—he lives with a roommate. What else did he forget to mention? Maybe this was a bad idea. I begin to look around. This place is cute.

"Well, I need to get in the shower and head out. Feel free to make yourself at home, and just yell if you need anything before I leave."

I barely hear the last part of that because my eyes were fixated on the collage of photos on the wall. Some are of my brother and this new guy, Taylor...Tyler...Kyler, whatever it was, and him with an older woman I assume is his mother. There are some empty nails with photos missing too. That's weird. But it's not the empty nails where photos once hung that catches my attention the most. It's the collage frame that includes photos of Zach and Emmett; Zach, Emmett, Haylee, and me; Zach and me; and even one of me and Emmett and from the summer before he died.

I won't cry, I won't cry, I repeat over and over. I start to take deep breaths in and out to try to prevent an anxiety attack. *Breathe in, breathe out. Breathe in, breathe out.*

"Holy shit, Dani, you're actually here!"

I hear my brother's voice from behind me. I turn around to see him standing in the doorway wearing black slacks and a white button-up shirt rolled at the sleeves. The edge of a tattoo is peeking out of one of his sleeve. Holy shit, my brother grew up. He sets his work bag and jacket down on the chair in the living room and runs over and throws his arms around me. I have to catch my breath. My brother is so grown up, he looks like an actual adult—and I missed the whole thing. I wrap my arms around him. God I missed him so much.

Pulling back, he places his hands along my cheeks to look me over. It's as if he's trying to memorize everything about me in case I run again. To be honest, I haven't decided if I'll be able to stay, but I'm willing to try.

He takes my hand and pulls me to the couch. "Have you been here long?"

I shake my head. "Your *roommate* let me in." I accentuate the word roommate.

"Oh, you met Ky. He's a good dude. We met freshman year of college. We hit it off right away." My mind drifts to his freshman year of college. Emmett. My lip begins to tremble, so I pull it between my teeth and bite down until I taste copper. I look back over to the wall where the photos are on the wall.

Zach catches me staring and opens his mouth to say something but is interrupted by Kyler walking into the room. "Hey, man, you're home." Zach nods.

"You headed out to—" Kyler starts, but Zach cuts him off to say, "Nah, I'm home tonight to catch up with Dani."

Turning to me, he asks, "Pizza for dinner work for you?" I nod. Zach turns back toward Kyler. "Ky, you want to join?"

Kyler is grabbing his keys off the table. "Thanks, rain check. I'm headed out to meet the twins. I'll catch you both later." Kyler turns to me with a smile. "Nice to meet you, Dani. Welcome home." And then he's out the door. Twins? Jesus, what a player.

Zach must be able to sense my judgment, because he playfully nudges my arm and laughs. "The twins are his older twin sisters, Lauren and Kate. They live here in town. They meet usually once a week for dinner. Sometimes they come out for karaoke night, so you might be able to meet them soon."

My eyes go wide at the mention of karaoke and meeting new people. I don't know about all that; I'm just trying to make it through the day on my own.

Zach slaps his hands on his thighs and rises off the couch. "Come on, I'll give you the tour and show you the guest room. It's yours for as long as you like. I'll order a pizza, and we can get you settled and catch up. Still prefer ham and pineapple?"

"Sounds great."

Zach's house is a rancher-style house. There are three bedrooms and two baths. One bathroom is attached to Zach's room, and the other is in the hallway between Kyler's room and the room I'll be staying in. I grew up with my own bathroom but shared one with Em and Zach when I would visit the apartment, so I'm sure I could share a bathroom with Kyler, or maybe I could ask Zach if I could just use his at times.

The kitchen is beautiful. There's a giant island with a marble countertop. I could see myself spending hours in here baking and making a giant mess. I'm sure my brother missed my baking. I have a lot of making up to do, so might as well start as soon as possible through his stomach.

Dinner arrives not long after we unload the last box of mine into my room. I prefer a minimalist lifestyle just in case I feel the need to pack up and leave quickly; all of my belongings fit in my Toyota RAV4.

Zach drops the pizzas on the island as I take a seat on a barstool at the counter, then heads to the fridge and grabs two beers. Setting one down in front of me, he laughs. "Damn, that feels weird giving you one, even though I know you're twenty-one now. Still weird. Another milestone we missed, huh." He quickly takes a sip of his beer and looks anywhere but at me.

He finally turns back to me, and his face grows serious. "Can I ask you a question?" I nod and set down my slice of pizza. "Why now? Why after all this time did you finally call?"

I knew this question would come up sooner or later when he didn't ask on the phone. "That's kind of a complicated answer to give. There were times that I had thought I would show up randomly at Mom and Dad's door. I even packed up my whole apartment once and got into my car to head home, but I couldn't turn my car on." I take a sip of my beer. I might need to ask for something stronger if I want to get through this conversation.

"Anyways, one night I had this dream...well, it was more of a nightmare, and I had woken up covered in sweat, which sadly wasn't anything new, but I couldn't get rid of this weird feeling and could remember the whole thing. Over the next week, I kept hearing the song 'Count on Me' by Bruno Mars. Like literally, everywhere. It played at the restaurant I was waitressing in, the local coffee shop I went to, the grocery store, and the car. It's not like it was a newer song. But it just felt like a sign. So, I finally found the strength to press Send."

I let my brother process that before I change the subject to break some of the tension in the room.

"So, what have you been up to the past four years?"

"Well." He pauses as if he is trying to decide what to say. "Well, when I graduated UPenn, I started full-time at the sports marketing firm in the city that I had interned at senior year. I really love it. I get to spend my days watching sports and get paid for it. Still have dinner with Mom, Dad, and the Hankses once a week, although with my work schedule we've been doing more brunches or early dinners. You should come. I know everyone would want to see you."

The mention of the Hanks family makes my stomach tie in a knot. I'm not ready to face them. The people who were my second family, my future in-laws...no, I can't.

My face must falter because he sets his pizza back on the plate and reaches for my wrist. "When you're ready, okay? I'm not going to push you. I'm just glad you're here."

Pulling me into another tight hug, Zach whispers into my hair, "God I missed you so much, Dani. I've looked at my phone so many times the past few days to make sure you calling wasn't actually a dream." His grip on me tightens as if he doesn't want to let me go, and I realize my grip on him is just as tight.

"I'm here. I'm not going anywhere," I respond, and I can feel him instantly relax. As long as I keep telling myself that I'm not going anywhere, maybe I'll believe it. I want to believe my words.

I stand and take my plate to the sink. "Well, it's been a long day. Is it okay that I take a quick shower and head to bed? We can catch up more tomorrow." I want to reassure him that I'll still be here in the morning.

He smiles, and I can genuinely tell my brother is happy to have me back. I'm still deciding how I feel about it. "Of course, we can talk more tomorrow." I wrap my arms around my brother's waist, and he kisses the top of my head. "Night, sis."

"Night, Zachy." I hear him laugh at the childhood nickname as I walk toward the bathroom.

I don't even grab a change of clothes from my room, but I'm happy that I placed my toiletry bag in there earlier this evening. I just need to feel the warm water run over me. I've been on my own for so long, it feels weird being in the presence of others, even if it's just my brother, someone I grew up with my entire life. Turning the water on, I strip out of my clothes and stare at my naked body in the mirror. When I see my reflection, I don't really recognize it. I miss how Emmett used to look at me and tell me how beautiful I was.

The first time he saw me naked, I was so nervous. He had seen me in bikinis for years, but being completely naked left me feeling vulnerable. I tried to cover myself up with my hands, and Em pulled my arms away and told me, "Never cover yourself up from me, baby girl. I love you—all of you—even the parts you don't like about yourself. I—" He kissed my forehead. "—love—" Then my cheek. "—all—" My neck. "—of—" My collarbone. "—you." And just above where my breasts were. We were fifteen and sixteen when we lost our virginity to each other. Em had been my first for everything: first crush, first boyfriend, first kiss, first...and only sexual partner, and first heartbreak.

I shake the thoughts away before I get lost in the tears. Now that I'm living with Zach and his roommate, I want to limit the times I cry in public. When I am alone in my room, all bets are off.

I pull back the shower curtain, which may I mention seems to be a little girly for being Kyler's bathroom. Hmm, maybe he's gay, although judging by the way he looked at me when I arrived, I'm thinking that is probably not the case. Knowing my mom, she might have decorated the whole house.

Aware that I am not living alone and not wanting to use up all the hot water, I try to take a quick shower. As the water runs over my face, I can't help but let the tears fall that I have been keeping in all day since I walked up to the front door. When I step out of the shower, I can hear Zach talking on the other side of the door. I'm not sure if he's on the phone or if Kyler has come back from his night out. I wrap the towel around me and run my fingers through my wet hair. I'm too tired to blow-dry it tonight, so natural waves tomorrow it is. It'll be a nice change from the daily messy bun I've been rocking for a while now.

I am lost in thought when I open the door and walk into the hallway straight into...Kyler. I yelp and almost lose my towel, causing me to grab on to it tight. His hands are on my arms in a heartbeat to steady me. Since I'm only five foot five, he looks down at me and directly into my eyes. "You okay? I didn't mean to scare you."

Catching my breath, I realize his hands are still on me, and my eyes drop to where he's touching my naked skin. He notices and quickly drops his hands, leaving one by his side and running the other through his hair, forcing some of it back in his eyes. My heart begins to beat a little faster. Why do I feel like I want to brush it away?

"Yeah, I'm fine, but you're kind of blocking my door," I snap a little harsher than planned, but I need a quick escape from his presence.

Living with Zach is one thing, but I'm not sure if I can handle living with a stranger. Kyler steps aside and I walk past him toward my room. I hear him say softly, "Good night, Dani," as he walks into the bathroom and closes the door.

I enter my bedroom and close the door behind me. Searching through the boxes for some clothes, I find one of Emmett's T-shirts and throw on a pair of shorts. Yes, I still sleep in his shirts. I know they don't smell like him anymore. I tried to go a while without washing them in hopes that they would never lose his scent, but then it started to fade and they started to smell, so I was forced to wash them. I look around at this room and decide I won't unpack much tonight, but I do browse some boxes in search of a few items I need to sleep: my phone charger, my iPod and headphones, and the photo of Emmett and me that is always on my nightstand. I plug my phone into the charger and set it down on the nightstand along with the photo, and unwrap my headphones from around the iPod.

I turn the light off and walk back carefully to ensure I don't knock over any boxes. Climbing into bed, I find it's definitely more comfortable than anything I've slept on in a while. I stare at Em's photo and kiss my fingers, placing them on his face in the photo. Tomorrow is another day, another day I have to wake up without him. I can do this. Deep breath in and deep breath out.

I set the frame back on the nightstand. "I love you, baby." I pause as if he were responding with *"I love you, Cupcake,"* then sink down into the covers and say, "Forever and always." I put the earbuds in my ears and turn on the song that has been on repeat to help me dream of Em at night, "Forever" by the Beach Boys.

CHAPTER 17
KYLER

I look over at my cell phone and it reads 2:00 a.m. Fuck! I've been staring at my ceiling for hours since I got back home from dinner with my sisters. My mind is racing with thoughts of that beautiful bombshell sleeping in the room next to mine. I've seen photos of Dani obviously—we have them all over the house—but they were from four years ago or earlier. She is simply the most beautiful woman I have ever seen. Opening that door and seeing her standing there took my breath away, like literally took it away. I guess in my mind I had still pictured the young girl in the photos, not the woman she has become.

I saw the way she looked at me, and if we were living in a movie or one of those silly romance novels Lauren is obsessed with reading, then I should have pulled her into my arms right there and given her a kiss to end all kisses. But this isn't the movies or a romance novel—this is real life. I'm well aware of her backstory. I couldn't image losing the love of my life at such a young age or, well, any age actually.

Zach and I met the second semester of freshman year in English Lit, just after the accident. I had moved into the apartment the weekend she up and left. Over the years, I've seen the struggle in Zach's eyes of dealing with Emmett's death and Dani being gone.

When Zach mentioned the other day that she had finally called, I didn't hesitate saying yes when he asked if I minded if she stayed with us for a little while. He broke down in front of me, explaining how he had hoped and prayed every day that it would be the day she would finally call. I didn't know why after all this time she called, and it didn't matter. All that mattered was that she was here, but she is now consuming all of my thoughts, causing me to still be awake at this hour when I have a shit ton of work to do tomorrow.

If I can get through growing up with Lauren and Kate, then I can get through living with Dani, although I didn't expect her to take residency in my brain. When Zach extended the invitation of staying around to join them for a pizza and a movie, I seriously thought about canceling on my sisters, but I think they needed time alone to talk and catch up, not to mention if I bailed on Lauren and Kate I never would have heard the end of it. They knew something was up with me when they got to the restaurant.

"What's up, asshole?" Lauren said as she slapped her hand on my shoulder before taking her jacket off and placing it in the corner of the booth. I stood up and kissed her cheek.

"Hey, where's mine?" her identical twin sister, Kate, said, coming up behind me and capturing me in a hug. My sisters and I are five years apart, and we weren't super close growing up. It wasn't till they had gone off to college that we got close, which seems silly since they no longer lived at home anymore.

I leaned back and kissed Kate's cheek too. "Always a joy seeing you both," I said, rolling my eyes as I took another swig of my beer. Kate and Lauren both took a seat across from me.

"What the hell has your panties in a bunch, Ky," Kate spat

out. *My mind went back to the sweet brunette who showed up at my door an hour ago, and unknowingly, a smile hit my lips.*

"Holy shit, that looks like a smile on his face. Little brother's in love!"

"Oh yeah, look at him blushing."

My sisters were ridiculous. Why did I meet them out again? The waitress came to the table and took their drink order. They may be identical, but their styles were completely different. Lauren was more of a girly girl and ordered a cosmo, channeling her inner Carrie Bradshaw—for the record, I never watched Sex in the City *but had heard my sister call herself that plenty of times before. Kate, however, was the opposite. She was an artist who danced to the beat of her own drum. Her short brown hair with pink streaks throughout started out as a rebellion phase to tell them apart but became her signature look. Kate also didn't believe in "girly drinks," which was why she ordered an IPA on tap and a shot of whiskey.*

Silence descended over the table, and I hoped they would forget and move on to a new subject. The waitress came back and brought their drinks and a refill for me. Kate threw back the shot and slammed it on the table. "Okay, little bro. Spill."

I took a sip of my beer. "It's nothing really."

Lauren cut me off. "Nope, not buying it. It's clearly something, or you would just come out and say it."

I took a deep breath. "Okay, fine. God you guys suck. Remember I told you that Zach's sister would be staying with us for a while?"

"His sister who ran away and he hasn't seen in years?"

I nodded. "She didn't just run away; her boyfriend died, and she wasn't coping, so she ran. I mean, I guess there are worse things she could've done. Anyway, she...Danielle...Dani arrived today. Zach wasn't home yet, so I let her in just before I left to come meet you guys."

"What's she like?"

"I don't know, I spent maybe ten minutes around her. She looks a lot like Zach; I can see how he said when they were younger people thought they were twins for real."

The waitress took our food order and left us alone again. My throat was getting drier by the second as I sat there thinking about Dani, but I had to pace my drinking. Couldn't be arriving back home drunk. Lord help me, what I might do then.

"So, what's the problem, then?" Lauren questioned innocently, but Kate was looking into me like she saw right through me.

The light in Kate's eyes got brighter as she realized. "You like her!"

"Ha! How could I like her? I don't even know her. But fuck... she is beautiful. I'm in trouble." I ran my fingers through my hair before placing my hands on the back of my neck and exhaling a long breath. I was in trouble for sure.

As our food arrived, Lauren spoke up. "Let me just say this, Kyler, because we love you and want what's best for you... Be careful. I don't know what she went through, but there's a reason she up and left without a word. You don't know if she is going to leave again or if she's even..."

Before I let her finish, I interrupted. "I get you looking out for me, but I'm not looking to marry the girl. Just going to live with her for a little while, while she gets her shit together. Just relax, okay? I'm a big boy. Thanks for the concern, Mom."

My sister's foot came in contact with my shin. "Ow! What the fuck was that for?"

Kate shoved a forkful of pasta into her mouth. "Because you're an asshole, a royal asshole."

We spent the rest of dinner discussing typical bullshit as we usually do. I loved meeting up with them, and I knew they meant well.

When I arrived home, I expected to find Zach and Danielle on the couch watching a movie. I hadn't been out too late, but when I walked in the front door, I found Zach spread out on the couch alone on the phone and Danielle nowhere in sight. He put his hand over the phone. "Hey, man, how was dinner?"

"It was good. The girls send their love, and Kate says whenever you're ready to get back on the market, you know where to find her."

He laughed, and I heard a mumble on the other end of the phone to which Zach responded, "Ky sends his love, babe."

I rolled my eyes and laughed. "Everything go okay here?"

He nodded. "Yeah, it was fine. Leftover pizza is in the fridge. Dani was tired, so she went to bed."

It was my turn to nod. "I'm going to take a shower and head to bed, too. See ya tomorrow, man."

"Later," Zach yelled as I headed into the hall toward our rooms.

I was too busy lost in my own thoughts and looking at the floor that I didn't notice the bathroom door swing open and Danielle walking out until she was pressed up against my chest. She made the cutest yelp, and I reached my arms out to steady her. Her skin was so soft, and holy shit she was only in a towel. Her hands squeezed the towel tighter since she almost lost her grip on it when she jumped. I had no intention of scaring her—I thought she had already gone to bed like Zach said, otherwise I may have been on the lookout for her. I needed to figure out what it was about this girl that made me so nervous. It took everything I had in me to keep my cock from being at full attention while she was standing in front of me in just a towel.

"You okay? I didn't mean to scare you."

I also didn't mean for my hands to linger on her naked arms as long as they did, but once I had my hands on her, I wasn't sure I could — or wanted to — take them off her. It was like her skin was setting me on fire, something I'd never felt before, and I'd had my hands on my fair share of women. Her eyes moved down to where I was still holding her, and I quickly released her from my grasp.

I ran my hand through my hair, having no idea what to do next.

"Yeah, I'm fine, but you're kind of blocking my door." Her tone matched her icy glare.

I stepped to the side to allow her in the guest room. I definitely needed a shower now. Making my way to the bathroom, I looked over my shoulder and said softly as she entered her room, "Good night, Dani." When I heard her door click shut, I finally relaxed.

Stepping into the shower, I let the warm water run down my body before my hand found its way to my hard cock. I imagined my hand was actually hers, stroking me before dropping to her knees in front of me and wrapping those luscious lips of hers around me, teasing me with her tongue. My hand wrapped in her hair, pushing her head to take me further till I came down the back of her throat. With each pump, I imagined her blue eyes staring up at me while she took me in her mouth, enjoying it as much as I did.

Trying to keep my sounds down, I made a fist and bit down on my knuckle, grunting as quietly as I could as I sent myself over the edge to my release, letting my load fall straight down the drain. Shit, that was intense. I placed my forehead against the cold tile. It hadn't even been twelve hours that she'd been here, and I'd already jerked off to fantasies of her.

I had gone straight to my room after the shower incident, thinking I would just crash hard, post-orgasm, and wake up feeling better, however this girl has somehow taken residency in my brain and I'm not sure what to do with that. Tossing and turning, I decide to go to the kitchen to get a glass of water. I don't bother putting on shorts or a shirt—everyone should be asleep, so I don't care if I'm walking around my house in just boxers. I quietly open my bedroom door and slowly walk past her closed door to the kitchen, grab my water, and slowly creep back. I place my ear to her bedroom door to see if I hear her awake, but I'm met with silence. I'm glad she is relaxed enough to have fallen asleep—that makes one of us. I tiptoe back into my room and finish my water knowing that I will probably have to take a piss at some point in the night, but whatever.

If I'm going to be anything but useless tomorrow at work, then I better cut this shit out and fall asleep. I find the remote on the nightstand and turn on Netflix. Maybe I just need some background noise to drown out my thoughts. Turning on an episode of *The Office*, I barely make it through one episode before I am off in la-la land dreaming of that beautiful brunette sleeping just a few feet from me. Maybe in some way, she is dreaming of me too and we can meet up in our dreams, in a world where her heart hasn't been crushed into a million pieces and could even fathom giving it to someone like me.

CHAPTER 18

Danielle

The past week, we have fallen into a groove. I cooked and cleaned up in gratitude for Zach and Kyler allowing me to stay here. I haven't found a job yet, but I have a few good leads to follow up on. Thankfully I was paid pretty well at my last job, so I was able to save up a good amount since I never went out, lived a minimalist lifestyle, and needed to prove I could support myself on my own. I also haven't reached out to my parents, but knowing Zach, they are well aware that I am here and alive and well. I honestly wouldn't put it past them to have done few drive-bys, but I'm sure it took an incredible amount of strength for them not to get out of the car and barge into the house and find me.

Haylee is another person I haven't reached out to yet. All Zach has told me is that she is doing well. I feel guilty that I haven't called her yet, but I was supposed to be her best friend and I just dropped her without a word. Asking about where she is and what she is doing in life almost feels like an intrusion. I figured when I finally have the courage to reach out to my parents, I will reach out to her too. Who knows, she might just tell me fuck off or hang up on me. If I were her, I would.

With my back to Kyler, I turn the water on to begin doing the dishes from dinner. Zach still hasn't arrived home yet, so I made sure to set aside a plate for him. Over the sound of the running water, I can hear the opening of the container that contained the cupcakes I had baked this afternoon—strawberry cupcakes with a champagne buttercream frosting. They became my signature cupcakes over the years. I always loved baking them when I was younger because I thought I was getting away with murder when Mom would buy me champagne for the frosting when I wasn't even old enough to drink. I loved baking —one day I had planned to open my own bakery where I could spend all day doing what I loved and spend my nights with the man I loved. Emmett could come home from a hard day's work at the office to dinner made and a fresh-baked dessert each night. We would need to find ways to make sure we kept all the extra pounds off from all the sweet treats, but with Emmett I couldn't resist that smile.

My breath catches as I try to push back the thought along with all the memories, hopes, dreams, and happily ever after. They all died four years ago along with Em. I can feel my eyes filling with tears, but I can't do this now, here. I refuse to let them spill over, especially not in front of Kyler. Kyler Lawson...I don't know much about him except for the fact he is Emmett's replacement in my brother's life.

To keep from crying, I go to my happy place. It's the only place that has gotten me through the past four years. Oh, how I wish I could just stay there and not in the bleak reality of life without him. My happy place is where I feel whole, not this sorry excuse of a shell. I envision Em standing next to me, putting his arms around my waist, his front to my back, rubbing his nose up and down on my neck as he inhales my vanilla perfume, kissing my shoulder before whispering...

"Mmmmm...I love you, cupcake."

CRASH!

I'm instantly pulled back to reality as I hear Kyler's foot-steps rushing over to me, avoiding the broken glass of the Pyrex casserole dish that I dropped. Glass is all over the counter and on the floor in front of the sink.

"Fuck! Dani, are you okay?"

I am in a trance still, frozen in space. Did I hear those words in real life? But how? I know they weren't just in my head this time, right? Maybe I'm losing my mind.

"Dani? Dani? Are you hurt? What happened?" Kyler is looking at me directly in the eyes, cupping my cheeks, trying to bring me down from my shock.

His eyes drift down my body, inspecting me. "Holy shit, Dani, you're bleeding." Taking my hands, he safely escorts me to the other side of the island and pulls out the stool for me to take a seat in. Kyler leaves the room and returns just as quickly as he left with a first aid kit in hand. Taking a seat next to me, he takes my left hand in his. There's a gash on my palm. Blood has always made me a little queasy but not in this moment.

"Dani? Look at me. What happened over there?"

Finally making eye contact with him, I cock my head to the side. "Why are you looking at me like I've got three heads or something," he asks me while cleaning my wound. It makes me flinch a little.

"Ow, that stings."

"Well, I'm no doctor, but I don't think you'll need stitches. It looks worse than it is."

If only he knew the awful pain that's on the inside. Studying him, I try to divert my attention away from my hand by looking into his eyes. Wow, they are the most beautiful shade of chestnut brown with golden specks in them. My gaze travels from his eyes down to his mouth. What would it feel like to press my lips against his? My stomach drops, realizing I just had that thought about another man. Someone not Emmett...what the hell is wrong with me?

While I'm distracted with my inner turmoil, I didn't notice Kyler finishing up with the bandage on my hand. He then raises my palm to his lips and presses a brief kiss over the bandage. It startles me to say the least. That is the first time another man has kissed me. Em was the only man to ever do any of those things.

"Ummm, thank you." I pull my hand back to my chest and take a moment to breathe before I go to get up off the stool. I must get up a little too fast because I am shaky on my feet when I stand. Maybe the thought of blood had made me weak after all.

Kyler grabs my arm and says, "Why don't you go lie down. I can clean this up."

I nod. Kyler heads to the mess I left on the floor while I make my way out of the kitchen. I glance over my shoulder, planning to steal one last look at this man who is messing with my head, but instead my eyes meet his as if we were magnetized. I swallow hard, wishing that I could explain this pull between us. His expression is intense and burning a hole right through me. He breaks eye contact first, and I make my escape, not looking back again.

KYLER

I am throwing away the last of the broken glass in the trash can, when Zach enters the kitchen, setting his keys and workbag on the counter.

"Whoa! What happened in here?"

He opens the fridge and grabs the leftovers of the delicious veggie lasagna Danielle had made earlier and two beers. He opens them both and passes one to me.

"Care to explain?" He tips his fork toward the dustpan and broom by the trashcan before taking a bite.

I shake my head. "Honestly, man, I don't have a clue. I mean, your sister and I had a nice evening chatting, she was standing there doing the dishes, and I just had to try one of those amazing cupcakes she made. That shit is heaven, like borderline orgasmic.

"I even confessed my undying love for the damn thing, telling the cupcake how much I loved it. The next thing I know, Dani dropped the Pyrex dish and it shattered everywhere. It scared the shit out of me. I ran over to her, but it was like she was paralyzed. It took me a few minutes to drag her out of the state she was in. She ended up cutting her hand."

"What? Is she okay?" His eyes widen with concern.

"Yeah, it was just a little cut. I tended to the wound, and she ended up going to bed. I guess it just slipped out of her hands, but her reaction to it...it was strange."

Zach turns to me with a confused look similar to mine. "What exactly did you say to the cupcake?" He lets out a small chuckle, taking another bite of lasagna.

Laughing, I look at him like *are you for real?* "I don't know, man. 'I love you, cupcake' or something."

Zach blows out a breath and puts his head down on his arms, mumbling something under his breath.

"Am I missing something here?" I take a sip of my beer and try to figure out the missing piece.

"It's not your fault, Ky. You didn't know."

"That she doesn't believe in love at first bite?" I ask jokingly. This whole conversation is a little weird. What am I missing here?

"Emmett." I'm still not following here. "Emmett used to call her Cupcake." He pauses. "He used to say 'I love you, Cupcake,' and she would respond, 'Forever and always.' God they were sickening."

I snicker. "Hmm, sounds like another couple I know."

He laughs and shakes his head. "Nope, not even close."

I settle into my seat and place my head in my hands. "She must think I'm the biggest asshole ever."

"Hey, don't worry about it. How could you know? She won't talk about it, about him." He takes a swig of his beer. "I guess I should be happy that she came home, huh."

He gets up and places his empty container in the sink and walks the empty beer bottle over to the trash can. It clanks against the shattered glass when he drops it in. "Sorry about all that, man. Thanks for cleaning this whole mess up and taking care of her hand." Slapping me on the back, he grabs his workbag and heads toward his room.

Danielle Jacobs really is the whole deal, beautiful and talented, but I have to remember that she is off-limits. She's so closed off, and while I wouldn't want to take Emmett's place, maybe one day she'll see me as something other than his replacement.

I finish tidying up the kitchen, grab another beer, and head toward the living room to watch some TV.

CHAPTER 19
KYLER

"What a fucking workout. I'm not gonna be able to move my arms for the rest of the weekend." Zach stretches his arms out after he parks his Jeep in the driveway.

"Hey, I didn't say I was gonna go easy on ya, ya fuckin pussy." I punch his arm as I pass him on the walkway to the front door. He winces and rubs his arm as he meets me on the front porch, while I insert and turn my house key into the front door lock. When we reach the living room, we're both stopped dead in our tracks by the most amazing voice I have ever heard. The shower was running from our bathroom. Dani must be playing some music or something.

"Wow, I haven't heard her sing in so long." Zach leans up against the arm of the couch and takes a drink from his water bottle.

Holy shit, that is Dani actually singing? "That's your sister singing? As in that's her voice?" He nods. We both stay in place, listening to the emotion in her voice while she sings. She must not have heard us come in.

I can hear her crying while singing. Shit, I'm on the verge of tears just listening to her. She has the voice of a fucking angel. We continue to listen in silence as she sings a second song. If you heard her voice, you wouldn't have been able to move either. The first song I only recognized because I saw Snow Patrol in concert once in college, but this one, I don't know that I've heard it before.

"Damn, she can cook, *and* she can sing. Is there anything your sister can't do?"

Zach's head is still down. "Yeah. Moving on."

"Huh?" I'm not sure what he means by that, but before I can ask more, he rises to his feet.

"Nothing, man. Just that song." He speaks so softly that if I wasn't really paying attention, I would've missed it. He looks back at the bathroom door and then walks to his room. I'm not sure what that was about. I hear the shower turn off, and my heart begins to race knowing that I will see her in just a few minutes. I've never been affected by a girl this way. I start to panic and try to figure out what I should do. Should I be sitting here and tell her I was listening? No, that sounds creepy. I can run to my room or the kitchen and hide till I know she is in her room. Before I can make up my mind, the bathroom door opens. Holy shit, she's only in a towel...*again.*

Damnit! Don't stare, dude.

She has her head down as she walks out, not noticing me standing there frozen. When she finally looks up, she yells, "Fucking hell, Kyler! You need to stop doing that." She tightens her grip on her towel. Wow, I'm having a bit of déjà vu here.

Her eyes are bloodshot and rimmed with red, a telltale sign that she's been crying. I go to step forward to comfort her and think better of it—one, that might be weird, and two, she is in a towel.

"I'm sorry, I didn't realize anyone was home," she says shyly once her breathing goes back to normal.

I don't want to embarrass her or myself for that matter since

I have been sitting here listening to her, so I decide the better approach is to say, "We just walked in the door."

Her eyes take me in. I'm covered in sweaty gym clothes; I know this shirt is sticking to my body in a possibly unappealing way. After a few moments, my ego starts to swell—and so is another part of my body with the way she's looking at me. Holy fuck, Dani is totally checking me out. I need to calm down or she's going to notice my excitement down below. Clearly, my dick doesn't want to listen to me and is enjoying the attention a little too much.

Bringing her attention back to me, I duck down to look her in the eyes. "Earth to Dani," I joke.

She snaps out of her trance. "What?"

"Can I get in there to take a shower?" I ask with a smirk.

"Oh yeah, sure. Let me just grab my things and the bathroom's all yours."

I watch her gather up her belongings, and then she slips by me and heads to her room. I let out the breath I've been holding and walk into the bathroom, shutting the door behind me. As I turn on the shower and strip from my gross clothes, I can still smell her vanilla scent. I wonder if that's perfume or body wash. It smells heavenly. What the hell is wrong with me?

I shake the thoughts from my mind before I need to rub one out here in the shower...again...with her just a few feet away from me. I'm thankful my post-gym routine includes a cold shower. It is definitely needed.

I WALK OUT OF MY ROOM AFTER MY WEEKLY CHECK-IN CALL with my mom and find Zach on the couch watching what looks like might be home movies. "Hey, man," I say, and he startles.

"Oh sorry, didn't see ya there. Have you been standing there long?" he replies.

"No, I just got off the phone with mama dukes." I take a seat next to him and see a younger version of him and Emmett in a tux—prom maybe?

I can't help but let out a laugh.

"Dude, what the fuck is in your hair? Is that shit flammable?"

"Fuck off," he says, punching me in the arm. He laughs and turns back to the TV. "That used to take me an hour to perfect the rolled-out-of-bed look."

On the screen, Zach keeps adjusting his collar, and he looks like he might want to be anywhere but there. Emmett playfully shoves Zach. "Knock it off, dude. Melissa isn't going to stand you up. She should be here soon."

"Ha! I'm not worried about that. She'll be here. She wouldn't miss what I have planned for us after prom, if you know what I mean." He elbows Em and winks. Wow, my best friend, everyone. Emmett playfully pushes Zach, shaking his head.

"Un-freakin-believable. Keep it in your pants, Jacobs."

"Whatever. I know you have something planned. Don't act like you don't. Just keep that shit to yourself."

They both laugh as he tries to shove him back. Emmett is bigger than Zach and he barely moves.

There is a throat clearing in the background of the video, and they stop their shoving contest to turn their attention toward the front porch of the house. Standing there is a younger version of Dani, the one I'm used to seeing in photos. Wow, she is beautiful, absolutely stunning.

"Dani, wave to the camera," I hear an adult male voice say. Sounds like its Mr. Jacobs's voice.

"Dad, you're embarrassing me," she says. "Can't you point that thing somewhere else?"

The camera quickly turns to show another couple. Oh shit! That's Haylee. Look at her all dolled up.

"That guy was such a douche bag. I can't believe she went with him." Zach leans his elbows on his knees and runs his fingers through his hair. He exhales a loud breath. "This is so stupid. I need to talk to her."

After a moment, the camera goes back to Dani. Sporting a smile from ear to ear, a smile she no longer wears, the camera zooms out and I see the reason for her smile. Emmett is walking up the front porch steps carrying a corsage.

"You look gorgeous, baby." He then dips her into a deep kiss. That's pretty ballsy to kiss his girl like that in front of her parents. Emmett places the corsage on her wrist. I really didn't think she could smile any bigger, but I was wrong. Fuck what I wouldn't give to be able to see that smile in real life. She smiles sometimes, but it's a sad smile, mainly forced. Dani and Emmett pose for a few photos. They look so happy, the poster couple for young love.

The song I didn't recognize earlier begins to play in the background.

"What song is that?"

"'Forever' by the Beach Boys. It was their song." Zach doesn't even take his eyes off the screen. I notice he is focused on the background and not his sister and Em slow dancing in the front yard. I totally see what Zach was talking about with the grossly cute shit. He's right, he is not *that* bad, but pretty close.

The video zooms in on them. "I love you, Cupcake."

He looks at her like she is his entire world. She looks right back at him with the same look.

"Forever and always," she responds before she kisses him.

We are in the zone when we hear a loud noise. "What the fuck are you doing?" I hear Dani scream. Her voice causes us both to turn our heads toward her.

"I said, what the fuck are you doing? How dare you," she spits out at her brother. Tears are freely streaming down her cheeks. I look over at Zach, who balls his fists together. I have a feeling shit is about to hit the fan. Dani stomps over to her brother, demanding the remote to turn the video off. He refuses to give it to her or turn it off.

"How dare I? Are you kidding me right now? How dare you!" Zach rises to his feet. "You act like you're the only one to have ever lost someone they love. You think you're the only one who lost someone that day? I lost my best friend, Haylee lost a brother, Natalie and Brian lost a son. I am so sorry that you lost the love of your life, I truly am, but what about the rest of us?"

I have never seen my best friend this angry. He is pacing the living room and running his fingers through his hair.

"Fuck! Danielle, I didn't just lose Em that day—I lost you too. I lost my sister. Haylee lost her best friend. We needed you and you were so fucking selfish living in your own world that you cut us all out too. We were all grieving, but you didn't care —it didn't matter. For fuck's sake, Dani, you fucking abandoned us! You just left us behind to put back the pieces of our broken world and try to move on. Do you think that's been easy?! I miss him—I miss him every godforsaken day. He was my best friend, my brother. Some days I have to just force myself out of bed in hopes that when I walk into the kitchen I'll see him sitting at the island drinking out of that ridiculous Batman mug, that when my phone chimes it's a text from him seeing if I want to get a beer after work, or that I would've gotten a chance to give a kick-ass best man speech at yours and his wedding so that I could spill all the stupid embarrassing things over the years. I started planning that speech at thirteen because somewhere deep down I knew you two were the real deal. Sounds ridiculous, doesn't it?"

I don't want to look over at Dani, but I'm afraid that if I don't she may just disappear into thin air. I quickly glance at her; I'm not even sure if she's breathing right now. I want to go comfort her, but I can't move. I need to let Zach get this out and remember this isn't my place to do that. I rise from the couch and walk into the kitchen to give them space. Zach's voice is loud enough that I can still hear him clearly in the other room.

"I can't say that I know what you're going through because I don't know exactly, but I hurt too. You can't even say his name. Emmett. Say it... *Em-mett*." He makes sure to enunciate each syllable.

"You, Dani, are still here. For some fucking reason that I'm still trying to figure out, he isn't. He was denied all his dreams and plans. He wouldn't want you to be living this bullshit excuse for a life that you are. He would want you to live, to move on. You can do that without forgetting. I do it every. Fucking. Day. You say you want to start over and move on, but look at you—have you even gone home to see Mom and Dad, visit the cemetery, or hell, even call Haylee? Yeah, I didn't fucking think so. So, dear sweet sister, if you want to talk about selfish, I suggest you look in a fucking mirror." I hear him walk to grab his keys followed by the slamming of the front door.

I wait three seconds...and return to the living room. Dani is no longer there. Oh shit, did she leave too? I didn't hear the front door close twice. Walking toward her room, I see that the door is opened a little, and I can hear her sobbing on the bed. Fuck, what do I do? I shoot a text to Zach to make sure he's okay.

ME: *You okay, man?*

ME: *Please don't do something stupid.*

ZACH: *Yeah, I needed to get out of there. Sorry to blow up like that. I'm heading over to Haylee's. I'll be back later or maybe in the morning. Idk.*

Okay, one Jacobs checked on. Against my better judgment, I push Dani's door open a little and walk into her room. There are lots of boxes still not unpacked, some open with clothes hanging out. Guess she wasn't sure how long she would be staying. Without saying a word, I walk over to the side of her bed and sit down. She is facing away from me, gripping a photo frame that I'm pretty sure is safe to assume is a photo of Emmett.

I sit on the edge of the bed and place my hand on her shoulder. We aren't that close—hell, we only met two weeks ago—but it's breaking my heart seeing her this upset. In the short amount of time I have known her, she has found her way into my heart somehow. I wait a few moments before I shift on the bed, planning to get up and give her some time to herself. She probably just wants to be left alone. She places her hand on mine to keep me in place. I nod, acknowledging I won't go anywhere, even though I know she can't see me. I take my hand from her shoulder and begin rubbing her back while she lets out what seems to be a nonstop flow of tears. When I hear her breathing even out, I assume she finally fell asleep. I decide to close my eyes and try to steady my breaths.

I wake up a few hours later—shit, when did I fall asleep? I look over to the side of the bed where Dani was, and it's empty. Where is she? Getting up from the bed, I walk quietly to the hallway. Zach's door is closed, and I slowly open it to see my best friend still hasn't returned. I see a light coming from the living room and hear voices. Man, I'm having a bit of déjà vu here from earlier today.

Quietly, I walk to the living room but stand back so I can give Dani privacy. Crossing my arms and feet, I lean against the wall. On the screen, I see what looks to be Dani and Emmett at an ice rink. Is that Backstreet Boys playing in the background? I remember my sisters arguing who was better, them or *NSYNC. Personally, I don't get the appeal or anything, but then again I'm a dude. Ha! Look at that little fucker, Zach, on the screen. Damn, I'm glad he grew out of that awkward stage. I'm not sure if I could be friends with him with all that gel shit.

I can't help but laugh out loud when I see young Dani and Emmett turn their heads when the camera moves to reveal Zach flat on his ass on the ice. With my laugh, Dani jumps and pauses the DVD.

"I'm sorry, I didn't know you were there." She wipes tears from her eyes. Shit, how many tears is one person allowed in life because I feel like this girl has had her fill for a lifetime, maybe even two.

"No, I'm sorry, I should've let you know I was there instead of standing there like a stalker. I'll go to my room and leave you be." As I go to turn, she quietly says, "No, please stay."

Turning back toward her, I walk to the couch and sit down. We watch more of the DVD in silence. Unsure what to say, I go with the first thing that pops in my head. "I'm sorry I didn't get to meet him. I transferred to UPenn the semester after the accident. Zach and I had freshman English together and hit it off. Next thing I knew we were best friends. I eventually moved into the apartment. I'm not trying to replace him, you know." Man, the words just keep spilling even though I try to tell my brain to shut the hell up. I don't seem to have a filter for words or actions around this girl.

Looking over at me with the saddest eyes, Dani just nods. Her eyes lock on mine. God, the hurt and pain she's gone through in her young life is just unfair. The pain they all suffered, I would do anything to take that away. I'm not sure exactly how long we stare at each other, but our attention is drawn back to the video when we hear everyone sing Dani Happy Birthday.

"There was no shortage of love, and Em was never embarrassed or held back how he felt even at only thirteen. I loved that about him so much..." She begins to choke on her words. I scoot over closer to her, wrap my arm around her, and rub her shoulders. She leans her head on my chest, and we sit in silence and finish watching the DVD.

Still wrapped in my arms, her breathing evens out. I think she's fallen asleep again. I wonder how many times she's cried herself to sleep the past four years. It breaks my heart to think that she shut everyone out from her life. That she went through all of this alone and didn't have someone here to hold her. I feel a weird sensation in my chest that I want to be the one to help her get through this. Does that make me an asshole? It's possible, but there is something about this girl that makes me hurt that she's hurting, or when I saw her smile in those videos, that made me smile too. Just being around her gives me peace. I kiss her temple and just hold her the rest of the night encased in my arms.

CHAPTER 20
Danielle

Thump. Thump. Thump. Thump.

I can hear the sounds of his heartbeat. I can feel the warmth of his arms surrounding me. I can feel the rising and lowering of his chest as he breathes, the hardness of his body pressed up against me. I lightly moan in appreciation that he is here with me as his arms tighten around me. That was the best sleep I've had in forever. It must have been because I was in his arms again. God it's been so long.

Wait, how is he here right now?

I quickly jump up out of his arms and off the couch. That's not Emmett—that's Kyler.

"Good morning," he says in a raspy voice.

Slowly he sits up and opens his eyes to find sheer terror on my face. I slept with another man.

Standing, he touches my cheek with one hand. "Hey, nothing happened, we just fell asleep. Why don't you see if Zach is back from Haylee's and I'll make us some coffee."

I nod. Wait, why would Zach be at Haylee's? As if he can read my mind, a look of panic crosses his face.

Just then the front door opens and there stands my brother. Before I can ask why he would be at Haylee's, I see that he is not alone. He walks in holding hands with none other than my best friend, or possibly former, I'm not really sure. I'm not sure that she would forgive me for how awful I was for leaving.

I look back at Kyler, then to Zach and Haylee and down to their hands. "Wait, why are you holding hands?"

I'm not prepared for what comes out of Zach's mouth next. Haylee grips onto his arm as if she is grounding him.

"Dani..." He pauses and looks down at her. "Hails and I are together. We've been dating for almost three years. I was waiting for the right time to tell you."

I plop down on the couch in shock. Yep, definitely did not see that coming. Silence consumes the room. Zach and Haylee? My brother and his best friend's sister? Zach and my best friend? Well, I guess hell has frozen over.

Haylee comes over and kneels on the floor in front of me and grabs my hands. She smiles at me, but I can see tears in her eyes. "Hey, bestie, it's been a while. About time you got your ass back here."

She then pulls me up into a hug. Kyler pulls on Zach's arm and says, "We'll be in the kitchen making coffee and breakfast and let the two of you catch up."

Still locked in Haylee's embrace, I am hit with memories of growing up with her. Happy memories followed by the emptiness of her face at Em's funeral. She rocked a blank expression for days, as did I. We were both empty and lost inside, and now she's with my brother? Are they in love? I don't even know where to begin, but for now I can feel her grip on me tighten. I hug her back. The past four years I have been without my best friend, and it's been difficult, but I also feel as though if I had stayed it would have been more difficult. I wonder what it was like for her here, but it clearly couldn't have been too bad if she found my brother.

I pull back. "So you and Zach?"

She blushes and smiles. I recognize that smile—it's one I used to wear. Not something I was used to seeing on Haylee though. That smile says it all: she's head over heels in love with my brother.

She sits on the couch and pats the spot next to her for me to sit.

I stare at the couch for a moment, the same couch Kyler and I had fallen asleep on, then take the seat next to her and pull my knees under me.

"I'm sorry, Hails, I should have called. I should've..."

How do I finish that statement? I should've kept in touch? I'm stuck in my own thoughts when Haylee finishes my sentence. "Never left."

Her words sting, but I know she is right. I hurt her—I hurt everyone when I left—but it had to be done for me. Losing Emmett, I knew I would be alone for the rest of my life, so it was inevitable that I would have to deal with it alone.

"I don't want to talk about that right now. Not before coffee at least," Haylee says, "Remember Mom used to say nothing good happens after 2:00 a.m. and before morning coffee."

Zach delivers us mugs full of coffee. We both say thank you to him, and he kisses the top of Haylee's head before he heads back into the kitchen. I readjust myself with my knees comfortably under me while Haylee pulls her feet up to sit Indian-style. It's clear the way they both looked at each other that they aren't just casually dating or fucking but are actually in love.

I can't take the awkward silence anymore, but Haylee must have the same thought because she goes to speak the same time I do.

"So you and Zach..."

"So me and Zach..."

We both giggle. I guess after all these years our brains are still in sync. Our moms use to joke that we shared the same brain because we were always known for saying the same thing or reaching for the same thing at the same time. I bite down on the side of my bottom lip. "You go first, Hails."

"Sure." She looks toward the kitchen and smiles, hearing Zach and Kyler goofing off in the kitchen while supposedly making breakfast. I've never seen this smile on her before. She is 100 percent in love, and it's weird that it's with my brother. Although when I think about it, I guess it shouldn't be too weird since the roles used to be reversed and she would watch me with the same look when I would look at her brother. But I mean, come on, this is Zach, the big manwhore in college—or well, at least he was in the first few months of his freshman year. I guess it's possible that he changed.

"So, I guess I should start from the beginning. When you left, Zach and I had both found ourselves in a darker place—we not only lost Emmett, but we also lost you. We didn't have answers. We didn't know where you were, if you were okay, or if you were even coming back. We had both lost our best friend, and yeah, I mean, you didn't answer my texts or calls, so I mourned you as if you had died alongside Emmett, and it was so hard."

Her voice catches and I reach out to comfort her.

"That summer, it was an adjustment for all. Zach stayed in Philly and I decided to stay local and attend UPenn instead of California. Zach and I found ourselves hanging out, seeking comfort in our friendship when he would come home. He even brought Ky back a few times. By the time I moved into the dorms, our friendship had blossomed into something new."

"And that's when you guys started dating?"

She shakes her head. "We were still just friends although my roommate was convinced otherwise. We hung out on the regular. We would help each other study, attend parties together, drive home together for holidays."

My heart breaks at the realization of all I missed.

"After Emmett's birthday I was having a hard time again, and your brother took me to a carnival. There was something that was happening that neither of us could explain. So, he got me on a Ferris wheel of all things and asked me on a date. I know we used to make fun of him because he didn't have a romantic bone in his body and his idea of a nice date back in high school was McDonalds and making out in the back of a movie theater."

I laugh at that memory of how awful my brother was, yet he always had a girlfriend—go figure. I'm actually impressed right now.

"But with me he went all out—well, he tried. He showed up at my dorm with flowers and had made reservations at a fancy restaurant downtown. Things didn't exactly go as planned, but things never do. When we got back to my dorm, he didn't try to invite himself in but kissed me good night. And oh my God." She starts to blush, and I feel nothing but love for them. I am actually happy for them.

"That kiss, Dani, was seriously the best kiss of my life. We've been kind of inseparable since, well, minus this one little misunderstanding." She smirks. "We healed each other. I mean, it's still quite a process, but we're doing it together. He makes me really happy."

"And you make me really happy," Zach adds as he walks in and sits on the arm of the couch next to her. I blink a few times just in awe at this.

"Why didn't you tell me," I ask more confused than ever now.

They both look at each other before Haylee says, "I didn't

want to overwhelm you with all of this. Zach wanted to tell you right away, but I was afraid that you would leave, and we're just getting you back. So, I told him to wait while you adjusted to being back."

She looks down at her feet. "I actually live here too. I have been staying at a friend's apartment who is out of town. I just didn't want to throw this in your face. A lot of things have changed since you left. I even made him take down photos of us." She points to the empty nails on the wall. I look over and remember how I thought that was odd upon my arrival, but I never remembered to bring it up to Zach or Kyler since then. I thought maybe it was like where photos of either of them and an ex used to be, but in fact it was Zach and Haylee. I don't know what to think now. This is a lot of information to process at once.

Zach clears his throat as I take another sip, finishing off my coffee, and place the mug on the table. "On nights when I said I was working late, that wasn't entirely the truth." I raise my eyebrows at him, and he holds up his hands as if in surrender. "Okay, that wasn't true at all...I was with Haylee. I didn't like hiding it from you, but I needed to respect Haylee's decision. But after our fight last night, I went straight to her place and told her I was done hiding. If you were going to be back in my life, then I wasn't going to hide from you, and if you couldn't accept that, then..." He trails off, but he doesn't need to finish.

I scoot closer to them and reach out to grab Haylee's hand. I pause, thinking of the words to say. "I'm sorry you felt you needed to hide this from me and that I made the past three weeks difficult for you by forcing you to sneak around. I'm here —I don't plan to leave either—so it's time I start making up for lost time and fix the mistakes I've made, starting with you both. I love you both so much, and I don't want to come between you two. So, I'm sorry for everything I put you through, but you found each other, so I guess maybe something good came out of my leaving. You guys look happy even though it may just take some time for me to get used to."

Haylee starts to cry, and I pull her into a deep embrace like we used to do. I want my best friend back. I've missed her and hate that Zach was right. I was selfish, incredibly selfish, trying to deal with my own grief, that I didn't think at the time how my actions would affect those around me. While still holding on to Haylee, I reach my hand over to my brother, and he takes it in his. I squeeze his hand and meet his eyes. Without using words, he knows I'm sorry for what I said yesterday.

Our moment is interrupted when we hear a throat clearing behind us. "Breakfast is ready," Kyler chimes in. Zach is the first to rise and follow him into the kitchen. As Haylee and I rise, I place my arm around her shoulder and she puts her arm around my waist.

"Okay, what do you say first thing after breakfast we put those pictures back on the wall," I say.

She nods and replies, "Sounds good. Then we can catch up when I go get my stuff and bring it back. Your brother has had enough of this separation. Looks like I'm coming home."

I find comfort in knowing that my best friend lives here too, that my brother wasn't alone, although it is definitely not something I expected. It seems like a lifetime ago since we spent time together, just us. We join the boys at the kitchen table, and I laugh when I look down at the for breakfast—cereal and fruit. Oh my, I think I moved in here just in time to save these boys and their *poor attempt* at cooking. They definitely have a lot to learn.

I sit down next to Kyler, and our knees accidentally brush under the table. I quickly pull my legs up, crossing one leg over the other away from him. Our eyes meet for a moment, and I remember what it was like to wake up next to him—or, well, I guess partially on top of him. His body was warm, and hard. I could tell that he works out. Well, I know he does because I've seen him with his shirt off, but to actually feel his body and have his arms around me... I don't know what I'm feeling about it. Our eye contact is broken when I hear my brother's voice.

"So are you going to see Mom and Dad soon?" Zach asks.

I slowly push the food in my bowl around. "I will. I promise."

Zach gives me a stern look, but Haylee smiles over at me and places her hand on mine. "It's okay, Dani. You'll go when you're ready."

I've crossed off reconciling with Haylee from my list. Next up, my parents. I know I can't hide from them forever.

CHAPTER 21
Danielle

*I*t's been a few days since the big reveal of my brother and best friend not only being together but living together. I guess a lot has changed while I've been gone. I'm happy for them, but it's still a little weird for me. I never would've put the two of them together, but they seem really happy. I truly hate that they felt they needed to hide this from me, though, as if I were a fragile bird or something. Who am I kidding—it would have definitely freaked me out, but I feel like my arrival may have disrupted their lives. If Zach and I hadn't had gotten into it the other day, would they have waited to tell me still?

The quiet here at the house is nice. There always seems to be a lot going on. It reminds me of growing up in our house; it was always busy. The quiet used to terrify me. I mean, it's still a little scary but a nice break from everything. Tonight, Zach and Haylee asked if I wanted to join them for dinner out and then a movie, but I graciously declined knowing they deserved time alone. Kyler was also out with his sisters. I haven't met them yet, but from the stories I've heard, I think we would get along. I think it's sweet he is so close to them.

I'm deep into my second scary movie, wrapped up under my favorite blanket, and my empty bowl from dinner on the coffee table, that I don't even notice the sound of the key opening the front door. I jump halfway off the couch when the door opens a little too quickly, hitting the wall behind it. Thankfully I had placed my glass of wine back on the table, otherwise it definitely would have spilled all over me and the couch.

"Jesus Christ!"

"Nope, just me!" Kyler throws his hands up in the air to claim innocence. "I didn't mean to startle you."

"You didn't startle me...you scared the shit out of me," I state a little too loudly, but I feel like I have to raise my voice so he can hear me over the sound of my heartbeat.

Kyler closes the door and takes his shoes off before striding over to the couch with a look of concern as I'm still clutching my chest, willing my heart to slow down. However, the closer he gets, the more it speeds up. I'm starting to think my rapid heartbeat has nothing to do with the act of being scared and more about being close to the one who did the scaring.

"Are you okay?"

I nod. "I'm fine." I wish he would stop asking me that. I know he doesn't mean anything by it, but every time he asks, that phrase puts my head back in a bad place of memories of everyone asking me if I was okay after Emmett died.

He looks around the room. "What are you doing sitting in the dark? I thought you were going out with Zach and Haylee."

"No, they needed some alone time, so I told them I wanted to stay home. Plus, I'm not really a fan of being the third wheel."

Nodding, Kyler lets out a laugh. "Welcome to my world."

I let out a low laugh too. "Yeah, now I know how my brother felt all those years ago back when..." But I refuse to finish that statement. Kyler must have assumed what I was going to say or at least that it had to do with Emmett, so he just quietly nods before getting up to grab himself a beer. Walking back from the kitchen, he takes a sip from the bottle before plopping down on the opposite end of the couch.

"So...what are you watching?" he asks, tipping his bottle toward the television.

I readjust myself on the couch after reaching for my wine-glass and take a sip. When I bring the glass away from my mouth, I look over and see that he is staring at me. Does he see something interesting? I am mentally going over my appearance: leggings and a comfy top that hangs off the shoulder, no makeup, and a messy bun on top of my head. Do I maybe have pasta sauce on my face or something? He jumps a little in his seat, and I remember he asked what I was watching. Right, that must have been why he was staring in my direction. *Get your shit together, Dani*, I replay in my mind over and over. I look up at his face, and he raises his eyebrows at me, still waiting for my response.

"*The Strangers.*"

"Huh?"

"You asked me what I was watching. It's called *The Strangers*. It's probably the scariest movie I've ever seen."

"Then why the fuck are you watching it, home. Alone. In the dark?" The look of confusion on his face gives it away pretty easily that he isn't much of a horror movie fan.

"How else am I supposed to watch it? I can't help it. I love horror movies."

Nodding, Kyler takes a sip of his beer. "Gotcha. Horror isn't really my cup of tea. I'm more of a comedy or action man myself."

I roll my eyes. "Let me guess, is *Die Hard* your favorite movie?"

He laughs and I notice he has a nice laugh. "Nope, although it's a classic. *Office Space* is actually my favorite."

"Ugh...are you serious, Lawson?" His eyes go big at my use of his last name, and it makes me giggle on the inside. "*Office Space* is seriously the worst movie ever."

Kyler places his hand over his heart in a fake dramatic way as if I have just offended him. "Are *you* serious now, Jacobs?" Raising his eyebrow, he shakes his head at me. "And to think we could have been friends. You break my heart saying shit like that."

I shrug and take another sip of my wine. "Sorry, babe, not my fault you have shitty taste in movies." I quickly cover my mouth my hand, realizing I called him "babe." In my peripheral vision, I see that he noticed it as well. I avoid his gaze, and after staring at me for a few moments, he turns toward the television and watches the movie.

We sit in silence for a while, both not knowing what to say, and end up watching the entire movie together. I laughed during a few moments when either he jumped, I jumped, or both of us jumped. Kyler even offered to refill my glass each time he got up to get a beer. I guess he's not so bad even though his taste in movies could use some work.

As we watch the credits go up, Ky clears his throat. "So now what?"

I turn back to him in confusion. "What do you mean?"

He nods toward the television. "I mean are we going to watch another movie?"

"Oh, well, technically I never invited you to watch the this one. You kind of just sat down and never got back up." I shrug and try to play it cool. Luckily the room is still pretty dark so he can't see me fighting back a smile. For once, it was nice to have quiet and not be alone. Also, knowing that this type of movie isn't really his scene but he still sat here watching it without complaint is nice too. Whenever I forced Zach into watching a movie of my choosing, he would talk and complain during the entire thing, and I would be so frustrated by the end that I would suggest he pick one that *he* wanted to watch so that he would shut up during it. Thankfully, Emmett never complained about things that I wanted to watch—at least I think he knew that he would earn his reward for going along, if you know what I mean. "Ummm...do you want to watch another one?"

"Yeah, that would be cool. I mean, if you want me to? I guess I did kind of just crash your night. I can leave if you want and leave you to your horror movies," he says as he starts to rise from the couch.

I quickly jump over to his side and reach out and touch his arm. "No, please, you can stay." I smile at him, and he sits back down. "If you want to pick the next one, you can...I mean, don't pick something super crappy though."

He looks down at his arm the same time I do, and I realize that I have not removed my hand from him. I quickly pull it back and drag myself back to my side of the couch. My mind quickly travels back to a few mornings ago when I woke up on this couch with his arms surrounding me, and it was the best sleep I had gotten in a while. Shit, maybe I should just say I am going to go to bed and run back to my room.

Kyler takes the remote and searches the on-demand movies. "How about this one?" I realize it's my brother's favorite movie, *Happy Gilmore*.

"Yeah, sure, let me just run to the bathroom real fast." We both stand at the same time. "I meant alone, ya know," I laugh as we both head in the same direction.

"Oh, of course. I'm headed to my room to change into something more comfortable."

"Oh, right, duh. I'll meet you back out there."

He nods and walks into his room, closing the door behind

him. I walk into the bathroom and close the door as well. After washing my hands, I look in the mirror. Oh my God, I look a hot mess. I let my hair down and run my fingers through my curls. I pinch my cheeks to add a little color to them. My pulse begins to race, so I grip the counter and take three deep breaths. *Get a grip.* I open the door and head back to the living room. I turn the corner and see Kyler sitting on the couch in gray sweatpants and a tight Philadelphia Flyers T-shirt. There's no hiding his muscles as his T-shirt clings to his body.

Come on, Dani, stop looking.

I also notice that he has a blanket partially over his lap. He catches me staring and smirks. "Everything okay?"

"Yep. Fantastic." I take a seat and pull my feet under myself and adjust my blanket. "Let's get this over with."

Kyler smiles as he presses Play. We watch the movie in silence, and he laughs more than I do. I eventually fall asleep, and at some point I feel myself floating and briefly open my eyes to realize that Kyler has carried me to my room. He places me on my bed and covers me with the blanket from the couch. I hear him mumble something as he leans over and places a quick kiss on my forehead before exiting the room. I am halfway conscious and still trying to figure out if I'm dreaming or not. I roll over and fall asleep without my headphones.

CHAPTER 22

KYLER

The following week, I find myself lost in my thoughts of Dani while sitting at my desk. My phone buzzes on top of the pile of papers I had neglected to deal with this afternoon.

LAUREN: *Still on for dinner?*

ME: *I am slammed at work.*

KATE: *You better not back out, asshole! We're not afraid to come down there.*

ME: *Okay. Okay. *Hands up in surrender* I'll be there.*

KATE: *So how are things at home* 😉

LAUREN: *Yeah, share all the juicy details.*

ME: *Things are fine.*

KATE: *ACHOOOOOOOOOoo! I'm allergic to that bullshit.*

LAUREN: *BULLSHIT!*

Wow, their twin sense is in full force. Some days I wonder how they even function together. I'm not sure I could ever handle having another version of me around.

KATE: *Great minds think alike, sis!*

ME: *Seriously?? Can't you both talk on your own time and stop bothering me while I'm trying to get work done? I've barely done shit today with other things on my mind.*
LAUREN: *Other things such as...*
KATE: *Maybe a cute brunette that lives 10 feet from you???*

I roll my eyes. This is getting out of hand. Maybe I can just ignore their texts so I can try to get my work done to get out of here soon.

KATE: *...And stop rolling your eyes at me. I know you too well!*

Fuck! Why didn't I just blow them off that first night I met her. I never should have said anything. But maybe I should talk to them about it. Not like I can talk to Zach. How would that conversation go... *Hey buddy, I know you just got your sister back, but I think she's beautiful and amazing and I'm enjoying getting to know her, not to mention can't stop thinking about her and jerking off in the shower to her. That's cool with you, right?* Yeah, I'm sure he would totally go for that. I roll my eyes at myself this time.

LAUREN: *I have an idea. Why don't you invite her tonight? I want to meet the girl who has my brother under her spell.*
ME: *FOR FUCK'S SAKE! I'M NOT UNDER ANYONE'S SPELL!*
KATE: *Yeah sure, keep telling yourself that. How many times have you jerked off to her since meeting her?*
LAUREN: *WTF Kate?! That's gross.*
ME: *I'm not answering that, ya freak!*
KATE: *Exactly! I rest my case.*

KATE: *But in all seriousness, you should invite her. Does she have other plans?*

ME: *I don't know. I don't know her schedule or anything. Maybe she has plans. She doesn't usually go out much though.*

I wonder if she has plans tonight. Maybe I could just text her and ask her. Wait, why am I even considering this? I would never want to voluntarily throw her to the wolves that are Lauren and Kate. If I ever thought I could potentially have a chance with her, it would completely go out the door once she was interrogated by the Lawson Twins. No, thank you!

LAUREN: *Just ask her... what's the worst that could happen? She says no? No big deal, not like you wouldn't be seeing her at home anyway.*

KATE: *Yeah, get your head out of your ass and grab the bull by the balls!*

ME: *What is wrong with you?! I'm starting to think I'm adopted.*

LAUREN: *If only you were that lucky *Kissyface**

ME: *You TWO can't go all crazy and scare her away.*

LAUREN: *Wait does that mean she's coming?!*

ME: *I haven't even asked her. I'm just saying in general.*

ME: *You both can sometimes be a little intense?*

KATE: *A little?!*

LAUREN: *I take offense to that!*

ME: **Eyeroll**

ME: *You both need to promise to be on your best behavior, DEAL???*

KATE: *...*

ME: *I'm serious! Zach will be pissed if you both are your usual selves.*

KATE: *Oh please, Zach loves me. It's okay!*

LAUREN: *And you call me cray-cray?! Pa-lease!*

ME: *I'm leaving this conversation, to get actual work done. I'm not asking her since you both didn't agree. Bye!*

LAUREN: *Okay. Okay. Little bro, keep your pants on! We promise to be on our best behavior!*

KATE: *Scout's honor!*

ME: *You know that only works if you were Scouts, right?!*

KATE: *Whatever*

ME: *K, seriously though I need to get work done so that I don't have to bail. See you both tonight. Love u.*

LAUREN: *you too!!!!!*

KATE: *ASSSSSKKKKKKKK HERRRRRRRRR!*

Sweet Jesus! These two are too much. I throw my phone into my desk drawer to avoid any other distractions. I have enough of those in my own head. But what would be so bad about asking her, besides exposing her to my crazy family? We're just friends—I can say it's my job as her friend to get her out of the house. Yeah, I could do that.

I grab the first paper in the pile and end up reading the same line four times. Okay, I'll just text her. The worst that can happen is she says no. As Kate said, grab the bull by the balls and text her. Shit, I'd love for Dani to touch my balls. *Fuck!* This is why this isn't a good idea. I place my head in my hands with my elbows propped up on my desk. What the hell is wrong with me?

After having a heated debate with myself and being distracted yet again from these papers, I take my phone out of my desk, pull up Dani's name, and type out a text:

ME: *Hey*

Really? All this time debating if I should text her, let alone invite her to join us, and all I say is hey? It feels as though an eternity goes by, but by the time my phone buzzes again, it has really only been about two minutes.

DANI: *Hi.*
DANI: *How's your day going?*
ME: *It's busy... too much work to get done.*
DANI: *Then how come you're texting me?*

Why am I texting her? Because I'm thinking about her? Because she's on my mind all the time? Because I care about her? No, I can't send any of those responses.

ME: *I needed a distraction.*
DANI: *So I'm a distraction? Lol*
ME: *Something like that* 😏
ME: *How's your day?*
DANI: *It's fine.*
ME: *Well, that's not very convincing.*
DANI: *No, it's fine. Really. I spent the morning baking.*
ME: *You're going to force me into working out a lot more with all these treats.*
DANI: *Shit, you figured out my master plan all along. Evil laugh.*
ME: *Do you have plans tonight?*

The conversation between us is so easy, I'm not sure why I was so nervous. But it's been a few minutes now since I sent that last text. Maybe I shouldn't have been so blunt. When I see the three dots indicating her response, my heart begins to beat a little faster.

DANI: *Ummmm... Zach called and has to work late and Haylee is studying. So... I'm thinking I'll be hanging out with my good friends Vada Sultenfuss and Thomas J*
ME: *Huh?*

Who are these people? New friends? I've never of them before. Are they hanging out at the house? Maybe I should cancel dinner and act as though I didn't have plans tonight and just go home.

DANI: **Face Palm* Seriously? My Girl! The two main characters. Come on, Ky, really?! I'm insulted. This is my ALL TIME favorite movie.*
ME: *Nope, never seen it.*
DANI: *Well shit! I'm not sure we can be friends anymore. Fuck! Where did this go all wrong?*
DANI: *I'm just kidding! Bet I had you there, huh?*
ME: *Is sarcasm and being a smartass a Jacobs thing?*
DANI: *Yep! Aren't you so lucky to have both me and Zach to deal with.*

If only she knew how lucky I felt.

DANI: *Do you have plans tonight?*
ME: *I'm meeting Lauren and Kate at Momento for dinner.*
DANI: *Oh. Cool. Well, have fun.*
ME: *I mean since you don't have any plans, you could join us.*

DANI: *Do you want me to join you?*

ME: *Do you want to join us?*

DANI: *Is there an echo in here?*

ME: *Echo! Echo! Echo!*

DANI: *Asshole.*

DANI: *About dinner. Idk. I don't want to intrude on your family bonding time.*

ME: *It's totally fine.*

ME: *I know from the stories you've heard, they can be a little...*

DANI: *Overwhelming?!*

ME: *Exactly. LOL. But they promised to be on their best behavior.*

DANI: *You already asked them?*

ME: *Yeah. It was actually their idea.*

DANI: *Oh...*

Shit! Shit! Shit! Abort! Abort! Now she might think I don't want her there.

ME: *You don't have to if you don't want to. I just thought you'd might like a change of scenery for once and get out. And lucky for you I have TWO sisters, so you wouldn't even be a third wheel.*

DANI: *I don't know.*

ME: *No pressure. How about this, since I need to actually get back to work if I want to leave anytime soon – thank you Miss Distraction – but we are meeting at Momento on Lincoln at 630. If you want to join us, we would love to have you. If not, it's ok and I'll see you at home.*

DANI: *Ok.*

That's it, just *okay*? Well, it wasn't a no, so maybe she will show up. I focus back on the paperwork on my desk, and when I look back up at my phone, I see that I have twenty minutes to get to the restaurant. Well, so much for knocking this pile out of the way. I gather up the stack and throw it in my bag, grab my phone and key, and head out the door.

Fifteen minutes later I'm being escorted to the table where my sisters are already waiting. Before I even have a chance to sit down, Kate rests her elbows on the table, propping her chin up on her balled-up fists. "So..."

Knowing that my silence is killing them both puts a devilish smirk on my face. Funny—do they know I don't have an answer for them? Because I have no clue if she is going to be here. I look around the restaurant and don't see her. I pull my phone out of my pocket and see no new texts from Dani, so I turn back to my sisters. "Well, I tried... I grabbed my balls as you said."

Kate makes a face of disgust. "I said the bull's balls, not yours."

I laugh, knowing exactly what she had said. I just wanted to fuck with her. "Meh, tomato tomahto."

Silence takes over the table while we decide what to order before the waitress comes. I look up from the menu and quickly glance over at the door.

My sisters notice something has caught my attention. Kate and Lauren both flip their heads around to see what or who I am staring at. Dani is standing there talking to the hostess, who turns around and points in our direction. My eyes meet hers, and she smiles and waves.

"Holy shit."

"I can't believe she came! She must be something special, Ky."

"Will you both shut up, you promised," I manage to spit out as Dani reaches the table.

I stand up and pull out the chair next to me for her. "You came."

She smiles at me. "I did." She shrugs her coat off and places it on the back of her chair.

As we both take our seats, I lean in to her. "To be honest, I didn't think you were coming."

She leans toward me and whispers back, "To be honest, I didn't think I was either."

A throat clearing across the table draws both of our attention in that direction. I laugh, shake my head, and give the twins a stern look.

"I'm sorry, my brother here seems to have forgotten his manners," Lauren chimes in.

"You're right, how could I have been so rude. Dani, this is Lauren." I extend my hand to indicate which twin is Lauren. "And this is my other sister, Kate." I do the same to point out the obvious.

Dani smiles weakly; I can tell she is nervous. "Nice to meet you. I've heard so much about you both."

"So have we, darlin'," Kate mumbles under her breath, almost low enough so that no one was supposed to hear her, yet based on Lauren's expression, my own look of embarrassment, and the redness of Dani's cheeks, I think it's safe to assume that everyone heard.

This is going to be a long night...but all that matters to me is that she is here.

CHAPTER 23

Danielle

The waitress approaches the table. "What can I get everyone to drink?"

Kate, Lauren, and Kyler all place their orders.

"And for you, miss?"

"Oh, umm." I frantically look around for a drink menu.

"Here you go." I look up and see Kyler holding it in his hand. I reach for it, and our fingers quickly brush one another. A shock spreads through me as our skin touches. I quickly grip the menu and yank it out of his hands. I didn't mean to do it so quickly, but that shock sent something through my body that I haven't felt in a long time.

I browse the menu knowing that the waitress is waiting for my answer. My lips curl upward as I spot my favorite wine on the menu. I hand her the drink menu. "I'll have a glass of the Kim Crawford Pinot Noir and a water."

Silence takes over the table after the waitress leaves. My leg starts to bounce anxiously. Maybe coming here was a bad idea. It's a little late to make an excuse to leave though. Maybe I can run to the bathroom and come back and say I was sick. I look around the restaurant for the bathroom, and my gaze catches Kyler. He's staring at me with his head tilted to the side. Maybe he can see right through me.

Kate and Lauren are whispering their own little conversation, not paying attention to us. "Are you okay?" he asks softly, his eyes full of concern.

I press my lips together and lightly nod.

The waitress returns with our drinks, my wine, a cosmo for Lauren, beer for both Kyler and Kate — along with shot of some sort of brown liquor that she places in front of Kate.

Kate holds up her glass. "A toast. To new friendships."

"To new friendships," we all respond in unison. I take a sip of the glass of wine, and it settles the butterflies in my stomach.

Ky mumbles something and shakes his head as he brings his beer to his lips. My eyes wander to his lips as they press against the glass. He takes a swig of the amber colored beer, and my eyes linger as I watch his Adam's apple bob when he swallows the liquid. *Jesus, Dani, stop staring.* I bite my lip hard enough to wince at the pain and direct my attention away from Kyler. I grab the wineglass so quickly that a little splash of wine spills over the top of the glass. I take a large gulp, and as I place the glass down, my eyes meet two pairs of chocolate-brown eyes just like Kyler's staring at me before giving an obvious look at each other and smiling. *Shit! They so caught me, didn't they?*

"Kyler, you told us she was beautiful, but you didn't say she was gorgeous." Lauren smiles at her brother and gives him a wink.

Kyler sprays his beer all over the table and rushes to the stack of napkins at the edge of the table. I blush at the compliment. Did he talk about me to his sisters? I mean, I figured he did since he admitted earlier that me joining them was their idea, but he called me beautiful? What else did he have to say? I'm not sure why that matters, but I want to know everything he said.

Our eyes meet as he cleans up the last of the spilled beer. He shrugs innocently, trying to brush off the statements.

Kate throws back the brown liquor in the shot glass and slams it onto the table in front of her before propping her crossed arms on the table. "So Dani." She pauses. "How long do you plan on sticking around for?"

My eyebrows raise in shock by her bluntness, but my attention is quickly diverted to my right when Kyler begins coughing uncontrollably. His body jerks.

"Ow!" I yell when I feel his foot come in contact with my shin.

"Oh my God!" Kyler turns to face me. Regret and remorse are written all over his face. "I am so sorry." I lean down, rubbing my leg. What the hell was that about? Kate and Lauren's mouths are wide open in shock. "I didn't mean to kick you. I was aiming for my sister."

Both sisters snicker. "Silly little brother," Lauren starts.

"Don't you know karma's a bitch?" Kate laughs as she finishes the statement. They high-five each other. Wow, these two are quite the pair.

"I really am sorry." He puts his elbows on the table and runs his fingers through his hair, exhaling a loud breath.

I reach out and touch his arm. "Ky, it's okay. Seriously. I'm fine." I meet his gaze and swallow before making a comment about how beautiful his eyes are. It's not until the waitress comes back to the table that I divert my attention from his.

"Is everyone ready to order?"

"Can we get a few more minutes?" Kyler responds to her.

"Yeah, we're still trying to decide what we want. Some of us just take a little longer to figure it out."

The waitress nods. "Take your time. I'll come back."

I look up from the menu in front of me to find both girls moving their gazes between both me and Kyler.

I avoid their gaze, glancing back down at the menu. I feel like the twins can see right through me. The same way Kyler does. It's like they are picking up on the things I'm not sure I'm ready for.

Wiping the sauce from my mouth with my napkin, I place the chicken bone back on my plate. These wings are delicious. "So Kate, Zach tells me you're an artist?"

She scoffs, earning an eye roll from both her sister and her brother. "Hmm, so Zach's been talking about me, huh?"

Lauren smirks. "Will you just give it a rest already?"

I look between the siblings, trying to find the missing puzzle piece here. Kyler leans back in his chair, stretching out, and his leg brushes up against mine. I quickly readjust in my seat. He doesn't seem to notice my movements; if he does, he doesn't show it on the outside.

"You see, my sister has this crazy idea in her head that Zach will ditch Haylee and be with her."

I laugh and look at Kate. "Oh. Wow. Okay."

My response earns a loud, deep laughter from Kyler.

Kate throws her hands up in the air. "I'm only joking, of course."

Lauren leans in. "No she's not."

"Well, I'd hate to break it to ya, but I don't know that he will break up with Haylee. I've never seen my brother act like this around anyone before. I mean, I know I missed a lot, but he's basically a new man."

Kyler reaches for the last chicken wing. "See, that's what I've been telling her, but she refuses to give up hope."

Kate folds her arms over her chest. "What can I say? I'm not a quitter." I laugh and she continues. "Hey, you never know, plans change."

My laughter abruptly comes to an end. I shake off that feeling creeping up my throat that tells me to cry. I know far too well that plans change, but I refuse to let that emotion show. I know Kate didn't mean anything by it. Kyler's thigh brushes against mine, pulling me from my thoughts. My skin heats at just that brief contact. This is insane to have that effect after an accidental touch.

I tuck a piece of hair behind my ear and steal a glance at Kyler from my peripheral vision and watch him carry on a conversation with his sisters. He smiles at something Lauren said. I am solely focused on him. My eyes drop to his lips again. I remember the other night and the feel of them on my forehead after he carried me to bed. That's now two nights since I have been back that I have slept peacefully and without headphones or wearing one of Em's T-shirts. That's just a coincidence, right?

Lauren clears her throat. "So what do you think, Dani?"

I jerk my head back toward her. Oh shit, I totally wasn't listening.

"I'm sorry, I sort of zoned out. What were you saying?"

Kyler leans in and whispers in my ear, loud enough that everyone can hear, "Don't worry, I block her out all the time too."

Lauren focuses on me but lifts her middle finger in her brother's direction. "I was saying that at the school where I work, we have a bake sale coming up, and I can't bake for shit, but we hear you're a goddess in the kitchen."

My cheeks heat at the compliment. A goddess? I don't know that I would go that far.

"I don't think those were the words I used," Kyler stutters.

"Oh you're right, those weren't the exact words. The exact words you used were, 'She is a freakin' goddess in the kitchen. Those cupcakes were literally the best thing I've ever tasted.'"

Kyler runs his hands over his face in embarrassment, but it earns a smile from me.

"So what do you say? Will you help us out?"

I think it over. Who am I kidding? A reason to bake and help kids? That is a no-brainer. "Of course, I'd love to help. I'll give you my number and we can go over all the details. I look forward to it." I turn to Kyler, who is chugging the rest of his beer. "And thank you."

He seems to relax now that he knows his comment doesn't bother me. I mean, one might think that would bother me but for some reason coming from him, it doesn't.

Lauren backs her chair up. "Excuse me, I need to use the ladies' room."

Kate scoots her chair back as well and rises along with her sister.

Kyler turns to his sisters. "What, you two can't go to the bathroom alone?"

Kate laughs. "Of course we can. I just thought you two would like some time alone—that's all." She winks and walks away to catch up with her sister. They lace their arms together and look back at the table. They are clearly up to something.

I take a sip of my water as the restaurant suddenly feels hotter.

"Look, I'm sorry about my sisters and their..."

"Directness? Abrasiveness? Lack of a filter?"

"Ha. Well, those are the polite ways to put it. I was going to say asshole behavior."

I sigh. Does it bother him? Does he think it bothers me? "Oh, they're fine, Ky. They're just looking out for their little brother. It's sweet."

"It's not sweet." He chuckles. "They just love giving me a hard time. Been doing it since I was a kid."

"Your mom must be a saint for dealing with the three of you."

He smiles. I know that he cares about his mom a lot, and I've learned they have a weekly call every week to catch up—that's sweet.

"You have no idea."

"You do remember who my brother is, right? We're only eleven months apart. I have a little idea as to what growing up in craziness is like."

"Touché." Kyler grips the back of his neck and I watch his bicep flex. "In all seriousness though, my mom seriously deserves a gold medal. I couldn't even imagine raising twins."

"And throw you into the mix, that poor lady."

He clutches his chest. "Your words hurt."

"Aww, poor baby, do you need a shoulder to cry on?" I push my shoulder in his direction. We both laugh at the comfortableness surrounding our conversation. I feel like I could talk to him about anything, even topics I'm not sure I would feel comfortable opening up to Haylee or Zach about.

He raises his glass in my direction. "To being the baby of the family and blaming everything on the older siblings."

"Now that I will cheers to for sure." We clink our glasses together. As I bring the wineglass down, I briefly look up, locking eyes with Kyler. My cheeks heat at the attention and the look in his eyes. I swallow deep. I realize our thighs are again brushing against each other. Our eyes stay locked, and my breath quickens. What is happening here?

A loud noise of a chair scraping the floor interrupts us, indicating his sisters have returned, and we both turn away from each other.

Kate smirks as she takes a sip of her drink. "Did we miss anything interesting?"

CHAPTER 24
Danielle

$\mathcal{K}$yler walks into the kitchen to find me gathering the ingredients I need to make cinnamon rolls to take to my parents' house tomorrow. I typically wouldn't make them the night before, but since we are leaving early, I wanted to get them done now instead of waking up even earlier in the morning. Part of me wants to fake sick and back out, but I know I owe it to my parents after all this time to visit. I've been here two months already, and I know they know that I'm here thanks to my brother's big mouth.

I am quite shocked they haven't stopped by yet, but they are probably just as worried as Zach that I will get spooked and take off again. I'm not sure who I am more nervous to see, my parents or the Hankses. It has been great rekindling my friendship with Haylee again these past few weeks, but I have kept away long enough. Talking with Haylee has helped a little, but I need to work on getting myself back to "me" and stop shutting everyone out. Of course, it's a lot easier said than done.

The hairs on the back of my neck stand up, so I know that he is staring at me without even turning around. That is another friendship I am oddly happy about its progression. I didn't really want to feel like the third wheel around Zach and Haylee,

158

so I have declined most of their offers of going out with them some nights.

What started out as a random occurrence has turned into a regular thing of watching movies over the past month on the couch with Kyler. We couldn't have more opposite tastes in movies, but we came to a compromise and alternate who gets to pick what we watch. That way we both are equal to suffering through the other's choices, although, I will admit to myself but not to him that I have enjoyed almost all the movies he has picked—all except *No Country for Old Men* because who the hell in their right mind would enjoy that movie. I have enjoyed getting to know him. He's a good fit for my brother; I can see why they became such good friends quickly.

"Can I help you make whatever you're going to make?" Kyler asks from behind me where he is sitting at the island.

"Ummm...I guess. Sure," I say, turning around and arching my eyebrow at him. "You don't have anything better to do on a Saturday night? I find that hard to believe."

With a smug smirk on his face, he plops his chin on top of his fists. "Nope, I'm all yours."

A weird feeling instantly comes over me. Are we still talking about baking? I would say yes if it wasn't for the way he was looking at me. It was as if he's looking right through me. We shared a similar look the other night at dinner with his sisters. If they had not interrupted us, would he have kissed me? Did I want him to? I'm not sure whether I should grab my stuff and run away, or maybe even worse, run toward him. Who the hell is this man who keeps creeping into my world one moment at a time?

I'm so lost in my internal argument that I don't realize Kyler has since moved from his spot at the island to right behind me. "Earth to Dani!" I jump back at his proximity and end up backing right into him, my back to his front. He places his hands on my shoulders to steady me.

"Whoa there, killer, I didn't mean to startle you," he says with a laugh. "I feel like I'm always scaring you." If only he knew it wasn't just physically that he scared me, but the feelings that I start to feel at times when I am around him scare me more. I've never felt this way about anyone that wasn't Emmett and am charting new territory. "I was just talking to you about what you were going to make, and you were lost in your own world, so I just wanted to bring you back to me."

"Oh sorry, I was..." Trying to come up with any excuse that's not *I was thinking about you and things I wouldn't mind you doing to me*, but instead I come up with "I was going over all the ingredients in my head to make sure I wasn't missing anything."

He nods, whether or not he buys my reasoning. He steps back so that I can take the ingredients to the island.

"So, you really want to help me?" I ask him, still feeling as though he's just messing with me.

"Well, yeah, I wouldn't have asked otherwise," he responds with a crooked smile. I can sense that Kyler is a little nervous as he takes in all the ingredients I have set out. I feel as though he may back out—in fact I am kind of hoping for it. I'm not sure I can handle him this close to me at the moment.

With a deep breath, he turns to me. "Okay, make me your bitch. Let's do this!"

I laugh. *Well, here goes nothing.* "Okay, well, first of all, we are going to make cinnamon rolls to take tomorrow to my parents' house."

"You're finally going?"

"I'm finally going. I can't keep putting it off."

"That's good. I'm proud of you. To be honest, I'm surprised your mom hasn't knocked down the door yet."

"I know." I snicker. "That is more her style. Do you maybe want to come with us?"

The expression on his face masks my own shock. Did I seriously just ask him that? I pull my lip between my teeth while I nervously await his answer. He must be able to sense my hesitation, because he places his hand on my wrist, giving it a reassuring squeeze.

"Are you sure? I don't want to intrude on this family moment." He hasn't removed his hand from my wrist and is now rubbing circles along my skin with his thumb.

"No, I would like that. I could use all the support I can get." I half smile. "And you can let everyone know you made these."

He lets out a hearty laugh and removes his hand, and I miss his touch. "Yeah, well, only if they're good. If they taste like shit, then they're all on you, sweetheart."

I tense at his endearment, but for some odd reason it doesn't bother me. In fact, it causes a weird feeling in my stomach, almost like butterflies. I reach for my apron, a Christmas present that Emmett had given me one year that reads "Lick my Frosting." Needless to say I was so mortified opening that in front of our families knowing the double meaning. He went an entire week without getting any—okay, so really just three days, but it felt like a week.

I turn my back to Ky. "Do you mind tying this for me?" He complies and swats my butt when he is done, causing me to jump. I sure wasn't expecting that. I feel a blush creep on my cheeks and completely lose my train of thought. *Fuck.* I look over my shoulder at him, and Ky is grinning ear to ear. My eyes meet his before looking down at his mouth.

I clear my throat and clap my hands together. "Okay, let's get started."

While I dissolve the yeast in warm water and set the bowl to the side on the counter, Kyler finds a playlist on Spotify and turns the music on. I smile because Mom always had oldies music playing in the kitchen when we would bake together. Dad would swoop her in his arms and spin her around the kitchen. She would swat at him, getting flour all over him, but he never stopped, and she would eventually give up the fight and embrace their dancing together.

Per my instruction, Kyler mixes milk, melted butter, salt, sugar, and an egg.

"Okay, now add the flour but do it slo—" Before I can finish my sentence, he has added some a little too quickly and it poofs up in a smoke ball. Flour covers us, and I let out a loud giggle.

"Thanks for the warning," Ky says as he joins in my laughter. I shrug, still laughing.

"Okay, now add the rest *slow-ly*." I make sure to enunciate the *slowly* part. Without looking at me, he flips his middle finger at me. I try to hide my smile because he's really trying to focus on this. His eyes narrow and wrinkles form on his forehead from his concentration. I then add the yeast mixture and the rest of the flour.

"What got you into baking? You just look so peaceful in your element. I don't think I've ever seen you so calm before."

I smirk to the side as I continue to monitor the mixing bowl, making sure all ingredients are mixed perfectly. "Emme…" I pause, not wanting to bring Em up with Ky—why I want to hold back, I'm not sure. "Haylee's mom got me into it. She was the best baker and cook I knew. I just always found comfort in the kitchen. Some people feel at peace on the field or in a dance studio; for me it's the kitchen."

"Fair enough."

I take a handful of flour and spread it over the counter and look over to Kyler, who has a seriously confused look on his face. I smile. "Now we have to knead the dough. It's going to get a bit messy."

Looking down at his T-shirt, he raises his eyebrows at me while I press my lips together in an attempt to hold back my laughter. "Okay, so this time we are going to be doing it on purpose." He sticks his tongue out at me, and I laugh. I carefully take the dough out of the bowl and place it on the floured surface. I tilt my head for him to walk closer to me. "You're going to do this part." He hesitantly touches the dough and makes a face like he is turned off by it.

"Oh my God, quit being a baby about it. Just go for it."

He places his hands on the dough and attempts to knead the dough, and I cringe at how awful he is doing it. I remember my first time; my mother told me I was a natural. Kyler, not so much. He looks very uncomfortable.

He notices my furrowed brow. "I'm completely fucking this up, aren't I?"

I smile back at him, knowing he is trying his hardest. For some reason he really wants to be successful at this and not mess it up, maybe so he can actually take credit for these. Hell, if they turn out, I will gladly give him credit. Whenever Zach or Emmett tried to help, I ended up having to redo the recipe. They were better at eating the outcome than trying to help bake it.

I nudge him out of my way with my hip, coat my hands with a light dusting of flour, and start to knead the dough. "See how I'm doing it? It's an art, not just punching it into oblivion."

"Ready to try?" I go to move out of the way, but Kyler has blocked me in. With his front to my back, I close my eyes and relish in the feeling of his body up against mine. I can feel the ripple of each muscle up against my back and am now remembering him the day we met when he wasn't wearing a shirt. My breathing hitches and I inhale his cologne. God he smells good. He slides his hands down my arms, leaving goose bumps in their wake. He squeezes my hands before coating his own with a little more flour.

I swallow, trying to refocus. Is he aware of what he is doing right now? Of course he is. Was this part of his plan? Must. Focus. On. Baking. Kyler threads his fingers through mine and begins to knead the dough as I had shown him just now. I should release my fingers and back away, but I haven't. My breathing is becoming shallow. The feeling of having him close has sent all sorts of feelings to my core. I bite my lip before I say or do anything I might regret. Do I make him as nervous as he does me?

Anxiety and nervousness run through my veins along with a little excitement. Only a few more minutes of kneading the dough before we set it aside to rise and I get some much-needed space from Kyler.

KYLER

I am so close to her right now I can smell her vanilla shampoo, and I have no shame to say I inhaled it to commit that scent to memory. It's one thing to smell it from the bottle in the shower, but to actually smell it on her is heavenly. My thoughts are all over the place, causing my heart to race. I take notice that hers is too. I'd be lying if I said I didn't enjoy the effect I'm having on her. I wish she saw how fucking beautiful she is. I really hope that she doesn't think I planned this all when I asked to help her, but now that I am so close to her, I don't want to back away. I may scare her away entirely.

"Am I doing this right?"

She doesn't speak, just goes, "Mmmm."

I take notice her hands fit perfectly in mine. This is definitely crossing that invisible line between friends and something more that we have been playing with lately. The long glances, the innocent touches, and the dirty thoughts — at least on my end — have all brought us here. I tighten my grip on her hands as we knead the dough together, and a small moan escapes the back of her throat. Now my mind goes there—would she make that same noise if she were underneath me, squirming and screaming my name with pleasure? I wonder what she would taste like—sweet, I'm sure. When I saw her put that apron on, all I could think of was "Yes, I want to lick your frosting."

My best friend would kill me if he knew I was having these thoughts about his sister. What the fuck is wrong with me? We have a moment, and as quickly as that moment happens, it's gone as she quickly straightens up and steps away from me, clearing her throat.

I quietly adjust my pants when she has her back toward me, placing the dough ball in a bowl and covering it. "Now what do we do?"

She turns around with flushed cheeks. Was she thinking what I was thinking? How easily I could step up to her, lace my fingers in her hair, and kiss her. I have a feeling, though, that one kiss just wouldn't be enough.

Dani closes her eyes for a moment, taking in a deep breath. When she opens them and her eyes meet mine again, she looks as though she is having some sort of internal conversation with herself. I didn't misread the signs of her flirting, right?

She turns her back to me and begins to clean the mixing bowl. "Well, we have to let that rise, and that can take about an hour, so I was just going to clean this up to prepare the icing and then sit and read on my Kindle. You can go do whatever, and I can let you know when it's ready, or I can just finish. I'm sure you have other things to do."

I step up to her by the sink. "No, you have my attention and help, so I'm gonna finish it."

I'm suddenly nervous to be invading her personal space again and look down at my feet. "Can I get you a drink? Maybe we can sit and talk? Would that be okay?"

Dani continues to wash the bowl, then sets it on the drying rack and dries her hands on her apron. She bites her lip, and that goes straight to my dick again. "Yeah, sure."

I walk over to the fridge and grab two beers and meet her in the living room. She says thank you as I hand her the beer. Our fingers brush lightly as she takes it from my hand, and suddenly my mouth is very dry. I quickly take a big swig of beer before sitting down. I see she is picking at the label on her beer. Must be a Jacobs thing; I've seen Zach do it on more than one occasion.

She takes a sip and winces. "Are you not a fan of beer?" I ask.

"No, this is fine. I just prefer wine or tequila."

"Oh shit. Sorry, I can go get you a glass of wine instead." I place my beer on the coffee table and go to rise to replace her drink with something she actually likes. She grabs my arm, her fingers barely reaching all the way around my bicep, and uses such a force that she pulls me back to the couch.

"You don't have to do that. This is fine."

I nod. I make a mental note that when I need a refill, I will grab her a glass. "Want to play a game?" I ask her.

She has a confused look on her face. "Ummmm, what kind of game?" she asks nervously.

Why did I suggest a game? What are we, twelve? I just want to spend time with her and get to know her better. I want to know *everything*, the little things, the big things, what makes this girl tick. I want to know it all.

Thinking, I suggest, "Well, we could play Twenty Questions or Never Have I Ever?"

"Can you play Never Have I Ever with just two people?"

"Sure, why not?"

She shrugs but doesn't say no. She takes a sip of her drink, then says, "Okay, you pick."

Hmmmm, which can I learn more about this girl with? "How about Twenty Questions, just so we aren't too drunk to finish up those cinnamon rolls."

Dani tips her beer in my direction. "Valid point. Would hate for you to not be able to claim you made them because you were too drunk to make something good," she says with a giggle at the end. That giggle—I could listen to that every day. I prop my feet up on the coffee table as she brings her legs underneath her. I love when I see her comfortable in our house.

"I guess I'll go first. Favorite food?"

She smiles. "Cheese fries, but they have to be curly fries."

"That's so specific," I laugh, and she interrupts me with, "And delicious. What about you?"

"I used to say my favorite food was pizza, but I definitely think it's that lasagna you make. That was so fucking good."

Dani blushes at my compliment. "Well, maybe if you are a good enough student with this dish, then maybe I'll teach you how to make that next."

Is she flirting with me? The little smile that greeted her lips at the moment and the look in her eye...yep, she is definitely flirting with me. Okay, game on, Jacobs. I adjust myself on the couch and break our staring contest. What I wouldn't do to reach out and pull her into my lap and press my lips to hers.

"So, Kyler...that's a different name. I only ever heard it in a book I read once. Is it a family name?"

This question always makes me laugh a little because I remember as a kid people always messing my name up with Tyler. "Well, it's pretty simple. My parents couldn't decide on a name when they were pregnant with me. My dad wanted Kyle, and my mom wanted to name me Tyler, so this was kind of their compromise, I guess."

Over the next hour, we go from asking simple questions like favorite books to what it was like growing up with twin sisters. We forget the limit of only asking twenty questions. Not only does our conversation constantly flow, but it's easy. The shy, nervous girl that arrived at dinner the other night is long gone.

"Well..." She slaps her hands on her thighs and stands. "I'm going to go check on the dough." She heads toward the kitchen but stops and looks back at me over her shoulder. "You coming?"

I nod and rise to my feet to follow her but not without letting my eyes drop down to her luscious ass as she walks away. *Get yourself together, Ky.*

The rolls smell absolutely ah-may-zing! Damn, who knew I would be able to pull this off? I'd say Dani is a fucking amazing teacher if these taste as good as they smell. I'll have to try to make these one day for Mom and the girls.

Dani takes one of the cinnamon rolls out and slices it in half, giving me one slice. I watch her slowly bring her half to her mouth and take a bite. She closes her eyes and moans. "Mmmmmmmm." That is seriously the sexiest sound I have ever heard. I want to make her make the sound again and not just with food I helped make.

She covers her mouth after taking a second bite. "Well...are you going to taste it or what?" I nod and take a bite. Holy fucking shit, they do taste as delicious as they smell.

"Fuck yeah!" I shove the rest of my half in my mouth and reach out and pick Dani up. She yelps as I spin her around. When I set her down, she looks more nervous than ever.

"Sorry, I just got so excited that it didn't turn out like shit. Guess I earned another lesson now with that lasagna, huh?"

She diverts her eyes and blushes, her cheeks now the rosiest shade of pink. As she looks down at the floor, I see there is a drop of icing left on her lips. "You got a little something right..." I drag my thumb across her bottom lip to get the icing at the same time as her tongue slides out to clean it off. The tip of her tongue grazes my thumb, and I am instantly aroused. Her eyes meet mine as she closes her lips around my thumb and sucks the spare icing that I had gotten. Her blue eyes darken like I have never seen them before. The way she's looking at me, I would say she wants me to kiss her, but maybe I'm just reading the signs wrong. Once this happens, there is no going back.

I can feel her breathing change, and her eyes move from my eyes to my lips a few times. Okay, yes, she definitely wants me to kiss her. We could cut the sexual tension in the room with a knife. Should I? Is she ready for that? Fuck, why am I having an argument with myself instead of making a move?

She doesn't move away as I place my hand on her hip to keep her steady.

"Tell me to stop," I tell her as I slowly close the distance between us. She doesn't say anything, so as I take her cheek in my hand and brush her soft skin, I say against her lips, "Dani, I'm gonna kiss you now. Tell me if you want me to stop." *Shit, please don't tell me to stop.* She wets her lips instead of saying no, so I gently press my lips to hers.

I can feel her hesitate at first as I kiss her, but then she kisses me back. As I lick her lips, she opens for me, and I explore her mouth with my tongue. She tastes sweet and I already know I won't be able to get enough of her.

The kiss starts innocent but quickly becomes heated. I increase the pressure as her hands grip my hips, and walk her backward a few steps, my hands never leaving her body, until she's leaning up against the island. I place my hands behind her thighs and lift her up onto it.

I spread her legs to stand between them while she sits on the counter. My hands slide up her thighs and come around to her ass and pull her toward me. As if on instinct, her legs wrap around me. Holy fuck, is this real?

I kiss her as if I'll never get to kiss her again, and who knows, this might just be a moment of weakness and I will in fact never get to kiss her or touch her again. She suddenly pulls back, completely out of breath. Her eyes look different, but I can't clearly make out what she might be thinking.

It's not just sadness in her eyes...it's something else.

CHAPTER 25
Danielle

*H*oly fucking shit! I must be dreaming. That was... that was...wow! I am at a loss for words. I go to open my mouth to speak but close it for the words haven't come together yet as to what I want to say. Part of me wants to slap him for doing that, but more importantly, I think I want to do it again. I avoid looking in his eyes and hop off the counter. We are still only standing inches away from each other, and I am tempted to jump into his arms, wrap my legs around him, and beg him to take me to bed.

What was I thinking? I can't do this again. People date and fall in love and then get their heart broken. It's not like it happens on purpose—I mean, sometimes it does, but in my case it wasn't.

The words finally hit my brain moments later and connect to my mouth. "I...I... Ummm...I should go." I point toward my bedroom. "To bed. Early morning tomorrow and all."

He's just staring at me. I can't read his expression. Maybe he regrets it or maybe he doesn't—either way, I need to get out of here like now. Leaving the house would be too obvious, so retreating to my room will have to do even though he is just in the room next door.

Kyler nods. "Yeah, sure. I'll finish cleaning everything up here and see you in the morning."

I smile at him before turning to leave the kitchen, but stop when Kyler says, "Hey, Dani." I turn around, and he closes the distance between us. I look up at him, getting lost in those chocolate eyes.

"I just wanted to say thanks for tonight and for asking me to go tomorrow." Oh crap. Right. I asked him to go with us to brunch. *Act cool, Dani.* That kiss is messing with my head. It's not like it was just a few hours ago that I had asked him. His eyes move back and forth between my eyes and lips. Is he going to kiss me again? Do I want him to kiss me again? He leans forward, and I close my eyes. He presses his lips to my forehead, lingering just a moment before he smiles. "Good night."

I open my mouth to respond, but he has already turned around.

I take a deep breath, run to my room, and quietly close the door. I slide down to the floor and let out a slow breath. Would it be so bad to kiss him again? To want to be in his arms?

Shaking those thoughts off, I pull my knees to my chest and lay my head on my elbows that are wrapped around my knees. Fuck, I'm in trouble because my mind is on overdrive thinking about Kyler Lawson, my brother's best friend...*again.*

CHAPTER 26

Danielle

$\mathcal{K}$yler offered to drive us to my parents' this morning for brunch, which I was fine with. When I mentioned to Zach and Haylee this morning that I had invited Kyler to join us, they seemed a little confused and gave each other a weird look before shrugging it off. I think everyone expected me to fake sick and cancel last minute, not invite someone to join us. I promised myself that I needed to do this. I have to see my parents. It's time.

But even though it's time, it doesn't mean I'm not terrified at the moment. Zach is sitting up front with Kyler, and Haylee joined me in the back. The giant Toyota Tundra that I saw in the driveway when I arrived, in fact, belongs to Kyler. For being a truck, the back seat is pretty spacious and comfortable. For most of the ride to my parents' house, I keep to myself, looking out the window at the passing scenery, tuning the conversations between Zach and Haylee and Zach and Kyler in and out. Living outside the city shortens our drive back by about thirty minutes. There are times I look away from the window or up from my hands wrestling each other with nerves and my eyes meet Kyler's in the rearview mirror. He doesn't say anything, just looks away or gives me a brief smile.

I am completely lost in my thoughts of being back home, of

seeing my parents and the Hankses for the first time in four years, to realize we have reached our exit on 50. Haylee reaches over as we turn into the driveway and squeezes my wrist, giving me a reassuring smile that lets me know it will all be okay. But will it? Kyler parks his truck in my parents' driveway, and I take a deep breath, looking out the window at the house I grew up in. Now or never, I say over and over, knowing that never isn't really an option, at least not for me. I wipe my sweaty palms on my jeans and pull on the door handle to exit the vehicle.

Zach looks at me with concern as I walk around the truck to where everyone else stands.

I shake my head. "It'll be fine. Let's go." I'm not sure if I say that more to reassure myself than anyone else.

In front of me, not only do I see the house that I grew up in, but I see all the memories surrounding my life with Emmett. Walking up the front steps, I see the porch swing where we made plans for the future, our future together.

Zach walks through the front door without ringing the doorbell. I'm still staring at the porch swing when Kyler touches my elbow and asks, "You coming?"

Shaking the memory away, I smile briefly in his direction. As I enter the house I am assaulted by more ghosts of memories past. I see the stairs Emmett would chase me up when we'd realize we had the whole house to ourselves. I see the couch where I made Emmett watch every episode of *Lost* and he never once complained, even though I know it completely mind-fucked him trying to determine where they actually ended up and searched for answers. I see the dining table where we would play footsie while doing our homework after school with Zach and Haylee.

When I can no longer take a walk down memory lane, I pause and close my eyes, pushing the memories away. When I open them, I look to my left and see Kyler standing there staring at me, trying to get a read on how I'm feeling and what I'm thinking. Before I can say anything, he grabs my hand and smiles. "You got this. If it gets too much we can leave, but I really want to share these amazing cinnamon rolls with everyone."

He then gives me a pleading face, and how can I turn that down? I feel better from his words and comforted by his touch. But my mind goes back to last night, the elephant in the room that we haven't discussed any further. Maybe he regrets it since he hasn't brought it up, or maybe he wants me to bring it up, I'm not sure—I'm not sure how to do all of this stuff. It's new territory for me. It was always so easy for me and Em.

As we approach the kitchen, I can hear a familiar sound that also brings comfort—"Ob-La-Di, Ob-La-Da" by The Beatles. Our parents were obsessed, like legit obsessed, with them. Obsessed to the point where I was shocked that Zach or Emmett weren't named Paul, Ringo, or hell, even Jude. Anytime a cover band came within a four-hour radius, they went and sometimes even dragged us kids along. I didn't mind it really; over the years I learned to appreciate all forms of music.

The four of us stand in the hallway leading to the kitchen and watch Dad and Mr. Brian spin Mom and Ms. Natalie around the kitchen. No signs of crying and sadness, just happiness and laughter. It's as if it's a normal day for them. If they can be happy, why can't I?

We stand there in silence, watching till the song ends, and Zach claps and yells, "Encore! Encore!"

My mom jumps and turns around, placing her hand on her chest. I stand back behind Zach out of her view. Her eyes go to Zach first, and when he moves to the side, she sees me and her eyes instantly fill with tears. I squeeze Kyler's hand, and his thumb brushes over my knuckles. Memories of all the calls and texts I ignored over the years come rushing back to fill my mind, and I can feel my eyes filling up as well. *Don't cry, don't cry*, I tell myself. My mind betrays me as tears stream down my face.

"Hey, Mama," I manage to get out before she sweeps me into a big hug. My mom always gave the best hugs. I don't know what it was, but every time I fell and scraped my knees, her hugs always made me feel better. Her shoulders begin to shake as the tears run down her cheeks. I release Kyler's hand and wrap my arms around her.

"I missed you so much," she says as her arms tighten around me. I look up to see Ms. Natalie in Mr. Brian's arms, and she is crying too. Oh my God, maybe me being here was a bad idea—maybe my being here is bringing up all sorts of bad memories for her. Taking my cheeks in her hands, Mom holds me as if she refuses to let me go. "When your brother said you were coming today, I almost didn't believe him because I didn't want to get my hopes up."

I feel a hand rub my back as I continue to cry in my mother's arms. I look up from the crook of her neck and see my dad standing there.

"Hi, Daddy," I say in between tears. I look at my dad's face —he looks older as well. Gray threads throughout the hair surrounding his face.

"Hey, baby girl," he says as he pulls me out of her arms and into his. Zach and Haylee have moved out of the way to the other side of the kitchen to hug Haylee's parents. Kyler sets the tray of cinnamon rolls on the counter and joins Zach and Haylee standing out of the way of this homecoming moment.

My father releases me from his hug but keeps his arm around my shoulders. Just like my mom, I guess he fears if he lets me go I'll slip away.

"I hope you don't mind that I invited Kyler."

My mom pulls Kyler into a motherly hug. "Of course not. What a wonderful surprise." He also shakes my dad's hand. It's crazy to see his interaction with my family. I forget that he has been around for years, while I haven't.

I know it's time to hug Natalie and Brian, but is seeing me too painful? Does it remind them of what they lost?

I cautiously approach Ms. Natalie while everyone stands back watching, but instead of anger or hurt, I see happiness in her eyes. The same look I saw on my best friend's face when I saw her for the first time in four years. Before I can say anything, she has me pulled into her arms and kisses my temple, just like her son used to. "About time you came home, sweetheart, don't you think?" she says with a smile. I relax in her embrace. I can feel Mr. Brian close by, but Natalie refuses to let me go so I can hug him. "Get your own Jacobs to hug—I've waited four years to hug this one."

So, he settles for a kiss to the top of my head and mumbles, "Welcome home."

Everyone laughs in the background as Natalie pulls back but doesn't let go of my arms. She places her forehead against mine. "No more running, right?" I nod, so she continues. "Because we're your family here, and I'm tired of just your mom's help in the kitchen. Haylee's useless."

"Hey!" Hails yells from behind me.

Zach puts his arm around her shoulders and kisses her head. "Babe, I love your cooking, but..."

Before he can finish, she puts her forefinger in his face. "Don't even think about finishing that sentence, Zachary Jacobs!" She narrows her eyes at him, and he playfully bites her finger.

Mom claps her hands together. "Okay, who's hungry? We've got a whole brunch spread made."

I'm still at Ms. Natalie's side with my head on her shoulder and my arms around her waist. God, I have missed these people. Mom walks over to the tray that has the cinnamon rolls on it.

"Oh I brought cinnamon rolls; they just need to be warmed up," I interject while wiping away my tears as she lifts the foil. Kyler coughs and raises his eyebrows at me. I smile and laugh, remembering our deal last night. "Kyler made them."

"Well, then I'm definitely not eating them," Zach says as he grabs a strawberry from the bowl and shoves it in his mouth.

Ky punches my brother in the arm and mumbles, "Asshole."

"Kyler! Language, please," my mother scolds, getting a rise out of Zach, who sticks his tongue out at Kyler. I'm not sure why I was so nervous about today; it feels as though I never left. Just like Haylee had, my parents and the Hankses seemed to welcome me home with open arms.

"They're quite a pair, huh," Haylee says, handing me a mimosa. It feels weird drinking alcohol in front of my parents, but we are all of legal drinking age now. I notice Kyler declined one since he's driving.

"I think Emmett would've loved him," she adds, grabbing my hand when she senses my body tense up at the mention of his name. "He's a really good guy—funny, smart, able to handle your brother's bullshit."

When she catches me staring at him, she elbows me in the ribs and adds, "Good-looking. I'm just saying." She grabs her drink and walks out to the dining room.

Did she know something happened last night? Maybe Ky had mentioned it to Zach and then he told her, but judging solely on the fact that Ky doesn't have any bruises or black eyes, I'm thinking he kept what happened last night to himself.

"Damn, dude, these are delicious," Zach tells Kyler as he plucks his second cinnamon roll from the plate and shoves it in his mouth. Not even waiting till he is done chewing, he continues. "I can't believe you've been holding out on me with your skills in the kitchen all these years."

"Zachary Brian Jacobs, I know I taught you better manners than to talk with your mouth full," my mother scolds, earning an "Oooooooooooo" from me and Haylee at the same time followed by us giggling.

"Nice to see you girls back to your ways," my dad adds.

Kyler grins at Zach. "Nah, man, I just had a good teacher." He looks over at me and grins. "Dani even told me that next time she would teach me how to make that amazing veggie lasagna."

"Oh, now that sounds delicious." Brian leans back in his chair across the table.

"It's no chicken Parmesan that Ms. Natalie makes, but it's definitely a top contender."

Natalie leans over with her elbows on the table. "Dani, we're all adults now—I think we are old enough that you can drop the Ms. and just call me Natalie."

"Okay."

"I'm happy to hear you're still creating in the kitchen though."

"Of course, it's my happy place. I found myself spending hours in my apartment creating new recipes and perfecting the ones you taught me over the years. I even used to make baked goods for two local coffee shops back in New Hampshire while I was waitressing."

"I'm not surprised."

"I would love to see these new recipes you've been working on." My mom sits up straight in her chair, wiping her mouth with her napkin.

"Maybe next time you guys can come visit us and I'll make something."

"I'd love that." Mom reaches over and touches my hand. Her hand seems so fragile. I finally notice the stress of the past few years has taken on my parents. When we were busy earlier with our reunion, I hadn't noticed how much time had gotten away from me until I look over at my father again. His once brown hair is beginning to gray. My mother and father both look well above their age.

As the conversation continues around me, I look around the room. Not much of the dining room has changed; in fact, the only difference seems to be an addition of various photos. As my eyes travel over the photos, I notice there are new ones of Zach and Haylee from the last four years, but the ones of Emmett and me all stop from age eighteen. It's as if time stopped for us. In my parents' and the Hankses' world, it did. They all lost a child. I can't imagine the pain either went/still goes through of not only losing a child in death but losing a child and not knowing where they are or if they are even alive. I only ever responded once just after I left, letting them know I was fine, but to go years without ever knowing anything, how are they still standing?

I feel the room getting smaller, and I gasp for air. I push my chair back quickly, needing an escape for some air. I run straight out the back door onto the deck overlooking the back-yard and pool. As soon as the Maryland air hits my face, I curl over with my hands on my knees and try to even my breathing. I close my eyes. Inhale. One. Two. Three. Exhale. One. Two. Three.

I hear footsteps on the deck behind me, and a hand begins to rub my back.

"It's okay, sweetie. Deep breaths. Can you do that for me?" My mom continues to rub circles on my back as I squeeze my eyes shut and begin to get my breathing under control. I stand but hesitate before turning around to come face-to-face with my mother's sad eyes. I fall into her arms and allow the overwhelming emotions to take over—the loss we endured, the pain I put my everyone through, the memories missed. It consumes me. I'm not sure how long my mother holds me when I back up and wipe my eyes.

She cups my cheeks. "Come take a walk with me."

I follow my mother down by the pool, and she takes a seat on one of the lounge chairs. I stand there with my arms wrapped around my stomach. She pats the spot next to her on the lounge chair. I sit down, and she places her arm around my shoulder and I nestle into her side.

"My beautiful Danielle. Want to tell me what's going on?"

"I'm sorry, Mama."

"For what? For a panic attack? You think I don't know one when I see one?"

"I...I..." I look up at her, both our eyes filled with unshed tears. I blink and allow them to run down my cheeks again.

"Talk to me, Dani. Let me help you."

My sobs grow louder. "That's just it. I should have let you help me. But instead, I ran. I'm so sorry, Mama. I was just so empty. I thought I was doing the right thing by leaving. I thought I could do it on my own. I hurt you all so much. And then I came back and expected everyone to hate me, but you all welcomed me with open arms as if I had just been away at college or out of town. No one was mad at me. But then I looked at the photos on the wall and time had stopped for Emmett and me, but it continued for everyone else. There were so many memories and events that I missed. I wasn't here for Zach or Haylee when I should have been. I put you and Daddy through hell. I wasn't strong enough to handle it. I'm still not strong enough."

My mother cuts me off. "Danielle Kathryn Jacobs, let's get one thing straight. You're correct—you did leave, and I wish I could say that it didn't break me. It did, for a long time. It still hurts to think of you being alone and felt you had to cut ties with us. Some days I would just pretend you were away at college, but that almost made it worse when your brother would come home to visit, knowing that you would've been right there with him. I hated it.

"But you listen to me and you listen good. Don't you ever say you are not strong enough. You, my sweet girl, are strong. Do you know why?"

I shake my head while wiping my eyes.

"Because you did come home. That took great strength and courage to do that. You made amends with Haylee and Zach, you're here with us. I know that it's hard, trust me, I have just as many memories of you all here as you do. I love you and nothing that you do or say will ever change that."

Her arms tighten around me, and I collapse into her chest. We sit quietly as I allow my tears to slow.

"God, I forgot how beautiful this view was here."

"Well, it wasn't always this good. I needed something to occupy myself to keep from going on a manhunt to find you, so Natalie and I drove the men nuts redoing both of our backyards. But I don't mean to toot my own horn, but damn it looks good, doesn't it."

A quiet laugh escapes as I sit up. "Yeah, it does. I really am sorry."

"I know you are. Just remember you are here now. And our door is always open no matter what."

"Promise?"

She places her forehead against mine. "I promise. Now what do you say we get back in there before your brother and Kyler have literally eaten everything including the kitchen sink. I don't know where they all put it."

That is a true statement. No wonder they're always at the gym. I have to cook double the amount of food because they eat as though they were eating for two.

By the time we make our way back to the house, the dining room has been cleared. Mom heads into the kitchen, I assume with the rest of the grown-ups while I head to the couches where Haylee, Zach, and Kyler migrated. I take the empty seat beside Kyler. Zach and Haylee are having a side conversation of their own.

My body is still full of tension as I process my mother's words. I am strong. I am home.

"Hey, you doing okay?"

"Yeah, I'm good." I slowly bring my gaze to Kyler's. His lips curve upward. I return his smile, but I quickly divert my attention away from him. I focus on the soft material of the couch.

I readjust myself on the couch, pulling my legs underneath me. My knees are leaning toward Kyler. He places his hand on my knee, giving it a gentle reassuring squeeze. Just with that tiny touch, the tension I have been holding on to finally releases, and I relax back into the couch.

When I turn to join in on the ongoing conversation, I see Haylee's eyes focused on me. The rest of her expression is unreadable, but if I had to venture a guess, she may be catching on to whatever is going on between me and Kyler.

"Are you sure you can't stay any later? You guys could even stay the night. We could spend tomorrow walking around downtown, maybe get some ice cream at Storm Brothers."

I pause, unsure how to politely decline. I know my mom just wants to spend more time with me after all this time.

My panic subsides when I sense Kyler approach me from behind. "We really should be getting on the road. I have a day full of meetings Monday I need to prepare for."

"I promise I'll be back and stay a long weekend," I add. *Baby steps, Dani.*

When my mother turns to hug Zach, I spin and mouth "thank you" to Kyler. He nods and winks at me before shaking my father's hand.

As I approach Natalie to say goodbye, she hugs me just as tight as she did when I arrived. "Now, if you try to leave again, I have no problem coming to kick your ass." I laugh, but with the serious expression on her face I don't think she is kidding.

"You'd have to get in line," Haylee adds as she hugs her mom.

Mom swoops me into her arms. "Nat and I will come up, and we can all do a girls' day like we used to."

"I look forward to it. I love you, Mama."

My mom's arms squeeze me tighter. "Oh how I've dreamed of the day that I'd hear you say those words again. I love you, Dani girl."

I take an extra moment while hugging both of my parents. Today has been a lot to handle, but it's at least a step in the right direction. It also helped having everyone there, including Kyler.

As I walk out of my childhood home, I remember the emptiness I felt the last time I left. I wish I could say I didn't still feel it, but now it doesn't feel as deep. Making amends with everyone allows me to feel as though I can breathe for the first time. Coming home was the right decision.

Kyler walks next to me down the steps and places his hand over my lower back as we walk toward his truck. He opens the back door on his side for me, and I pause as I get in, then lean in and kiss his cheek. He blushes, taking his palm to his cheek. "What was that for?"

I smile at him, hoping he can see all the words I am trying to say with my eyes. "Thank you for coming with me today."

Before I allow him to respond, I hop in the back seat next to Haylee. He looks at me, unsure of what to say. I see a slight smile appear on his face as he closes the door and gets in his seat. I don't know what it is about him, but with trying to move forward, I think maybe I'm not afraid to see what's next...especially if I have him by my side to help me.

CHAPTER 27
KYLER

"How on earth did you guys find this place?" Dani asks as I hold the door open for her to our favorite restaurant/bar, Lucky's. They have amazing food, and yeah, it's a total dive, but those are usually the best places. Tonight was $2 taco night and $5 margaritas. It also happens to be karaoke night. I have a few tricks up my sleeve to get Danielle up on the stage—I just haven't shared that with her. I had hoped I would hear her sing again since that day we had overheard her in the shower, but no such luck. She seriously has a voice of an angel. I figure good food, great company, and a little liquid courage should be a good combination to get her up there.

I spot Zach and Haylee over at our usual table and place my hand on Dani's lower back to escort her over. She doesn't flinch at my touch now. I'd say that's a good sign, right? Things were a little tense at first, post-kitchen-kiss, but things have gotten better. Neither of us has brought it up though. I don't know about her, but I sure as hell want to do it again. That kiss...that kiss was better than I dreamed.

"You going to join us, or are you just going to stand there all night like a coatrack," Zach jokes. I realize that Dani has had time to sit down and I'm still standing here at my seat, lost in my thoughts of my mouth on hers.

"Asshole," I mutter under my breath but loud enough so he can hear me, and everyone laughs as I take a seat next to Dani. I look over to her, and she seems nervous. The cool, calm, and collected girl that was with me on the ride over here has been replaced by the nervous, closed-off girl I had initially met. Is it because we're out in public with Zach and Haylee? I see her hands fidgeting in her lap, so I reach over to her hand and give her a smile and wink, showing her that it's okay, but she gives me only one of those weak smiles. Oh no, that just won't do. But on a positive note, she doesn't pull her hand away. So that's progress.

The waiter comes over and we order the usual: two pitchers of margaritas and a variety of tacos—chicken, shrimp, fish, steak, barbacoa. While they aren't huge, they aren't small either. I am proud to say I know how to get down on tacos. Haylee was extremely grossed out by how much we ate the first night Zach brought her with us. She told me she couldn't look at me for a week—hell, I couldn't look at me for a week either.

The waiter brings us our pitchers and four glasses. "I propose a toast," Zach says as he holds up his glass. I can't help but notice the choice of words he used there. I know for a fact that Zach has been carting around an engagement ring to ask Haylee to marry him, but he held off when Dani randomly appeared back in his life. For her, he has put it off while she adjusted getting used to them being together. I guess he doesn't want to freak her out so she runs away again, which I can't blame him for because I'm not ready for her to leave.

"How lucky am I right now to have my girl"—he smiles at Haylee—"my sister back, and my best friend out on the town. To love, family, and friendship."

"Cheers!" we all say in unison as we clink our glasses together.

Dani's eyes go wide, and I can't help but let out a laugh at her expression when the waiter delivers our food. We probably have about twenty tacos, and I'd say there won't be any leftovers by the end of the night. Dani grabs a steak taco first and puts extra sour cream on it and a little salsa before taking a bite.

"Mmmmmmmmmm. Oh my God." She moans.

"Good, huh?" Haylee laughs, covering her mouth after taking a bite of her shrimp taco. That girl can get down on some seafood, let me tell you. Our last trip to Baltimore, we had steamed crabs at this restaurant, and I thought for sure she'd put them out of business. I have no idea where she puts it all, although I'm sure she works it all off—sadly, I have had the pleasure of hearing her and Zach at times.

We sit a few minutes without speaking, but the silence is quickly overtaken when the head bartender, Scott, steps up to the stage and everyone cheers. Dani looks around, a little confused as to where we brought her.

"Hey, hey, how's everyone doing tonight?" Scott yells into the microphone. "Thirsty Taco Night wouldn't be the same without our favorite part of the evening...karaoke!"

The color drains from Dani's face, and she begins to shake her head as if we just asked her to get up there. Little does she know that I do have a plan to get her up there. She takes a big swig of her margarita and laughs. "Well, this night just got a little more interesting."

She's playing right into my plan. "Yeah, I don't know why anyone would ever want to get up there. That's just ridiculous."

Zach and Haylee both chuckle, catching on to my sarcasm since Zach and I get up there every time, sometimes even more than once in a night. However, Dani doesn't do that. I give Zach a look in hopes he can read my mind as to what I'm thinking and not rat us out.

"Yeah, you'd never get me up there." Yet I don't really believe Dani when she says that since she's looking at the stage as if she wants to get up there really bad. *Here goes nothing...*

"You couldn't even pay me to get up there and make a fool of myself. What about you, Zach?" I stare into his eyes to play along.

"Ha! Yeah, I don't think so, not me. I don't do that shit."

Haylee is hiding behind her glass, trying to fight back the laughter as she watches this unfold. A devilish smirk emerges on Dani's face, and I realize she bought right into my plan, knowing how Zach told me they used to be so competitive as kids.

"I dare you to get up there, Zach. What are you afraid of? Huh? Is poor little Zachy scared?" She sticks her bottom lip out in a mock sad face—shit, what I wouldn't give to bite that lip of hers. *Damnit, Kyler, get your mind out of the gutter and let this plan unfold.*

Zach narrows his eyes at her. "Fine. I'll get up there if Kyler gets up there. I'm not making a jackass out of myself alone." He turns his gaze to mine.

I tilt my head as if I'm thinking it over. Duh, of course I'm going to do it, but I can't let Dani know I'm giving in right away. I hold my index finger up. "I will on one condition."

"And what's that?" she questions.

"If we get up there, then *you*"—I point my finger at her —"get up there and sing something too."

She turns her attention from me to the stage, back and forth; she is thinking hard about it. I stick my hand out to shake on our deal, but she just looks down at it before once again turning to the microphone on the stage. She looks at her brother, who has a super-nervous expression in hopes she will buy it.

Finally, she extends her hand and we shake on it. "Deal.

You both get up there, then I will, but judging by my brother's expression, I think he might throw up those delicious tacos before getting his ass up there on stage, so looks like you're gonna lose."

With her hand still in mine, I pull her closer and say, "We'll just see about that," and give her a half smile. I pull my hand back reluctantly and take a swig of my drink. These 'ritas seriously are delicious and go down so smooth, which can be super dangerous. See, what Dani doesn't know is that Zach and I were already signed up for karaoke, and I'm super pumped that this all unfolded before Scott called our names up there.

"All right, Lucky's, what do you say we bring up our crowd favorites," Scott says into the microphone. The crowd is cheering, which only makes Zach's and my smiles larger. Oh, Dani is so going down.

"Everyone, welcome to the stage, Zach and Kyler!"

"Well, darlin'—" I turn to Dani as I get up from my chair and smirk. "—guess you better start thinking about what song you're gonna sing." Her smile instantly falls when she realizes this was all a ploy to get her up there.

"Why don't you watch how the professionals do it, little sis." Zach takes one last swig, and together we head to the stage. We have our backs toward the audience till the music starts and dramatically turn. I have no shame that we have planned-out routines for all of our songs. We are both completely comfortable with our sexuality and attraction to women, but men can love to get up there and shake their ass at times too—it's fun. I tip my head in Danielle's direction as I start to sing. I know when I get back to the table, I'll probably be in trouble, but I'm going to enjoy this. Maybe even a little too much.

Danielle

"Oh, I was so set up, wasn't I." I take my palm to my face in embarrassment.

Haylee lets out a loud laugh. "Yep, you definitely were. I had no idea this was part of the plan, but it's even funnier they didn't tell you. They usually kick off the night with some ridiculous duet. I can't decide if my favorite was when they did 'Ain't No Mountain High Enough,' 'You're the One That I Want,' or wait, no, I think it was 'Islands in the Stream.'"

At that image of them being Dolly Parton and Kenny Rogers, I can't hold back my laugh. "Which one was Dolly," I ask in between my laughter.

She shakes her head. "The best part about it was that they both wanted to be her and ended up flipping a coin to see who was."

I snort from laughing, and instantly tears are in my eyes—not sad tears, but for once happy tears.

Zach and Kyler continue their well-rehearsed singing and dancing to Kenny Chesney and Uncle Kracker's "When the Sun Goes Down." They have the crowd eating out of the palm of their hands, clapping and cheering.

"She thinks Zach is sexy when the sun goes down," Zach sings and winks in Haylee's direction.

"Uncle Kyler's hotter when the sun goes down," Kyler sings, elbowing Zach in the ribs.

When the song ends, they take a rather dramatic bow and

Kyler has a wicked grin on his face. He realizes that I know I just got played.

"You're pretty proud of yourself, huh, asshole?" I poke at Kyler as he takes the seat next to me.

Pretending to be completely innocent, he takes his hand to his chest as if I had just offended his mama. "Who, me? Why, Jacobs, I am truly hurt that you would think I tricked you into this deal."

I look to Zach, who can't hold back his laughter. "Yeah, sis, I think we just got lucky or something." He shrugs it off and takes a swig of his drink.

"Oh hmm," I say playfully, placing my hand on my chin as if I'm in deep thought. "That's funny, since Hails here told me you guys do this all the fucking time."

Haylee chokes on her drink, almost spitting it out on the table. "Hey, don't bring me into this!"

I narrow my eyes at her, then at Zach, finally landing on Kyler. I shake my head knowing that a deal is a deal. Fuck, I haven't sung in front of a crowd in over four years. I don't know if I can do this.

I walk over to the bar and browse the book with all of the songs listed. I feel someone hovering over me. "So you make your choice yet?" Kyler asks, leaning up against the bar.

"I can't believe you tricked me," I say, still focus on the song listings. "How do you know I don't suck and ruin everyone's night?"

Kyler steps closer. "Can I confess something?"

I roll my eyes at him. "Oh, now you want to start being honest with me tonight?"

He throws his hands up in surrender. "Okay, I deserved that." I pause. "But in my defense, I just wanted to hear you sing again."

I whirl in his direction, tilting my head in confusion. "What do you mean *again*?"

Kyler looks down and shuffles his feet, so I repeat, "Kyler, when have you heard me sing before?'

His brown eyes meet mine as he confesses, "So that day you and Zach got into your huge fight..." I raise my eyebrows at him to continue. "Well, we may have arrived home from the gym earlier than what I had told you when you exited the bathroom.We may have caught your show that morning."

My hand goes to my mouth. Oh my God, oh my God, they had been home and heard me singing in the shower. I close my eyes in horror—I just want to escape the reality of my embarrassment, but I feel Kyler's grip on my wrist pulling my hands from my face. His hand then goes to my cheek, pulling my attention back to his.

"Hey, you are really good, like *really* good, and I just wanted to hear you sing again. Zach said you haven't sung in a long time, so I figured you wouldn't just get up there if I asked you. So, I'm sorry—really, Dani, I am. But they are going to love you out there. Trust me, if they can like your dumbass brother's and my routines and want more when we can't carry a tune to save our lives, then they are going to actually enjoy your performance."

He smiles at me, forcing me to smile back.

"Okay, let's do this."

"So what did you have in mind to sing?"

"Well, I saw they have a section dedicated to *The Voice*, which I absolutely love, so I think I'm going to sing this one." I point to Ashley De La Rosa's version of "Foolish Games." It was originally sung by Jewel back in the '90s, but I love this edgier rock version of the song.

Nodding his head, he lets Scott know of my selection and

whispers in my ear, "Go get 'em, killer," and winks before heading back to the table.

I wait at the bar since Scott said that I would be next. Holy shit, I can't really be doing this. As I look at the lady on stage currently attempting to belt out "Sometimes" by Britney Spears, I can't help but laugh. Well, at least I'll be better than her...and Zach and Kyler for that matter.

I was challenged and while I'm not like Zach and Haylee who can't refuse a dare/challenge, I need to be able to prove to myself that I can do this—turning over a new leaf. So here goes nothing.

My palms are beginning to sweat.

Scott takes the stage ahead of me. "All right, everyone, let's hope talent runs in the family. Give it up for Zach's sister, Danielle."

I wipe my palms on my jeans as the music begins to play, but I am frozen in time. The words appear on the screen, and I go to open my mouth, but nothing comes out. I look around at the crowd and find our table. My eyes land directly on Kyler, and he smiles. I nod and turn to Scott, asking to restart. I take three deep breaths as the intro begins again. I close my eyes and open my mouth, and this time the words spill out. I feed off the crowd cheering me on—they are actually cheering me on, not booing me off the stage. This rush is amazing. I haven't felt this alive in so long.

I get a bit ballsy and decide to take the microphone off the stand during the second verse. While I don't have choreographed dance moves like Kyler and Zach, I try to get lost in the music and feel the emotions coming off me. The cheers get even louder as I sing the last high note at the end of the song, and I can hear Haylee's loud whistling. I feel sorry for the guys because I have been in close proximity when she's done that, and it is loud as fuck. As I finish the song, I am frozen, out of breath, and full of smiles. The small crowd yells their praise as I set the microphone back on its stand and exit the stage, headed back to the table.

"Holy fucking shit, Dani! Where the hell did that come from?" my brother asks as he pulls me into an embrace, and I shrug.

"That was so amazing," Haylee adds before pulling me from my brother's arms and taking me into her own.

Kyler hasn't said a word. As I come around to our side of the table and sit back in my seat, I reach for my margarita that has surprisingly but pleasantly been refilled and take a sip. I place it on the table and catch Kyler still staring at me from the corner of my eye. I place my elbow on the table and prop up my head on my fist. "Don't you have anything to say, Lawson? Are you happy now?"

He still hasn't responded. Zach ends up throwing a napkin at him and he finally snaps back out of it.

"Wow, just wow, Dani. That was...I don't even have words. I am so not sorry I tricked you into getting up there now."

I smile back. "Good. I'm not sorry either. In fact, thank you. I hadn't felt that alive and good in a long time."

KYLER

I'm not sure if it's the tequila flowing freely in Dani's veins (she's on her third margarita), the adrenaline from getting up there to sing, or being in close proximity to me—I'm hoping it's the latter, but whatever it is, I'll take it—but this is the most relaxed I have seen her since we met. I place my arm over the back of her chair, and she instantly leans back into me...win for me! She makes it seem like a natural reaction as if she has been doing it for years. It makes me wonder if that kiss has been on her mind too. I mean, how could it not be? It was mind-blowing.

Leaning closer to her, I whisper in her ear, "Dance with me."

She tilts her head toward me, and we are just inches apart. If I bend forward I could press my lips to hers, but I don't want to make her uncomfortable or anything. Dani looks around. "But no one is dancing."

I fight back a laugh. "So? There's music playing—what more do we need?" I place my other arm on her leg to envelop her fully in my arms. She looks down at my hand but doesn't move it.

Leaning back into me, she laughs. "Umm, really bad music."

I look up on the stage and see someone butchering Billy Joel's "Piano Man." There's always that one person in the crowd who attempts to sing this song, but no one compares to Mr. Joel. I cradle my head in her neck and run my nose up and down, inhaling her scent. She always smells so good. I can hear her breath catch, and her pulse begins to race just as it did the other night in the kitchen.

"Dance with me, Dani." It's not a question but more of a request or a demand. She turns in her chair to fully face me and swallows hard as she looks directly into my eyes.

"Okay."

Just one word and I'm a goner. I am grinning ear to ear. I stand and extend my hand, and she takes it and stands.

"We'll be back."

Zach turns his attention away from Haylee. "Where are you guys off to?"

"The dance floor."

"The dance floor? Where the hell is there a dance floor in this place? I think you've had a little too much."

I wave my hand toward him, showing him that I don't care as I lead Dani to the cleared area we pretend is an actual dance floor. The liquid courage pushes away all thoughts I've had lately about Zach not being okay with this. After all, this is just one dance. I pull her close to me as I wrap my arms around her waist. She links her hands together around my neck and looks anywhere but at me.

"Hey," I say, gaining her focus back on me. "It's just a dance, not a marriage proposal." She giggles at my comment. Damn that sound is seriously heaven. I could spend every day of the rest of my life making sure I heard that sound and die a happy man. Fuck, I sound pussy-whipped already and this girl isn't even mine, at least not yet.

I reach up behind my neck, grabbing one of her hands, clasping it with mine, and pulling it to my chest. We move side to side, getting lost in the music and lost in ourselves. Her nerves quickly dissipate, and I can feel her relax against me. I need to be careful because if I pull her any closer at the moment, she will know exactly what she does to me. I'm trying to keep her away from the semi I've been sportin' all night, but fuck if I don't love having her this close to me.

As she relaxes, she places her head on my chest and says softly, "Your heart is beating crazy fast."

I smile, but she doesn't lift her head to see it. "Well, you do that to me."

She doesn't respond to my comment. I wonder if she even

heard it. We continue to sway to the awful tunes of a one drunk Mr. Thomas Hughes, but I wouldn't change a thing.

Dani looks up at me and doesn't move her eyes away. Is she feeling this too? She has to be. Here's my chance to kiss her again. I'm taking a big risk, and I'm not even 100 percent sure she wants me to kiss her until she takes her bottom lip between her teeth and diverts her attention back and forth between my eyes and my lips as if she's asking for permission. I swallow and wet my own lips, which in kissing language means "hell yeah." The space between us closes as I get closer to her mouth. I think she might pull back, and I open my heavy-lidded eyes one last time, asking her permission without words. She just nods moments before my lips crash on hers. My hands thread through her hair and pull her even closer to me.

Yep, there is definitely no hiding what she does to me now. Her hand releases from my neck and grips my shirt, like if she lets go she'll fly away. I am keeping her grounded. She tastes of tequila and deliciousness as my tongue slips into her mouth when her lips part for me.

My hands leave her hair and rest on her hips tightly before pushing her back, knowing that if I don't stop right then, I might take her on the dirty floor here at Lucky's, and in front of her brother no less. We are both breathless, and her lips are swollen from kissing me. She has never looked more sexy... Wait, nope, that's not true. The first night she got here as she bumped into me in only a towel in the hallway is tied for first place right now. She looks nervous as if she's done something wrong, so I grab her hand to keep her from running and place one last chaste kiss on her lips.

"Hi."

"Hi."

"We should probably get back before your brother storms over here and drags me off the dance floor like in a cartoon."

Dani smiles and glances over at our table. Her cheeks are flushed and her hair a tad messy from my grip.

"Oh my God he's on his way over here."

My entire body tightens, and I jump at the thought of this potentially going the wrong way. The slight smile Dani had before is now a full-blown smirk.

"I'm totally kidding."

"Smartass." I nod in the direction of the table and extend my hand to her. She takes it and we walk back to the table. Her hand never leaves mine. Once we approach the table, I see Zach helping Haylee into her coat. "Leaving already?" I ask, a little confused.

"Yeah, well, I found myself ready for bed all of a sudden," Zach replies with a grin from ear to ear, giving Haylee a wink. She gives a little drunk giggle and fake yawns. It's pretty clear neither of them are tired. I clearly underestimated Zach's reaction because there was no way he missed that little display of affection out there, and I am still standing. Maybe he would be okay with it after all, or possibly he has had more to drink than I thought and he is at the stage where he is nonchalant about everything. "We're gonna head out. Bill is paid—you got next time."

I nod at Zach. "Thanks. See you at home?"

"Nah, I think we'll be staying at Cami's tonight. She gets back in town tomorrow so we're going to take advantage of her place for one more night." He winks at me now. "See you both in the morning," he says pointing between the both of us as Haylee drags him out by his jacket. Shit, I would hate to be that Uber driver, I think, laughing to myself.

I turn to Dani, who is biting her lip, probably nervous as to what comes next as she realizes we will be alone together in the house tonight. Of course, that is pretty normal for us although we've never made out like this before, so to be honest, I'm not really sure what happens next. She reaches for her jacket on the back of her chair, and I quickly grab it from her and hold it up to help her into it. She slips her arms in the sleeves but doesn't move from my grasp right away.

Leaning down, ignoring the next poor karaoke victim attempting to perform Journey's "Don't Stop Believing," I whisper in her ear, "Do you want to get another drink somewhere, or are you ready to go home?"

She takes a moment to think and looks over her shoulder in my direction and says the last thing I expect her to say: "I think I want you to take me home."

She says it not in a way meaning that she wants me to take her home and leave her the fuck alone. No, she says it in a seductive tone, inferring that I might just get to feel her in my arms again tonight. With that, I place my hand on the lower part of her back and escort Dani out of Lucky's while we wait for a car to take us home.

CHAPTER 28

Danielle

The ride home from Lucky's is silent. I sit right next to Kyler with our fingers intertwined as he rubs his thumb against my knuckles. I don't want him to sense that I am nervous even though I am. I want him—I want this. The car drops us off in front of the house, and Kyler scoots out first and offers me his hand again. I take it. We slowly walk to the house, and Ky takes out his keys from his pocket. I walk into the house first after he unlocks the door. Here goes nothing.

Once the front door is closed, I press Kyler up against the door, startling him with my forcefulness. I crash my lips onto his and take his bottom lip between my teeth, causing him to release a soft groan. He slides his tongue into my mouth while his hands land on my ass, and he gives it a squeeze, pulling me closer to him. We are making out like two starving teenagers. In an instant he spins us around and slams me into the door, pressing his body against mine so that I can feel how turned on he is. His hands snake down my body to find the hem of my shirt, and he pauses as if asking for permission. I open my eyes and look at him and nod. His eyes have gone much darker than usual, eyes that are filled with desire. There is no questioning if he wants me or not especially judging by the bulge in his jeans.

Kyler pulls my shirt over my head and drops it to the floor

by our feet. He looks down, staring at my purple lace bra and my breasts that are spilling from it. "Holy shit," he mutters under his breath.

That deep voice makes my panties even damper. Leaning down, he trails kisses from my jaw to my chest, leaving little nips along the way and caressing the skin with his tongue as if licking the wound. His hand travels down and rubs me through the front of my jeans. My breathing is already so fast, but then panic starts to overtake me. I'm going to have sex. Why is that scary to me?

I want this gorgeous man in front of me, and all I can think of is what if I'm not good enough. As if he can sense that my body tensed under his touch, he pulls back. Oh no, I can feel my eyes beginning to fill up.

"Baby, what's wrong? Did I hurt you?" Kyler asks as he runs his thumb along my damp cheek, wiping away the runaway tears. I shake my head. He must think I'm seriously pathetic.

"I...well...I've..." I try to speak.

Brushing the hair out of my face, Kyler asks, "You what?"

Mustering the strength from the proximity of our bodies, one of his hands on my hip and the other now on the back of my neck, I whisper, "I've only ever been with one man." He knows who without me having to say his name. "What if I'm no good at this?"

He takes my cheeks in his hands, briefly places a kiss on my lips, and pulls back just enough for me to see a smile on his face.

"Not possible."

He is so close that I feel like I'm drunk on his scent, a mix of cologne, tequila, lust, and want. And that last part scares the shit out of me.

"We don't have to do anything you're not ready for or don't want to do, but please, baby, don't push me away. How about you come with me and we'll put a movie on and you let me hold you all night?"

I lean into his touch and nod. "Yeah, I'd like that."

We walk down the hall toward our rooms. I stop in front of my door, and Kyler stands behind me. He places his hands on my shoulders and kisses the base of my neck, resulting in an embarrassing moan on my end. I can feel his smile without turning around.

"You go get changed and do whatever you need, and then meet me in my room. I'll get the movie ready. I believe it's your turn to pick."

I shake my head. "No, you pick it tonight."

Kyler raises an eyebrow at me., "Are you saying you like my taste in movies, Miss Jacobs?"

I laugh as I enter my room. "Nope, not saying that at all, Mr. Lawson."

With that I close my door. I need to take a few deep breaths and compose myself. No need to freak out—he already said I was in control, that we would only do what I wanted—but honestly, what is it I want? He is the first man I allowed to touch me intimately since Emmett. Hell, to even touch me in general besides a few hugs from my father, Zach, Mr. Brian, or people at the funeral as they gave me their condolences. I spent the better part of four years doing my own thing, little contact with anyone really.

Funeral. Emmett. Fuck, what am I doing? I can do this, right? I look over at the photo of Emmett on my nightstand.

Please don't be mad at me.

We're just going to watch a movie, that's all...and maybe I'll let him kiss me again. I can feel myself blushing at the thought of what happened moments ago as we walked into the house. Those thoughts have my head spinning. I couldn't stop thinking about our first kiss in the kitchen—how the fuck am I supposed to forget tonight? *Maybe I don't want to...*

I shake that thought from my head for now, throwing my hair in a messy bun and changing into a pair of purple cotton shorts and a black tank top. I make a pit stop in the bathroom to wash my face and brush my teeth. I'm not concerned about Kyler seeing me without makeup like I'm sure most girls would be. If he's seen me crying my eyes out, barely breathing and in full-blown panic attack and yet he still didn't run in the opposite direction, I would say that means something. I stare at myself in the mirror for a moment and give myself one last "you can do it" pep talk. I'm sure I'm way overthinking this.

With confidence that I can do this, I exit the bathroom and head next door to Kyler's room. His door is partially open, but out of habit I knock.

"Come in," he says from the other side. I open the door and see Kyler sitting up in his bed, shirtless, a full-blown fucking Adonis in front of me. My eyes follow the hard lines of his chest.

"Holy shit," I mutter softly, but judging by the smile that creeps on Ky's face, I'm thinking I may not have said that as quietly as I thought.

"I was beginning to think you were gonna stand me up."

I shake my head but still haven't moved from his doorway.

"Are you just going to stand there gawking at me all night, or are you going to join me?"

I flip him off as I move toward the bed. He senses my hesitation. Ky throws back the covers and opens his arms for me. I see he is wearing teal gym shorts—phew, at least he's not just in boxers. I climb into bed and into his arms as he adjusts the covers over us. I wrap my arms around his waist and inhale his manly scent. God, how does he still smell so good without showering? I snuggle into him, and he kisses my temple. As soon as his lips touch my skin, all my nerves fade away and I relax into him.

I take a breath to enjoy the moment before asking, "So which shitty movie are you going to make me suffer through this time?"

Grabbing the remote from the nightstand, he presses Play. As the title appears for *Office Space*, I groan. "Oh no! Are you fucking serious right now? This movie is awful."

Leaning away from me, his face goes serious. "One"—he holds up one finger—"you said I could pick the movie tonight and two"—he holds up two fingers—"you better take those words back right now."

I can see the playfulness in his eyes, and I play along. "And if I don't?" I push up on his chest, and his eyes drop to where my breasts are spilling out of my tank. He grins and leans closer to me. I suck in a breath, thinking he's going to kiss me, or well, that I *want* him to. As his mouth approaches mine, I lick my lips. Yep, this is going to happen—I'm going to kiss Kyler in his bed.

When he's close enough that I can feel his breath upon my lips, he says, "Well, then I'm just going to have to make you."

I close my eyes, preparing to kiss him and feel his hands on my sides but jump when he begins to tickle me. I squirm under his touch, trying to get away. Fuck, why do I have to be so ticklish!

"Okay, okay, please stop," I say in between giggles.

He doesn't let up from tickling me. "Do you take it back?"

"Nope."

He continued to tickle me, and tears fill my eyes from laughter this time. "Kyler," I say breathlessly as he hovers over me. "Okay, you win, I take it back."

He smiles his devilish grin. "Thank you. Now I can do this."

He closes the space between us and presses his lips to mine. My hands grab the back of his neck to pull him closer as I part my lips. He takes that as an invitation to deepen the kiss, and I welcome his tongue in my mouth. He settles between my thighs, and I grind my hips into his growing erection, forcing a moan from my lips that he swallows up while kissing me. I take his bottom lip between my teeth, and Ky growls at me. Here we are in our twenties, dry humping like two crazed teenagers. I want him and just as I'm about to give him full permission, he pulls back.

Staring into my eyes, he pants, "If we don't stop now, I can't guarantee I will be able to. Plus, you need to suffer through this movie, as you so gently put it. I'll reward you only if you like the movie."

I groan at him, unsure if it's the fact that we're stopping or the fact he's still going to make me watch this movie.

Ky pulls me back into his arms and restarts the movie. He sets the remote back on the nightstand and turns the bedside lamp off. We watch the movie, and I will admit to myself—but of course not to him—that the movie was funny. There were a few times that I couldn't hold back my laughter, and he just went "Uh-huh" but didn't say an "I told you so" which was surprising.

I'm half-asleep when the movie ends and feel Kyler kiss my forehead and softly say, "Good night, Dani," before I fully fall asleep wrapped in his arms. And it was the best night of sleep I had gotten.

 KYLER

I wake up half expecting Dani to be gone since I don't feel her against me, but as I open my eyes, I see her next to me with her back to me and her hair spread across the pillow. I don't want to be a creeper, but I can't help staring at her. She is absolutely beautiful. I'm not ready to let her out of my bed just yet, so I drape my arm over her hip and pull her closer to me. She makes a slight moaning noise, not ready to wake up, and that sound goes straight to my dick. I wrap her in my arms and nuzzle my face in her neck.

"Good morning, beautiful," I whisper in her ear and kiss her neck. Her hand lies over mine, trapping it there on her stomach where her tank top has ridden up a little bit. Her fingers lace with mine. I see that her eyes are still closed. I kiss her shoulder and back up her neck and nibble on the sensitive spot behind her ear that I discovered last night, which creates another moan. Shit, this woman is going to kill me this morning.

"Good morning," she mumbles back with her eyes still closed, but she is smiling.

Her hand tightens on mine for a moment before she unclasps our hands, and I assume she's going to push me away, but she doesn't. Instead she leads my hands north on her body under her tank top to her chest. As I reach the underside of her breast, I lean in and whisper, "Are you sure?" I then kiss that sensitive spot again.

She nods. "Yes, please," she says in a needy voice. I could

come in my shorts right then the way she said that, as if she needs me to touch her to breathe. My girl doesn't have to tell me twice. My hands travel up her breasts to her perfect peaked nipples and brush one with my thumb. She jumps a little before leaning back into me. There is no way to hide my morning erection now. I love the way she reacts to my touch, and I want to see more. I take one breast in my hand, massaging it before moving to the other one. I work her nipples between my fingers, but shit I want to taste her, tease her with my mouth. I've fantasized about her breasts and the things I could do to and with them since the first day I met her.

Dani takes her arm and reaches behind my neck to pull me closer to her. She grips the back of my head, her fingers digging into my scalp. The sweet little noises she makes is driving me crazy.

"Do you have any idea what you're doing to me?" I growl in her ear.

Dani grinds her ass against my hard cock. "Mmm," she responds.

I think it's safe to say the nerves she had last night are gone, but I'm not going to push her because I'm worried about pushing her too far. But right now all I can think about is getting her naked and squirming under my touch. I press against her as she continues to grind against me. What is this woman doing to me? Dani is already panting and out of breath and I've barely touched her. Dani looks back at me through her eyelashes, and I need to taste her, so I pull her face to mine and dive into her mouth, assaulting her tongue with mine. She kisses me back just as fiercely.

She rolls over so that she is facing me and wraps her leg around my hip. We are making out and dry humping like a bunch of wild animals. Her sweet little moans are enough to make me come in my shorts, but I want to make her feel good this morning. Still kissing her, I roll her onto her back and hover over top of her. She opens her eyes and stares at me with those beautiful baby blue eyes that are filled with want and desire, biting her bottom lip as she feels my hand trail from her chest to the top of her shorts. Her eyes begin to close as my hand keeps going, and she doesn't stop me.

Sliding my hand into her shorts and into her panties, I find her soaking wet. "You're so wet for me, baby," I say against her lips before biting that bottom lip myself. I slide a finger inside her, and she grabs on to my shoulders, digging her nails into my skin while I explore her pussy, taking my finger in and out. I know she said she has only ever been with one man, so I plan to take my time and explore her and her needs and show her how good it can feel. Dani begins to writhe under me, and I know she is enjoying it, so I insert another finger and press my thumb to her clit to push her over the edge. I can feel her walls begin to contract around my fingers as I slide them in and out and circle her clit, applying the perfect amount of pressure.

"Oh shit, Kyler...I'm gonna...I'm gonna—don't stop!"

I know I can push her over the edge by pulling her top down, exposing her breasts, and I draw circles around her nipples with my tongue. Her moans get louder as her hands leave my shoulders and fist the sheet under her. Her back arches and her pussy swallows my fingers as she comes around them. The way her body jolts by my touch makes me want more, but I need to let her breathe and come down from her orgasm high. I am so mentally high-fiving myself right now though. Dani's breathing starts to even out, but I haven't moved.

I pull my fingers from her, and I can tell she is disappointed by the loss of me inside her. She finally opens her eyes and watches me pull my wet fingers to my mouth and lick them clean.

"Mmmmm, I didn't think there was something I'd like the taste of more than your cupcakes, but shit I was wrong."

I pull her close to me once I lie back down. Her hand travels down my shorts, feeling the outline of my hard cock, but I pull her hand back and lace our fingers together. I'm definitely giving myself a case of blue balls, but I need to show her it's not just about sex here.

"Baby, this morning was about you. We have plenty of time for me later. I want to explore this thing with you and get to know you more and see where it goes. Will you let me take you on an official date?"

Looking up at me through hooded eyelids, she leans in and kisses me softly.

"Is that a yes?" I ask as she pulls back smiling.

"Yes, but only if you do that again."

"Oh, you can bet your sweet ass we will be doing that again...that and more," I reply, winking at her. "And see, I told you last night you'd be rewarded if you liked the movie, so you basically just admitted that you loved the movie."

She doesn't say anything because I know she enjoyed both last night's movie and this morning's encore.

CHAPTER 29

Danielle

"So..." Haylee starts as we climb into her car. I knew it—here it comes. I've been waiting for it since she and Zach arrived this morning. After a long morning in bed, Kyler and I finally decided to join the real world. When we walked into the kitchen, we were greeted by a giddy and smiling Zach and Haylee sitting at the island sipping coffee. They watched us as we made coffee without saying anything. I knew Haylee would be pressing for details later.

After a hilariously awkward moment between the four of us, Ky and Zach headed to the gym. Haylee later found me in my room rummaging through my entire closet trying to find something for Kyler's and my official first date. She eyed the pile of clothing spread out all over my bed, and when a wicked smirk appeared on her lips, she didn't ask what I needed clothes for, instead clapped her hands together and said, "Looks like we need to go shopping," which brings us to this moment.

"So..." I say back as I buckle my seat belt and place my hands in my lap.

"You and Kyler, huh?" She thinks she's being funny knowing damn well what she witnessed last night at Lucky's. I blush, looking out the window as I remember me and Kyler...

what it was like to have his hands and mouth on me last night and this morning and sleeping curled up next to him all night.

"Mmmhmm," I mutter, but it comes out more of a moan.

Hails throws her head back in laughter as she starts the ignition. "Oh, I think lunch might need to be added to our shopping date, and that lunch may need to include cocktails because you better damn well believe you are spillin' all the details! But first things first, we need to set the mood."

"What!" I squeal as I see her pull our favorite Katy Perry CD out of her center console and put it in the CD player.

"You have no idea how long I've waited to be able to jam to this CD with a Jacobs and not feel like I'm being judged. I have watched your brother and Kyler do some crazy and stupid shit over the years, but there is some serious judgment in his eyes when I play this in his presence. It's like he didn't even know who I am, even though he's seen us perform these songs all the time. I guess it was different once it was his girlfriend doing them? I had to channel my inner Katy, all by myself. Now...let's go get you all hot for your date!"

I smile as I think of this morning when he had told me that he wanted to take me on our official first date. I mean, I guess baking in the kitchen and watching movies a few nights a week doesn't exactly count as dates. But what do I know? It's been four years since I went on a date, even longer since a first date. I feel like I need to brush up on what dating consists of now.

As we head toward the mall, listening to the tunes that made up our teens, I can't help but wonder what she must be thinking. Is this weird for Haylee seeing me with another man? I push those thoughts to the side because I want to be able to give Kyler a chance, and I can't keep having Emmett hang over us. I am finally trying to get the fresh start that everyone had pushed on me years ago. It wasn't that I didn't want to, it was just that I wasn't ready. I don't know that I'm fully ready in this moment, but I am willing to try and give it my best.

We walk almost the entire mall, going in and out of stores. By the time we are done, we both have our hands full of bags, with sore feet and rumbling stomachs. We pile the bags in the trunk and head over to the cute little bistro nearby and are seated on the water.

Haylee and I both order a mimosa and a salad—Caesar with chicken for her, and a steak salad for me. While waiting for the waiter to bring our drinks back, she places her clasped hands on the table and looks at me, scrunching her eyebrows.

"What?" I say as she looks me over.

"I'm trying to figure out who you are and what you did with my best friend?"

I laugh. "What the fuck is that supposed to mean?"

She smiles and sits back in her chair. "Well...it means, look at you, Dani! Look at how far you've come recently. You're opening yourself up to not only us but to Kyler. After all that time away and shutting us out, you actually saw your parents and mine—my mom has not stopped talking about how excited she is about having someone to help her in the kitchen, so thanks."

I let out a loud giggle and shrug—not my fault she sucks in the kitchen. She continues. "But in all seriousness, D, I'm proud of you. I mean, look at you...actually going on a date, and *hello*, that kiss last night." She fans herself as if she's on fire.

I can feel my cheeks redden as I remember not only that kiss but all the others. I nod in agreement that I have come a long way.

The waiter brings our drinks and salads. I begin to push the food around on my plate. My stomach is full of nerves, but I know I need to eat something, so I eventually take a bite. "To be honest, Hails, I'm not sure how to feel. There is something about Kyler that, I don't know how to put it in words..."

She quickly cuts me off. "You don't need to put it in words because you just smiled when you mentioned his name and that, I think, is enough."

And Kyler did feel different, not that I spent much time around other men, but I feel different around him, as if he can make me whole and fill all the broken parts of me.

"Can I be honest?" I ask while taking a bite of my salad, and Haylee nods. "I have no idea what I'm doing. I mean, I've only ever been on one first date and that was when we were thirteen. What if I'm no good at it or Kyler realizes how much of a mess I am? Then it'll just be awkward."

Snapping me out of my word vomit conversation freak-out, Haylee raises her glass at me, nodding for me to pick mine up as well. "I know you are scared, but that's how these things go. I knew Zach my whole life, but I almost threw up from nerves before our first date."

I let out a giggle, and she gives me a stern look back, knowing I am thinking of the time she threw up in his gym bag from the dare. Deep down, though, I feel a little bit of sadness knowing that I wasn't here for her to calm her nerves and help her get ready.

"What I'm trying to say is just take it one day or date at a time, okay? Now cheers, bitch—to us being back together and being able to gossip about boys and it not be my brother."

I go to open my mouth to interject that her stories these days *do* include *my* brother, but I keep my thoughts to myself. "Now spill all the juicy details of Lawson because I am dying to know!"

We cheers and I fill her in on everything that has been happening over the past few weeks—our first kiss, hanging out, and of course last night and this morning's activities. The waiter clears our plates and brings the check.

Haylee claps her hands together after finishing the last of her drink. "Kyler would kill me if I got you good and toasted before your date, so let's head on out and I'll help you get ready, just like old times."

Old times... That catches my breath for a moment as I think of all the dates with Em that Haylee had helped me get ready for.

She can sense my hesitation as I rise from my seat, and walks around to my side of the table and places her hands on my arms. "Whatever you are thinking—stop it. There's no need to overthink this. He's a good man, Dani. Zach loves the guy, and so do I. Your brother wouldn't be okay with this if he didn't think so, and last night the entire ride home he was giddy as a fucking schoolgirl over the thought of you two finally getting your heads out of your asses. Anyone in a three-foot radius could feel the tension between you guys. We've watched it go down for weeks just waiting for it to explode."

Maybe we weren't as secretive with our feelings as we thought, if Zach and Haylee picked up on something between us. I guess I'm doing this—I'm really doing this. Time to go get ready for my date.

HAYLEE HELPED ME CURL MY HAIR AND APPLY A LITTLE BIT more makeup than I typically wear. I went so long with not caring about my appearance that it feels good looking in the mirror and seeing myself dressed up like this.

I turn around to Haylee staring at me. "What? Does it look okay? It's too much, right? Maybe this was a bad idea."

Haylee jumps up from where she's sitting on my bed. "Oh no you don't. You look amazing. Kyler isn't going to know what hit him, and I have a feeling dinner and whatever he planned may be cut short because I'm sure once he sees you in this outfit, the first thing he's gonna want to do is get you out of it."

I can feel a flush creeping up my neck at that thought. Haylee had convinced me to buy some matching sets of lingerie —"Just in case," she joked—a set that I happened to have put on under my clothes tonight—just in case, of course. But I'm not sure I'm ready for sex yet. Kyler meant what he said last night that we can take it one step at a time, but this morning...*holy shit*, I had forgotten what it was like to be touched to orgasm by a hand that belonged to someone besides myself, to be craved, and now that I've had a reminder of what that all feels like, I'm not sure if I want it to go away.

I apply a little bit more lip stain on my lips and fluff my curls one last time as Haylee shouts, "I'm going to check on the boys. See you out there, D!"

Before she can fully exit the room, I call out, "Hey, Hails." She turns to me with one hand on the doorframe and one by her side., "Thanks!" I don't need to explain what my thanks are for —she knows. That's the thing about my best friend: we don't always communicate with words.

Grabbing my purse, I smile at my reflection and swallow big before heading out into the living room.

CHAPTER 30

KYLER

*H*aylee walks out of the bedroom first and meets me and Zach in the living room. She is looking at me funny, and I don't know if that's a good thing or not. Haylee walks over to where Zach is sitting in the chair and sits on the arm, putting her arm around him while he reads something on his iPad.

"Everything okay?" Zach asks Haylee without even looking up.

"Yep, everything is great. She'll be right out."

Okay, well, that settles the question of whether or not she was going to bail on me, but I still don't know what's up with that expression on Haylee's face.

Why am I so nervous? It's not like I haven't gone on dates before. I need to act cool. *Be cool, Ky! It's just a date! You guys have been out before—just this time it's without anyone else joining us. Shit, you've already tasted her pussy, why be nervous all of a sudden?* In the middle of my ridiculous pep talk I hear the clicking of heels against the floor, and my eyes slowly lift to see her.

I hear Haylee whistle in the background, and I'm thankful it's a low whistle and not her eardrum-bursting one she usually does. I don't turn around to see their reactions. My eyes are trained on Dani, this absolutely beautiful creature walking toward me. I'm the luckiest bastard in the world for getting to take this girl—no, *woman*—out tonight.

My eyes travel up her body, first noticing the black heels on her feet, and I hope one day to get her naked wearing just those. After I notice her fuck-me heels, I travel up her sexy, toned legs in skinny jeans that fit her in all the right places. Would I be a total pig to ask her to spin around so I can check out her ass? Damn! As I continue up her body, my eyes stop on her tits that are spilling out of her fancy-looking top thing. Dani doesn't usually wear low-cut tops, so I can't help but wonder if she is doing it on purpose just for me. Either way, I'm sure as hell not going to complain. I need to stop thinking about taking that top off and dragging my tongue along her breasts to suck on her hard nipples or I'm going to A) make this all super uncomfortable having a major hard-on in front of my best friend, B) end up taking her out here on the couch with an audience, or C) need to go back to my room and change my pants.

I try to think thoughts of the least sexiest things...dead bugs, road kill, grandparents getting it on... Okay, that last one was definitely not necessary and makes me shiver a little, but at least it did the trick and I can feel my dick deflating and at a pretty quick rate. It works until my eyes meet Dani's. She looks so shy right now, but she smiles big at me. A real genuine smile that makes my heart skip a beat.

It's not until Zach clears his throat behind us that we are both knocked out of the trance. I walk over to her, and she bites her lip, looking a little nervous. When I reach her, I place my hand on her cheek, brushing my thumb up and down in hopes of calming her nerves. She leans into my touch.

"Hi."

"Hi."

"You look beautiful."

She blushes at my comment and leans into my palm. "Thank you."

"You ready to go?" She nods her head yes. I remove my hand from her cheek and take her hand, intertwining her fingers with mine.

Zach stands and goes into protective-dad mode, thinking he's so funny. "All right, you kids have fun. Be sure to have her home by 10:00, or I'll be on the porch cleaning my gun or maybe send a search party out for you."

Haylee smacks his arms. "Dumbass. You guys have fun. Don't worry about this assclown. I'll make sure he's nowhere near a gun or the front porch." She rises from the seat and waves goodbye as she walks into the kitchen.

Both Dani and I roll our eyes as we walk past Zach and head out the front door. When we get to the passenger side of the truck, I push her against the door lightly and meet her lips with mine. Her mouth opens, welcoming my tongue...and we're back to my dick getting hard again. As our lips lock and kiss hungrily, she wraps her hands around my neck and pulls me closer. I know she can definitely feel my erection now. I pull back, knowing that if we don't stop now, I might not be able to. When Dani finally opens her eyes, the blue is sparkling even in the darkness.

"Sorry, I wanted to do that ever since I saw you walk into the living room." I open the truck door and wait for her to get in.

"I wouldn't have complained if you had." She gives me a devilish smirk before she climbs in and closes the door.

I adjust my pants for what seems like the millionth time lately and walk around to the driver's side. When determining our date, I thought about doing something fancy and heading into the city, but that might have been a little over-the-top. So I really racked my brain and came up with the perfect idea. There's a small music festival down at the park tonight with food trucks and music. There are also some vendors too. Now that the weather has gotten warmer, there are lots of cute events put on in town.

The ride to the park is a little quiet, but I think we both have a little bit of leftover nerves—mine brought on in hopes she likes this, and hers I'm sure are because she has no idea where we are going or what I am leading her into. I gave no hint whatsoever as to the details of our date.

When we pull up to the parking lot of the park, she looks around, trying to figure out where we are going. Before I can tell her to wait for me to walk around and open the door for her, she gets out of the truck the same time I do. She is clearly excited to see what I have planned. I originally hadn't planned on this being our first date, since I just asked her last night, but I remembered seeing the event posting before and was going to see if everyone wanted to go anyway. It just worked out perfectly.

"Where are we going?"

"You'll see. Just this way." I place my hand on the small of her back and lead her toward the area where the food trucks are sitting. Her eyes widen when she sees the trucks all lined up, surrounded by lights and picnic tables. On the outskirts of that area is a stage where a band is currently playing. I think they're local, playing country music, and people are even dancing in front of it. What a great setup. I think I've even impressed myself with this date; hopefully she is impressed as well.

She turns to me and places her hands on my hips. "Oh my God, this is awesome!"

"Really? You like it?"

She nods and places a quick kiss on my cheek.

"Well damn, if I knew this was the reaction you'd give me, then maybe I should've taken you out a long time ago."

"Don't push your luck, Lawson." She turns around and looks at all the different food trucks. There's a burger truck, Italian ice, taco truck, falafel truck, and then I spot it... "It's So Gouda"—the everything cheese truck. "So, what are you in the mood for?"

I reach for her hand, lace our fingers, and pull her in the direction of the cheese truck.

As we get closer, her eyes light up and I bet her mouth is watering because there is a huge sign on the side of the truck that says, *"Voted best cheese fries three years in a row!"*

She stops in awe, and I step behind her, wrapping my arms around her middle, and lean down closer to her ear. "How do cheese fries sound?"

She lets out a little moan that lets me know I made the right call with this.

"And, not just any cheese fry, but I happen to know they use curly fries."

She moans again and this time as she does it she leans back against me, her ass rubbing up against my dick. I don't think she does it on purpose, but I'm not fully sure.

"Is that a yes?"

Dani turns around and is smiling from ear to ear. "I will always say yes to cheese...especially if it's on fries. I'd put that shit on everything if I could. Well, maybe not everything." She looks lost in her thoughts, probably thinking of foods she wouldn't put cheese on, when I reach back and pinch her ass. She jerks forward.

"What was that for?"

"Sorry, just trying to get your attention...and can you blame

221

me for wanting to have my hands on that ass? Damn, you know how to fill a pair of jeans."

Busting out in a fit of giggles, she shakes her head at me and turns around, pulling my arm to get in line to order.

After enjoying a large plate of cheese fries, a chicken quesadilla, and a small order of fried mac and cheese along with two raspberry lemonades, we both are stuffed to the brim. I love a girl that can eat. Nothing sexier than a girl with an appetite—true, I ate most of the food, but my girl can surely get down on some cheese fries. I was so turned on watching her lick the cheese off her fingers.

We spend the rest of the evening walking around, browsing the little stands set up, and I even get her onto the makeshift dance floor for a few dances.

When we arrive back home, we sit in the driveway for a few moments, unsure of how the night will end. I've never taken a girl I lived with out on a date. Do I kiss her at the front door? Do I kiss her inside? Do we just go our separate ways? Do I walk her to her bedroom?

I am surprised when Dani leans over the center console and grabs my cheeks in her hands, pulling my face to hers, and devours my lips. What started out as a simple kiss has turned into heavy breathing, hands groping, and private parts grinding. I'm not exactly sure at what moment Dani climbs over into my lap, but hell, I'm not complaining. When she pulls away, I miss the contact already. Her cheeks and chest are both flushed, and I bet if I reached into her panties I would find them soaking wet.

"We should probably get inside. I'm worried Zach is spying out the window or something."

I laugh because sadly I know my best friend is not above pulling some shit like that just to be funny.

This time, I tell her to wait there. I quickly jump out of the truck, adjust my pants, and run around to her side of the truck and open the door for her. As she slides out of the truck, she is in close proximity, her chest pressed up against me.

"Yeah we should definitely get inside, like *now*," I breathe against her skin.

"Uh-huh." If anyone was looking, they could probably see the sparks flying between us with the sexual chemistry. What I wouldn't give to push her up against the truck and slide my cock deep inside her. *Calm down, Ky, before you both get arrested for indecent exposure.*

I wrap my arm around her shoulder and pull her close. She puts her arm around my waist, and we walk up the walkway to the front door. As we get to the front door, she starts to giggle.

"What's so funny?"

"Nothing. It's just like, do we say good night here and do that awkward walk where you say goodbye and then keep going in the same direction as that person...or do we just walk in? I'm sorry, I'm rambling, I'm just nervous. I mean..."

I stop her words by bringing her mouth to mine, plunging my tongue forward, not even waiting to ask for permission. I thread my fingers into her hair, pulling her to me as if she were my lifeline. I'm starting to realize that maybe she is. She lets out a noise that goes straight to my dick. This is one hell of an ending to the perfect date. I'm a little worried that she will think I'm expecting something more to happen once we go back inside.

"For the record, I don't plan to say good night now, but I just had to give this date a proper good-night kiss. And then I plan to walk you inside, take you to one of our rooms, wrap my arms around you, tell you that I had an amazing time tonight, and fall asleep with you in my arms."

"Are you sure you're real?" She looks up at me with hooded

eyes—eyes so full of want, desire, and lust. This girl...my girl... continues to surprise me more and more each day.

Jokingly, I touch my chest, stomach, arms, and lastly run my hand over my cock that is extremely hard. "Hmmm...I seem to be pretty real."

Dani runs her pointer finger from the base of my neck down to the bottom of my shirt. "So it seems."

I place a quick kiss on her forehead, take her hand in mine, fingers laced together, and run my thumb along the top of her hand while I use the key to open the front door. This seriously has been the best date of my life.

CHAPTER 31
Danielle

Sitting in the front seat of Kyler's truck, I watch him load our bags in the back before slipping into the driver's seat next to me. We are headed to my parents' house for Mom's birthday weekend. I had offered to help prepare all of Mom's favorites. I couldn't wait to be back in the kitchen with my mom and Ms. Natalie. Zach and Haylee would be joining us later.

I see Kyler look over to me from the corner of my eye. "You okay? You seem quiet."

I play with the hem of my shirt. "I have a confession. I sort of haven't told my parents that you and I are..." I motion between the two of us.

"Dating."

"Yeah. I'm not trying to hide us or anything, I just wasn't sure how to bring it up exactly. It's not like I could be like 'Hey, Mom and Dad, hope you're having a great day. Oh, by the way, I'm dating my brother's best friend.'" I gasp and quickly cover my mouth, realizing what I said.

Silence fills the truck. Leaning across the center console, Kyler reaches for my chin and turns me to face him. "Hey. It's okay. We can wait to tell them when you're ready or we can tell them together. I get it, this is new territory for me too. But if we're making confessions, I have one too. I kind of already told my sisters—well, they figured it out at our dinner this past week."

I laugh. Knowing that Lauren and Kate know, I'm surprised they haven't purchased a billboard yet. The night I had met them for dinner, they were anything but subtle now that I look back on it. At the time, I didn't really think about it, because even though I was attracted to Kyler from the moment I saw him, I kept myself closed off. Little by little, he is bringing me out of my broken shell.

He drops his hand to my thigh, giving me a reassuring squeeze. "We don't have to tell anyone this weekend. Let's just enjoy celebrating your mom's birthday." He leans over the center console and places a kiss on my cheek. He returns to his seat and starts the truck. "You ready to go?"

I give him an honest smile. "Yep. How 'bout some tunes for the road?"

He smiles back at me. "You got it, babe."

My heart warms at the nickname. It doesn't make me nervous anymore. Kyler flips through the stations, and I hear the beginning beats of New Radicals' "You Get What You Give." He goes to change the station again, and I quickly place my hand over his to stop him. "No, I like this song!"

He lets out a small laugh at my quick enthusiasm. I mean, I did basically yell at him not to change this song. Noticing that my hand hasn't moved from his on the radio dial, Kyler flips his hand over so our palms are facing and laces our fingers. Over the past few weeks, I am starting to feel like myself again, although I am still figuring out who that is exactly. The me that arrived on their doorstep would have quickly pulled my hand back at the point of contact, but not the new me. The new me welcomes his touch.

I squeeze his hand a little tighter as he places it over the center console, and turn the volume up with my free hand as Ky backs up out of the driveway. This will be the first time since our first official date that we are both going back to my parents' house. There was one weekend where they came to us, but Kyler had been out visiting his mom and sisters and missed it, and another time I was actually sick and not just making up excuses to miss out.

After a quick stop at the Starbucks drive-thru and a few rude comments from Ky asking how I can drink my coffee with almond milk—that's apparently unheard of for him, but I give as good as he gives—we are officially on our way to Annapolis.

Pulling up to my parents' house, I can't tell if the sudden pain in the pit of my stomach is nerves about spending the night in my childhood bedroom for the first time since I left or being here with Kyler given our new relationship. What will my parents think? The Hankses? Haylee and Zach seem to be cool with this, thrilled even, but will it be weird for Ms. Natalie and Mr. Brian to see who they thought would be their daughter-in-law with another man?

Bringing his truck to a stop and putting it in park, he lifts our joined hands to his mouth and kisses the back of my hand. "Don't move," he says and then steps out of the vehicle before hurrying around to my side and opening the door.

"M'lady," he says with a bow as he opens the door wider for me to exit the truck.

I curtsy. "Oh, thank you, kind sir, how chivalrous of you."

Kyler closes my door and leans into me, forcing my back against the door panel. "Well, you'll see that I am very chivalrous, and I know how to make my woman happy." He places his hands on my hips, and his thumb rubs the sliver of skin that shows as my shirt rides up a little. "If I remember correctly, I was very chivalrous with you last night," he whispers in my ear in a hushed and breathy voice. My heart instantly picks up its rate, feeling as though it's going to jump out of my chest.

"Oh, is that right," I manage to get out as he leans down to kiss my neck.

I can feel his hot breath on my skin. "Yes, that's right," he says, kissing his way up my neck to my mouth.

His mouth claims mine before I can protest for kissing outside my parents' house. I wrap my arms around his neck and get lost in his kiss—so lost that I don't even notice the footsteps approaching us until we hear a light throat clearing and jerk away from each other only to come face-to-face with a smiling mom and Ms. Natalie. I can feel a blush cover my entire body.

"Busted," Kyler says as he winks to me and turns around. "Hi, Mrs. Hanks, Mrs. Jacobs. You ladies are both looking lovely today."

Leave it to Kyler to suck up to them after being caught sucking up to me. I bury my head in his back in embarrassment.

"Well, I guess we don't have to ask how the drive was for you kids, now do we," my mom says to us, and Ms. Natalie giggles. "Kyler, we had made up the guest bedroom for you, but if you would rather..."

I interrupt my mother before she can finish that sentence. "Mooooooooommmmmm," I shout, feeling like I'm back to being a mortified teenager.

Kyler chuckles, and I can feel his whole body vibrating against me. "Thank you, Mrs. Jacobs, the guest room is just fine." I let out a breath in relief, but I can't help but also feel disappointed that we have been sleeping in the same bed and this weekend we won't be.

"I've told you all these years, please call me Kelly, or Ms. Kelly. Mrs. Jacobs is my mother-in-law."

"Oh, and God forbid you are put in the same category as that woman." Natalie smirks as my mother glares in her direction before turning back to us.

Kyler turns and places a kiss to my temple, then reaches around me to the back to grab our bags. "Well, we better get inside and start this celebration. It's birthday number twenty-nine, right?"

Mom places her arms around Kyler's shoulders as we all turn toward the house. "I knew I liked you." We all laugh as we walk toward the front door. Here goes nothing—our secret is out.

Later in the afternoon before dinner, after we had settled our bags into our respective rooms, I find myself alone on the front porch, rocking in the swing. Running my hand up the chain it hangs off of, I am brought back to the many memories over the years with Emmett, from the first to our last. I look up when I hear the creak of the front porch to be greeted with a different Hanks, Ms. Natalie. I smile at her as she approaches me.

"Can I join you?" She smiles at me as I nod for her to sit, and I scoot over. She pats her hand on my thigh as if she is about to have a serious talk.

"What's going on with you, sweetheart? You've been quiet ever since you were caught earlier. Cat got your tongue? Or maybe Kyler does." She lets out a loud laugh. It's been a long time since I heard that laugh, but it puts a smile on my face and a blush on my cheeks at her comment. I cover my face with my hands in embarrassment.

"Dani, it's nothing to be embarrassed about. Your mom and I were just caught off guard a little because you've never mentioned it, so the last thing we expected to see pulling into the driveway was you all over each other. It reminds me of a few times back..." But she closes her mouth and looks off into the distance. My hand quickly finds hers as I see a tear stream down her cheek. I bite the inside of my cheek to prevent tears of my own from falling.

She takes a deep breath, links our fingers together, and places her other hand over top, pulling them into her lap. "It's okay to miss him and feel sad at times. Each moment of happiness is always paired with sadness knowing it was something Emmett was missing...but just remember he is always with you and always in your heart. You just have to take one day at a time and one step at a time."

I look up at her and try to form the words I want to speak but end up spitting out, "But how did you just move on?"

She squeezes my hand a little tighter. "It's not that I've moved on, sweetie, because losing a child isn't something you move on from or get over. I ask myself how parents are supposed to go on after burying their child. I have to remind myself to breathe. People have told me that I'm so strong, but that's only on the outside. On the inside, my heart is forever broken. But I'm strong because I don't have a choice. There are some days that it will hit me at the most random times and I have to struggle to compose myself. I see people on the street and I hate them, I actually hate them without even knowing them because they have what I lost. I let my grief get the best of me the first year and a half. I know I'll see my son again one day, but until then I need to live my life so that when I do finally see him I can fill him in on all the good, the bad, and the ugly. There is no timetable or calendar that says when you're no longer allowed to grieve or feel sad, but wallowing in the pain and emptiness..." She pauses. "That's not what he would want. Em only ever wanted you to be happy, and I've watched you with Kyler and I think he makes you happy... Does he?"

I smile, a true smile not a forced one, and nod. "Yeah, he does...at least I think he can. I'm still trying to figure this all out and take it slow, which is why I haven't mentioned anything about us until today. I didn't want to make such a big deal out of it just in case things didn't work out. This is all so new to me."

Unclasping our hands, Ms. Natalie wraps her arm around my shoulder and pulls me into her. "I'm so proud of you, Danielle, and you should be too. You fought your way to get here." Ms. Natalie wraps her other arm around me into a strong embrace and kisses the top of my head. I close my eyes and remember the last time Emmett had done that. She leans her head against mine. "Plus you know Kyler is very good-looking—don't think I hadn't noticed. If Haylee wasn't taken, I would definitely push her his way."

Ms. Natalie lets out another one of her laughs, alleviating the somber mood that overtook the porch just moments ago. "Oh my God," I laugh and push her away. She lightly pushes me back jokingly, and we both burst into laughter.

When I look up from wiping the tears of laughter from my face, I am greeted with Kyler's smile as he stands in front of us on the porch. When Ms. Natalie notices, she pats my leg and pushes herself up to standing.

"Well, I'll get back in the kitchen before the birthday girl slave driver comes looking for me. Come join us whenever you're ready."

I nod, and she smiles before walking away toward the front door, placing a gentle hand on Ky's shoulder. I'm unsure what that was supposed to mean, whether it was an "it's all okay" pat or a "hurt her, I'll kill you" protective grip.

Kyler walks over toward me and puts his arm out as if asking if he can sit. I smile and scoot over. Gripping my chin with two fingers, he angles my head toward him and places a brief kiss on my lips.

"You doing okay? I know that's not exactly how we wanted everyone to find out, but it's out in the open now."

I nod. "Yeah, I'm fine...although I have a feeling we won't be living it down all weekend or possibly longer. Ms. Natalie already made jokes about it."

He throws his head back in laughter before wrapping me in his arms and pulling me closer. "That's funny. I assume they filled your dad and Brian in on what happened because they've been given me *the look* all afternoon."

It's my turn to let out a loud laugh, and I lean into him a little closer. As we sit there in silence, just the sound of our breathing together, hearts beating, and the swing squeaking as we rock back and forth, I realize that I am happy. I never thought that I would feel like this again, and it's all thanks to this man next to me. I will be forever grateful he has stood by me and has helped me through this. I begin to wonder if things had worked out differently and I hadn't left, when we had met, would we have ended up here?

My brow must be scrunched in thought because I feel Kyler's knuckles brush my cheek ever so slightly, drawing my attention to him. "Where's that pretty little head of yours at?"

"I was just thinking if I hadn't cut off contact with my brother, do you think we would have met and hit it off?"

"Hmmm, well, I know for sure we would have met, it would just have been a matter of when. We would have met sooner if you had ever visited him, but Zach brought me to your family's Fourth of July barbeque a month after you left. Eventually, coming back with him and Haylee became a regular occurrence."

"Why do I feel like there is a but in there somewhere...?

There's always a but."

He looks down at me and smiles. "Well, there's not *always* a but, and if it's as nice as your butt, I wouldn't be complaining." His hand slides down my side, and he pinches my butt, causing me jump closer to him. I smack his chest jokingly, and we both laugh.

"But...if we had met then, I would have definitely been attracted to you. That much was clear the moment I opened the door when you were standing on the porch, but you weren't ready then."

"And you think I'm ready now?" I sit up straight and turn my head toward him, looking deep into those chocolate-brown eyes. Seriously, those babies should be illegal.

Kyler cups my face between his palms, stroking his thumb along my cheeks, and brings his lips closer to mine. I can feel his hot breath against my skin. "Yes, baby, I think you are. It's not always easy, but no matter what, I'm here for you to get you through the good days and the bad. I'm not going anywhere."

Then he presses his lips against mine. This kiss is anything but friendly—it's feverish, demanding, and passionate. After a few moments of our tongues fighting for dominance, we break apart knowing that either my parents or the Hankses could be watching, ready to make their next smartass comment.

Ky presses a sweet kiss on my forehead before rising. He reaches for my hand to pull me up from the swing. "What do you say we head in and I get to watch you in your element cooking with your mom and Natalie?"

I let out a little giggle as our fingers interlock and we walk toward the front door. "You're just saying that because you don't want to be stuck sitting with my dad and Brian."

"Shit, yeah, that's 100 percent correct."

I let out a loud laugh as we walk through the front door.

CHAPTER 32

KYLER

When Kelly had let me know that she had made up the guest room for me for the night but I could stay in Dani's room if I wanted, I could feel Dani tense up, unsure how to react. I wasn't sure if it was because her family, besides Zach and Haylee, finally knew about us or if it was because I would be the only other guy who'd been in her room besides Emmett. I didn't want to pressure her; I hadn't since we met, nor would I in the future.

When I met Zach and his relationship with Haylee turned more than friendship, I didn't mind at first being the third wheel, but over time I started to envy him. I had hoped one day someone would look at me the way Haylee looked at him and vice versa. I just never expected her to show up on my doorstep and be related to my best friend...the girl just two doors down right now in her childhood bedroom.

After we had had a simple dinner with her parents and Haylee's, we hung out for a little bit longer, had a few drinks, and then decided to turn in. Not long after we went upstairs did we hear the front door close, indicating Brian and Natalie had gone home. I had kissed Dani good night standing in her doorway before leaving her there and walking down to the guest room. It was weird leaving her. This was the first time that I would be sleeping without her since that night after karaoke.

I can't sleep and end up pacing the room back and forth trying to talk myself out of walking down to her room or talk myself into doing it. As is tradition, my mind is having an internal argument that I choose to silence by reaching for the doorknob of the guest room, taking the thirteen steps to Dani's bedroom door, and knocking lightly, not wanting to disturb her parents, who I assume are downstairs still. I take a deep breath and hope that she hasn't fallen asleep.

The door quickly opens, and I find my beautiful girl standing there in a purple tank top and black sweatpants. She quickly looks out in the hallway before reaching for my hand, yanking me into her room, and closing the door softly so as not to disturb anyone else left in the house. She brushes her lips against mine ever so slightly and wraps her arms around me, pressing her chest to mine. Shit, it's only been maybe two hours and I missed her already. Why did I wait so long to walk over here?

She breaks the kiss and reluctantly releases from me. I mourn the loss of her body against mine. Unexpectedly, she grabs my hand and pulls me toward the bed, pushing me down and crawling up to meet me. I pull her down and wrap my arms around her.

"Hi."

"Hi back, beautiful. That was quite a greeting."

This is much better. It's crazy that I haven't been sharing a bed with this woman all that long, but I feel better and at home with her in my arms. We haven't even had sex yet—I mean, I've done things to her, but I haven't pushed for anything else, just spent plenty of time jerking off in the bathroom—but this is what I have been looking forward to after a long day at work.

Coming home to find her on the couch or in the kitchen, kissing her senseless, spending our evening together laughing, and then falling asleep wrapped up in each other's arms.

I run my fingers down her hair and feel her body relax into me. "Is it weird that I'm in here? I know I told your parents I would stay in the guest room but..."

Dani cuts me off, seeking my lips. Her tongue licks the seam of mine, begging for entrance. She moans the sweetest little moan as my hand grips the back of her head, securing her closer to me, and I pull her bottom lip between my teeth before licking the sting away. Her hips push against me when I let out a deep growl from the back of my throat.

With one last sweet kiss, she speaks. "No...honestly, I was tossing and turning trying to sleep without you, and I was actually already standing at the door when you knocked, about to walk down to the guest room and sneak into bed with you."

My heart feels fuller knowing that she couldn't be without me either. My heart isn't the only thing that feels fuller though —my shorts are starting to as well, with her this close to me.

"Oh, you were, were you?"

"Uh-huh." I wrap my arms tighter around her. This is exactly where I want to be, with my girl in my arms. I kiss the top of her head, and she sighs against my chest.

While Dani is lying on my chest, I look around the room. The light purple walls, the empty bulletin board, bookshelves that look as though they haven't been filled in years. There is no personal touch of the personality of the girl I have gotten to know over the past few months.

"So, this is where you grew up, huh?"

"Yep."

"I pictured it...well, I'm not really sure how I pictured it, but differently than this."

Dani tenses a little under my touch before she props herself up against her elbow and stares at me. "When I left after graduation I packed it all up and took it with me. There was nothing left here for me, yet I couldn't handle the thought of leaving my belongings behind. It's stupid I know."

I press my forehead against hers. "No, baby, it's not stupid. I'm sorry for bringing it up. I just always pictured your room being super girly and bubbly. I've heard plenty of stories of you and Haylee over the years to get an idea of what you were like growing up."

"Please don't apologize, Ky. That was a time I am certainly not proud of my actions. I was young and didn't know how else to deal with reality, but I'd like to think that maybe there was a reason for me leaving."

I'm not exactly sure what she means by that, but I am not given the chance to ask when her lips press against mine. Her kisses are urgent as if she needs my air to breathe, my lips and arms to keep her grounded, and my kisses to keep her alive. Who am I to refuse my girl? I try to hide my surprise when one of her legs travels over my body, planting itself on the outside of one of my thighs, and I feel her hot center press against my already growing cock. Whoever invented gym shorts and sweatpants should be pushed down an elevator chute, because those are some of the layers standing in the way between our bodies connecting.

I refuse to push the topic of sex, but my mind goes to only that when I feel Dani grind her hips against mine, making the softest purrs. I'm pretty sure I've jerked off more times in the time that Dani has lived with us than I have in all my horny teenage years.

Her mouth trails from my lips to my jaw, kissing me against the few days' old stubble. I had planned to shave the other morning, but Dani had walked into the bathroom just before-hand, saying in a sultry voice that she wished I would keep it. "Beard burn is a great feeling," she'd said.

"Kyler..." she says now, panting against my skin as she continues to grind against my throbbing cock. "I want to taste you."

Holy shit, my heart is racing. My dick is painfully hard. My eyes spring open and meet her usual sparkling blue eyes, and they are filled with so much want. I can feel the heat coming off her body. Shit, she is so fucking sexy like this. Before I can even say anything, she is already sliding down my body, pressing her lips against my chest, stomach, and down my happy trail, and stops just above my gym shorts. She settles between my legs and looks up at me, and I swear she has seriously never looked sexier. Her hands tease the elastic band of my shorts, slowly dipping her fingers in before dragging them back out. Her hand rubs against the outline of my cock, stroking me through my shorts, and I thrust forward. *Don't come yet, don't come yet*, I keep telling myself now that I am actually going to have her touching me. I have been dreaming about this for so long.

She looks up, her eyes meeting mine, seeking permission one last time. I nod and watch her as she bites her lip while reaching up to the waistband and drags both my shorts and boxers all the way down and tosses them to the side of the bed. Her eyes grow wide, taking in the size of my cock. She bites her lip so hard I worry that she might draw blood. She licks her bottom lip, and I'm unsure if it's to ease the sting or if she is ready to take my cock deep in her mouth. I reach down and stroke my cock a few times and look her deep in the eyes.

"Baby, I can't wait to look down and see those pretty plump lips wrapped around my cock."

That lights a fire in her eyes, and she doesn't hesitate as she leans over, her long hair tickling my thighs as she replaces my hand with hers and begins to stroke me up and down. Her tongue reaches out and teases the tip, and she swirls it around before taking the head of my cock in her mouth. Holy shit her mouth is like heaven, so warm and wet. I keep my eyes on her as I watch her lips move along my shaft, taking me deeper into her mouth, her hand stroking me up and down. With every moan she makes, I feel the vibrations of her mouth, and that feeling goes straight to my balls. I know I'm not going to last long. I can't believe this is finally happening. All the times jerking off in the shower to the image of her with my cock down her throat is nothing compared to the reality of it.

This feels so good. My body begins to tense up, and I know I'm close.

"Baby, I'm so close. Holy fuck! Your mouth feels so good."

She moans again before pulling her mouth off me and dragging her tongue down my shaft and back up. She looks up at me through hooded lids; she is so turned on right now, I bet if I reached down and spun her around so her pussy is straddling my face, she would be glistening with desire and dripping into my mouth without me even touching her yet.

I lace my fingers in her hair and press her head down farther on my cock, and she opens for me, taking me deep into her throat. My balls tighten ready for release. I close my eyes tight.

"Dani, I'm gonna..." But before I can even give her warning, I come down her throat. She swallows it down, making sure to suck me dry, not wanting to miss a single drop. She takes one last lick up my shaft, and I jolt because I'm so fucking sensitive.

The popping noise her mouth makes as she takes my dick out of her mouth is quite possibly my new favorite sound—just kidding, it's second to the sound Dani makes when she comes. I reach over and grab my boxers and shorts from the floor and quickly slide them back on.

Dani wipes her mouth and brushes her hair out of her face before crawling back up to me. I wrap my arms around her, my thumb lightly stroking her stomach.

"Was that okay?"

I place a chaste kiss on her sweet lips. "Dani, that was more than okay. I came so fucking hard, I just about blacked out, but my heart was racing so fucking fast that it kept me from fully getting knocked out."

"Oh yeah?"

"Yeah." My brain is complete mush right now that I can't even come up with more words than *yeah*. I guess my word limit has been reached. She twists in my arms so her back is to my front. I lean down and kiss the back of her neck in a postorgasmic bliss after the fucking best blow job of my life.

I had been dreaming about those plump lips of hers around my hard cock since we met, but no dream could ever even compare to the reality of it. Fuck! I need to stop my thoughts from thinking of her doing it again before my dick wakes back up and presses into her back. Her hands tighten around my arms, as if she doesn't want me to be able to leave and head back to the guest room. She has nothing to worry about; now that I'm here, there's nowhere else I'd rather be. I close my eyes and relish in the feeling of this girl in my arms...my girl. I laugh to myself at the stress I felt radiating off her earlier this day when we were caught kissing in the driveway versus this girl right now, wrapped up in my arms.

The next morning, I wake up with my girl still in my arms, our legs tangled and my morning wood digging into her ass. I lean farther into her hair, inhaling her shampoo scent. There's something about it that brings a sense of peace and calmness.

It's like it's embedded in my brain, and even if she isn't with me I can smell her, and it brings me to my knees. I don't want to wake her yet, but I know that there's going to be a house full of people shortly and she might want to get up before someone comes busting through her bedroom door and finds us in this compromising position. I mean, I personally don't mind—I would be rather content staying in bed tangled up in the sheets with her all day—but this is the first birthday that her mom gets to spend with her in years. Shit, this is going to be the first of many events and holidays that Dani will be around for.

I gently place a kiss to the back of her head and run my fingers up and down her spine. She makes a slight moaning sound that goes straight to my dick, and if I wasn't already hard as a rock, I would definitely be now. "Baby, I'm going to go shower. Is it okay if I use yours?"

Dani grunts a noise which I am going to assume was a yes and laugh to myself. This girl is definitely not a morning person.

I lean in to whisper into her ear, "Feel free to join me if you want."

As I get up from the bed, Dani rolls over, taking up most of the bed. "Bed hog," I mutter.

"Heard that."

I quietly tiptoe to the guest room and retrieve my bag and walk back to Dani's room without running into anyone in the hallway. As I step back into the bedroom, I see that Dani has made no attempt to move, so I quickly shuffle into the bathroom and shut the door. Damn, it would have been awesome to have grown up having my own bathroom. Having to share one with one sibling would have been brutal, but try having to share one with twin girls, especially when they were teenagers.

I turn on the shower and let the water adjust before stripping out of my clothes and stepping in to allow the water to run over me. My mind travels to the events of last night, the reality of her lips on my dick way better than any fantasy I had dreamed of. I have no clue if Dani is planning to surprise me in here, and the last thing I want her to find me doing is...well, myself...especially in her shower. The only other option I have, and I am definitely not a fan, but I don't have much of a choice. I silently curse as I reached for the temperature handle and crank the water to cold. Biting my lip to the point where I can almost taste blood, I yelp like a little girl. I shut my eyes, my dick and balls shriveling up into oblivion, and pray no one else heard my shriek in the house—hopefully no one in the neighborhood even.

I slowly turn the water back to a warmer temperature and finish up getting clean before turning the water off. I reach for a towel, drying off my body, and wrap it around my waist. I realize my bag is just outside the door. I don't want to disturb Dani, so I try to be quiet opening the door. When I step out into the bedroom, I'm greeted by the most beautiful woman I have ever seen sitting on the edge of her bed with her legs crossed, staring straight at me. Her eyes peruse up and down my body. I lean down into my bag, grabbing a pair of boxers, and watch her out of the corner of my eye continuing to watch me. She drinks me in as she lifts her coffee cup to her lips. I take my time getting dressed, knowing that this is probably turning her on, and if I walk over there and put my hand underneath her panties, I could guarantee she would be dripping wet.

After pulling my boxers on, I run the towel through my hair quickly to dry the excess water off it. It's left a mess, but I know that's how Dani likes it. She always loves to run her fingers through it and massage my scalp, which I have no shame in admitting I love too.

"See something you like, sweetheart?" I ask her after I throw the towel into the hamper outside the bathroom door and stalk toward her. She uncrosses her legs and stands, meeting me at the end of the bed. She sets her coffee down on the desk next to another filled mug, which I assume is for me, and then presses her body against me, running her hands up and down my chest. I chuckle as she continues her exploration. "You do realize that if your lazy ass got up out of bed sooner, you could have joined me in there."

She whines as I run my fingers through her hair this time. "But my bed was so comfy. I missed that bed...and it was even better with you in it."

I release her hair from my fingers and gently swat at her butt. "Oh, you do not want to start this, babe."

She begins to back up with a hint of passion in her eye. I quickly catch up to her with very few steps and grab her waist, pulling her to me before pressing a searing kiss against her lips, her mouth opening for me to allow my tongue to seek hers. We both moan at the back of our throats. I need to stop before I throw her down on the bed and have my way with her. I don't care who is in the house and why we said we would take things slow—her body makes me react in a way no other woman has before.

I continue to kiss her until my phone on the nightstand begins to buzz. Reluctantly I pull away from our kiss and press a brief one on her forehead, still needing the contact of her, and walk to retrieve my phone. I sit on the side of the bed as I open my text messages.

ZACH: *We ended up getting in late last night and stayed at Haylee's parents' house. Headed over now, dipshit. Wake the fuck up or I'll come steamroll your ass.*

ZACH: *Oh and heard the rents found out about you and Dani. Just couldn't keep your hands to yourself could you. *SMH**

ZACH: *Well, hopefully the image of you with your tongue down her throat *GROSS* will be a better image for the moms than well... you know!*

I feel the bed dip as Dani climbs over toward me, her front to my back, and wraps her arms around my shoulder. She begins kissing my back, to my shoulders, up my neck, and she sucks and nibbles on my earlobe. Who is this vixen, and what did she do with my Danielle?

I lean back and claim her lips with mine, molding my hand to the back of her head, keeping her there a moment while I savor this moment. "Baby, as much as I want to keep doing this, that was your brother and they are headed over in a few minutes from the Hankses' house. He also threatened to steamroll me if I wasn't out of bed, and let me just say the last time he tried to do that in college, I ended up taking a knee to the balls. It was fucking awful. Worst way to wake up."

Dani groans, clearly not wanting to get out of bed, but she doesn't want her brother to come running in here either. She gets up and grabs the coffee mug I assumed was for me and walks it over to me.

"Here, I got this for you. Hopefully it's still warm." She leans down and kisses my cheek before walking back to the desk to grab hers and then heads in the direction of the bathroom. She pauses for a moment and turns to look back at me. "Oh, hey, babe?"

I look up after taking a sip of the coffee. "Yeah?"

"You shriek like a teenage girl, by the way."

I grab the pillow behind me and throw it toward her, but she quickly shuts the door. I can hear her giggles on the other side before the sound of the shower drowns them out. I hear Zach's Jeep pull up outside, and I decide to get dressed and meet them downstairs.

Later that day, Kelly has her birthday cake in front of her that Natalie and Dani had baked, with a few candles lit—of course, not as many as her age, although Zach had suggested it and asked if we should call the fire department.

"Make a wish, Mom." Zach leans back in his chair with his arm around Haylee.

Kelly looks around at everyone gathered around her: Adam, Natalie, Brian, Zach, Haylee, me, and then her eyes land on her daughter's. She smiles the biggest smile I have ever seen Mrs. Jacobs smile. "There's nothing else I can wish for because it has finally come true. All I have wanted the past few years was for my family to all be together again, and here we are. I couldn't have asked for a better birthday."

Dani leans over and kisses her mom's cheek before her mom blows out her candles.

CHAPTER 33
Danielle

"Mmmmmmmm...that feels good," comes out more as a breathless moan as Kyler applies more pressure as he massages my feet in his lap. We've spent the last few hours curled up on the couch watching movies. Tomorrow is Kyler's birthday, and he asked for a relaxing night in with me tonight since we are headed out with his family and mine tomorrow. What my man wants, he gets—little does he know he will be getting a lot more later.

I spent part of the morning shopping with Haylee picking out the perfect lingerie to surprise him with. This man has been so patient with me that it's time to take our whatever this is—relationship, I guess—to the next level. I am finally ready. It's been a few weeks since our night at my parents' house. I had definitely thought about going all the way then, but I didn't want our first time to be at my parents' house, a quickie, and in a bed that I had shared before with another man.

I have been giving little hints all night. Of course, each movie picked had a sex scene that got my pulse racing. If I don't move soon, I may end up taking him right here on the couch. I want to feel his hands on not just my feet but on my whole body. I love the way he touches me; he brings my body alive in so many ways. I didn't think I would ever feel that again. True, it scares the shit out of me, but there is just something about this man that makes me want more.

I slowly pull my foot out of his grasp and lift it over his head to the back of the couch to trap him between my legs. He looks up at me with lustful eyes, before rising to his knees and hovering above me. My feet settle behind his calves to lock him in place. He dives his head into my neck where I can feel his hot breath on me as he drags his nose along my skin.

"So, almost birthday boy, are you about ready to open your present?"

Placing kisses up my neck and jawline toward my mouth, he whispers against my skin, "Baby, I told you not to get me anything. Just spending it with you is enough."

I reach down and pull his face to mine so we are only inches apart. "I know, but this isn't just for you..." I cut myself off by closing the distance between us and locking my lips with his. The kiss starts off slow and timid but quickly gets deeper. I press my center that is already pulsing with need and ready for him against his growing bulge. My hands slide in his hair, gripping tighter as anticipation for what is about to happen surges through my body. A deep, almost growl noise comes from the back of his throat. My hand travels down his body from his strong shoulders to his defined stomach down to the top of his shorts. I tease him by dragging my finger along the top of his shorts without fully letting my fingers go in. He breaks the kiss and places his forehead against mine and bites his lip.

"So what were you saying about this..." He loses his train of thought as my hand reaches into his shorts fully and my thumb rubs the tip of his cock through his boxer briefs.

"Hmmm...what was it you were saying, Ky?" I slowly pull my hand back out of his shorts and trail my fingers back up his body under his shirt this time. I run my nails down the hard planes of his chest, knowing that it turns him on.

He swallows and looks into my eyes before his lids fall heavy. "You said something about my birthday present. As long as its unwrapping you, I'm happy."

I grab the back of his neck and pull him to me, pushing my tongue in his mouth to massage his own, and bite his bottom lip as we pull apart, continuing to grind on him. "Why don't you take me to bed or lose me forever," I say, quoting *Top Gun*, which he had first picked out for us to watch. In a flash, he is up, scooping me off the couch into his arms and sprinting to his room.

"Wait, baby, wait." I press my hands on his chest when he gets to my bedroom door. I have been spending most nights in his room, but I want to surprise him with the outfit Haylee talked me into buying, which I have on my dresser in my room.

"But..." he whines as I force him to set me on the ground and grab the door handle to let me inside. I press up to my toes and run my tongue along his favorite spot on his neck, trailing to his ear.

"I have to get your present, so you go get on the bed and I'll be right in." I bite his earlobe, forcing another deep moan from him. He pushes me against the door and kisses me, leaving me longing for more when he walks past to his room. His eyes never leave mine as he walks away, and I slip into the confines of my own room.

I rush over to the pink Victoria's Secret bag that holds the black lace bra, matching thong, and lace knee-highs, and I grab the black heels from the closet. Quickly changing out of my leggings and T-shirt, I know this new thong will simply be ruined. My mouth has been dry ever since Kyler left me at my bedroom door, all wetness gathering between my legs.

Sliding the knee-highs on, I look in the mirror and don't even recognize the vixen standing in front of me. With Emmett, we had young love—the most I would dress up was a tank top and sexy boy shorts or a thong. I never went all out like this. I adjust my boobs that are now spilling out of this bra and rush over to my cosmetic bag to grab the bright red lipstick I picked up today as well. The salesperson said my lips were "totally fuckable in this shade." He said it's also what his boyfriend said to him the night before. I giggle at the memory as I adjust my hair and slip on my high heels. I take a deep breath. Yep, this is happening—no turning back now.

I walk the few feet from my bedroom to Kyler's, thankful that Haylee and Zach are out with her friend Cami tonight and they won't walk in on me in this outfit. I will have to thank Haylee later. Kyler's bedroom door is open, and I peek in to see him sitting in his bed against the headboard. He's lost the shirt and is now only in his gym shorts. Holy shit that man's body is amazing. I am forever grateful for the hours he and Zach spend at the gym. I am pretty sure I am about to get a workout of my own.

He hasn't noticed me standing in the doorway yet—I'm surprised because I was anything but quiet walking in these heels. I think my nerves might have finally set in.. Kyler is looking off at something, deep in thought, facing the opposite direction of me. He hasn't shaved the past few days, so his chiseled jaw is lined with stubble, and it is the sexiest thing ever. I love to feel his stubble against my thighs. His hands are clasped together by his mouth—maybe he is trying to figure out what the present is. We had agreed that I wouldn't get him anything, but I'm not sure that letting him sink deep in my pussy counts as getting him a present. Maybe an orgasm courtesy of something other than my hand or mouth counts too.

I wait a few moments and adjust my stance in the doorway, leaning my back against it with my left foot propped up against the frame, showing off my elongated legs. I clear my throat, and his head whips around so fast it's impressive that he doesn't get whiplash.

"Holy fucking shit, baby! Is that my present?" He rubs his jaw with his palm as if his mind is racing with dirty thoughts of what he wants to do to me. I step into the room so that he can admire my body fully and nod. I lock my eyes on him as I walk toward the corner of the bed.

"Come here."

He pushes off the headboard so he can join me at the edge of the bed. I step forward into the space, spreading his legs apart a little farther. His eyes browse the black lace covering my body —or, well, partially covering. His hands slowly ride up the outer part of my thigh to my ass where he squeezes it in his hands.

"You did this all for me?" he asks between kisses up my stomach to my breasts.

My fingers trace his arms and land on his shoulders. "Do you like it?" Can he sense my nervousness and hesitation? I am completely out of my element here.

He places his hands on the small of my back and pulls me toward him. "I love it. You are so fucking sexy—I feel bad though." My sexy smile drops, and I am instantly regretting the outfit choice. "Oh no, no, Dani, it's not what you think. I feel bad, because I want to tear all of this off you right now and get my hands on you."

There it is—the encouragement I needed. I climb into his lap, straddling his thighs. I trace my fingers from his shoulders up the back of his neck to play with the messy pieces of hair that hang there. I massage into his scalp, and he lets out a deep groan.

Grinding my hips against his, I attack his mouth hungrily, tightening my grip on his neck to pull me closer. While Kyler trails kisses down my jaw to my neck and across my collarbone, I look over at the alarm clock on the nightstand and see it reads 12:03 a.m. I pull back on his hair to bring his attention back to me. He looks confused as to why I want him to stop, assuming maybe I'm still not ready. The sides of my mouth turn up in a devilish smile, and I rub my already soaking wet undies on him. It's my turn to trail kisses along his cheek, his jaw, his neck, his shoulders, and chest before making my way back to his lips.

"Happy Birthday, Kyler...now make love to me."

He can see by the tone of my voice that I'm serious but still asks, "Are you sure?"

I bite my bottom lip before answering, "Yes. I want you inside me. Make love to me, Ky. *Please*."

In a quick movement, Kyler flips me on my back and scoots us up to the top of the bed. "Oh, baby, you don't have to beg, and this is quite possibly the best birthday ever."

Kyler starts kissing me, our tongues tangling, fighting for control. He grabs my wrists and pushes them over my head. His fingers trail down my arms, teasing me, leaving goose bumps in their place. My skin feels like it's on fire, and that fire is leading straight to my core. That's how Kyler makes me feel...alive. I've waited so long to feel anything but emptiness, and here this man comes barging into my life and I welcome him into my arms, into my bed...into me. His hot breath trails from my neck to my collarbone. The room is silent except for our heavy breathing.

"Kyler..." I don't even know what I want to say, but all thoughts leave my mind as his mouth continues his journey across my body. He bites the sensitive spot where my neck and shoulder meet before licking the wound and blowing hot air on it to soothe the sting. It's a combination of pain and pleasure, something I never thought I would want, but he makes me want more. My nipples are instantly hardened, almost painfully hard, in this bra that is becoming too tight and needs to be gone. I arch my back, forcing my breasts to rub against his chest, begging for more. Ky kisses down my shoulder to my chest, sliding one bra strap down before kissing his way to the other side and sliding that strap down. His hand reaches around my back and gently unhooks the clasp holding my breasts in.

"As sexy as this is...I like it better on the floor," he says, leaning into my ear. He drags the bra down my body and tosses it to the floor. My breath becomes labored with anticipation. Kyler kisses and licks his way down my ribs. He presses back on his knees, resting on his feet and giving me a glimpse of the giant bulge in his shorts that's dying to break free. His fingers trail fire down my thighs to grip the lace edge of the stocking.

He bites his lip in an attempt to hide the ravenous look in his eyes that makes me dripping wet. He is trying to control himself. Slowly he drags the knee-high down my leg and tosses it to the floor to join my bra. Starting at my ankle, he licks his way up my legs, stopping just before where I need him most. He shifts to the other thigh, making the same movement to remove that one and toss it to the ground. He inches upward, licking and nibbling my inner thighs, causing me to let out a loud moan. Hovering over my sex, he hooks his fingers into the lace strips holding my panties to my skin.

"Ky," I breathe, needing him to touch me before I combust, thrusting my hips in the air, needing more.

"It's my birthday, baby, and I want to savor you even though it's killing me not to just be deep inside you already." His words and sharp tone almost make me come alone without his touch. My panties melt off me, joining the pile of clothes on the floor.

Kyler's smile widens when he sees my pussy soaked with

my juices craving to be touched and licked by him. His fingers drag up my inner thigh, stopping at the apex; I shiver at the sensation. I need friction and I need it now. Just as I am about to push him to his back and straddle him to create the movement I need at that moment, he makes his move for the promise land. His fingers finally graze my clit, my body tightens, and my back arches, waiting for release. One finger circles my clit, and he applies more and more pressure with each circle. I can feel the pressure starting to build in my toes. My hips jolt against his hand.

"Mmmmmmmm, you're so wet. I love you dripping wet for me, that my touch does that to you." His eyes close as he continues to slide his finger in and out, curling to hit the right spot, and that's when I let go and let the impending orgasm take over my body.

"That's it, baby, come for me."

I grip the sheets as the wave of pleasure takes over, and I scream out Kyler's name. Yep, definitely glad that we have the house to ourselves. Sending me plunging over the edge and coming on his fingers, Kyler bends down and takes my swollen clit in his mouth, adding to the pleasure by swirling his tongue around it. My legs try to close, but his free hand presses my knee down, forcing them open. When the pleasure finally surges, my whole body is shaking.

I open my eyes to find Kyler's deep brown eyes staring at me, into me, through me even. "Happy fucking birthday to me," he growls as he takes in the view of my flushed body in its postorgasmic state. I press up on my elbow, and my finger curls upward, motioning him to come here. He slides his gym shorts and boxer briefs down his legs, freeing his erection. I can feel the heat radiating from it. He reaches over to the nightstand and grabs a condom from the drawer. I bite my lower lip and run my own tongue across it to relieve the sting, never taking my eyes off him as I reach for him and wrap my fingers around his shaft. He sucks in a breath as my grip tightens on him, moving up and down.

The sound of the foil package opening draws my attention back to reality as he grabs my fingers and removes them from him to cover himself with the condom before crawling over to me. Ky repositions himself between my legs, spreading them wider. The sexy girl ready to pounce fades, and nerves begin to kick in. It's been four and a half years since I've had a man inside me, and my breathing escalates almost in an anxious way.

Cupping my cheek with his palm and stroking his thumb up and down, Kyler smiles. "It's okay, Dani. We'll go nice and slow, and if you need me to stop, just tell me, okay?"

I nod. I want this. I want him.

Kyler moves his hand from my cheek to the back of my neck, pulling my lips to his. This kiss isn't fast and crazed like before; this kiss is slow and sensual, calming my nerves in a way only Kyler would know how to do. I moan into his mouth and press my fingers under his arms and into his back as I feel him slowly inching inside me. He pauses, and I nod to continue.

Once fully inside, Kyler breathes out, "Fuck, baby, you feel so fucking good." His hips begin to pump into me as I wrap my legs around his waist to encourage him to thrust deeper inside me. My fingers dig into his back, leaving marks, my mark, in his skin, claiming him as he claims me.

Kyler leans over, taking my nipple in his mouth while still thrusting, and I can feel my insides start to tighten again. "Don't stop. Fuck. Don't stop," I manage to get out.

"Oh baby, I don't plan on stopping." He takes his hard cock out before slamming back into me, then leans over to the other breast and swirls his tongue around my nipple. My head pushes back into the bed, and I meet his every thrust with my own. I am so close. As if he can sense it without me saying it, his hand finds its way down to my clit and feverishly rubs it in circles, and I'm done for. My legs tighten around his waist, and my pussy tightens around his cock, sweat now dripping down my forehead and back.

"Shit, right there, Dani." After two more pumps into me and a loud moaning sound from him, deep within, he finds his own release and collapses on my chest, both of us heavily out of breath and spent. My eyelids flutter closed while trying to find words to say...any words at all.

Finally, Kyler lifts his head, causing my eyes to open and meet his gaze. "Wow" is all he can manage to get out, his brain clearly in the same state as mine. Still buried inside me, Kyler props up to his elbow and hovers over me, brushing his lips gently across mine. I run my fingers through his damp, sweaty hair and take comfort in his touch. I mourn the loss of him inside me as he slowly backs up out of me and off the bed toward the bathroom to dispose of the condom. I roll onto my stomach and stretch my limbs across the bed. I place my head on my bent arms and breathe contently and allow my eyes to close.

I feel the bed dip and a smack on my butt. "Hey!" My eyes open and my head shoots up off my arm. I am met with a genuine smile from Kyler. Damn, I thought he was hot before, but post-sex Kyler is even sexier. His cheeks are flushed, a light coating of sweat covers his chest, and his already messy hair is all over the place. Without even looking I'm sure there are red marks on his back where I dug my nails in. At some point he put his black boxer briefs back on, and he is currently sitting on the edge of the bed with one leg bent on top of the bed and the other on the floor. My body is definitely taking up most of the bed, but I am in such a blissful state, I don't want to move. Kyler tilts his head to the side, indicating for me to scoot over, and instead of complying, I smile and shake my head no, laughing, and duck my head under the pillow.

"Scoot over, babe," he says with another smack of my butt. I scoot over about a half inch and continue laughing. "Oh, it's gonna be like that, huh, and on my birthday." He fakes taking offense and moves away. I come out from under the pillow and groan and scoot over far enough to allow him on the bed. He smiles at me knowing he just won and climbs into bed, reaching down for the blanket to cover us but stops what he is doing as I continue to scoot toward the other side. I'm quickly tugged by the hip. "Oh no, babe, where you think you're going?" I'm met with a sexy smirk on his face.

"Ummm, allowing you room on the bed." Kyler pulls me closer to him and twists me around so that my head is on his chest. I'd be lying if I said this hasn't become my favorite spot to be. I wrap my leg around his and lay my hand across his waist. Even though he has his boxer briefs on, I am still completely naked. He pulls the covers up and settles into bed.

My fingers trace his chest while he runs his fingers up and down my arm with his lips pressed against the top of my head. Nervously I ask, "So did you enjoy your birthday present?"

He lets out a laugh. "Is that a trick question? Dani, that was amazing." Pinching my chin with his thumb and forefinger, he raises it so that I look at him. "I mean it, that was...I don't even have words. I would have waited for as long as you needed, but now that I've had you, all I can think about is when can I have you again? Are you sure we need to still go with everyone because I'd much rather just spend my birthday in bed with you."

I let out a giggle and brush my lips gently against his. "You're incorrigible."

He kisses me again before pushing a stray piece of hair behind my ear. "But are you okay?"

I think about it for a moment. Yes, I'm okay—better than okay, really. I nod, "Yeah, I am. In fact..." Before I finish my sentence, I shift my leg to straddle to him. My core, already wet and craving more of him, lines up perfectly over his already growing cock. "What do you say we continue celebrating your birthday just us."

He smiles. "I think that can be arranged," he says, before pulling me down closer to him to kiss me passionately. I can already tell we will need extra caffeine for going out later, but like he said, it is well worth it.

CHAPTER 34

KYLER

*B*efore I even have the key in the door, I can hear the music coming from the house. It reminds me of being back in college and showing up to a frat house for a party. Finally putting my key in the door, I hope I don't open it to find a bunch of college kids dancing with beers in hand. This could get a little awkward if that's the case.

Luckily, when I open the front door I am greeted by an empty living room, but I can hear the voice of an angel along with the loud music coming from the kitchen. Even though we are at karaoke just about every Friday, I never tire of hearing that voice.

I quietly walk to the kitchen where I can hear Dani singing, but nothing prepares me for the sight in front of me. I have come home plenty of times to Dani cooking in the kitchen, but here she is with her back toward me, wooden spoon in hand as a microphone, shaking her ass and pretending to be onstage. She either hasn't heard me approach or just doesn't want to stop her performance. I recognize the song to be "Like A Prayer" but have never heard this version. Maybe she is practicing a new routine for karaoke.

She is in the zone, and who am I to disturb her? I just stand and watch her. Hearing her voice reminds me of the time Zach and I had arrived home from the gym and heard her singing in the shower. There was so much power and emotion behind her voice, and while I still hear that same power and emotion, she is not the same girl. It has only been a few months, but there is such a difference in her from the first time she knocked on the door to now, in the kitchen, making that spoon her bitch.

I have no idea what she is cooking, but it smells delicious. As if my stomach is on the same page, it grumbles and I'm lucky that the music is too loud for her to hear it over the tunes. I'm not ready to stop staring at her just yet.

It's in that very moment when I realize that this girl...this girl is everything...my everything. She is my world. I would do anything for her. I need to make her smile, to make her laugh, to make her feel that she is enough. I want to fill all the cracks in her broken heart and pray she never has to know that kind of pain again. I want to go to sleep with her every night in my arms and wake up the same, kissing her and showing her what she means to me. I want to dance with her around the kitchen like her parents and for her to teach me more about her being in her element of cooking and baking. What is this feeling? I can't make it out exactly, maybe because I've never experienced it before. I... I... I think I love her. Yep, I do. I look at her the way Zach looks at Haylee. I love the way she looks in our kitchen, dancing around as if she's auditioning for a girl band. I love the way she fits in my arms, in my "nook" as she calls it, how she is honest and isn't afraid to speak her mind.

I want her...all of her...forever. I just need to figure out how to tell her that.

"Hi, handsome." She finally turned around and noticed me standing here, leaning against the wall with my ankles and arms crossed. She reaches over to her phone and turns the volume down from the source instead of walking over to the Bluetooth speaker.

"Hey, baby." I smile at her. I could tell her right then and there, but nope, it's not the right moment. I stride over to where she is standing at the counter, wrap my arms around her waist, and press my lips to the spot where her neck meets her shoulder that causes her to shiver. She leans back into my touch and turns her head to look up at me before pulling me in for a quick kiss.

"Mmmmmm, a guy could get used to this."

"What can I say? I aim to please." She winks and sneaks out of my arms, heading over to the fridge, and my excitement goes straight to my dick. She is quite the sassy little vixen. I adjust my pants before walking over to the island and pulling out a stool to sit down on.

Dani brings over two water bottles and hands me one.

I take a sip and look around the kitchen. "What's all this?"

She laughs. "Dinner."

"Thank you, Captain Obvious. I meant what are you making."

She scrunches her nose up at me, a face she makes often when she is trying to be a smartass. I've learned many of her expressions, like when she is pretending to be mad but is fighting back a laugh, when she is sad but trying to hide it from me, when she is annoyed with her brother, when she is about to come. That last one is my favorite expression of hers. Her cheeks and chest get so flushed, her eyelids start to flutter, and she will chew her lip on the left side to try and keep from crying out at first. I am completely in my own world reliving each of her expressions that I don't hear her talking until I feel—

"Owwww! Did you just tweak my nipple?"

With a devilish smirk on her face, she says, "Yes, yes I did.

You clearly weren't listening, so I had to get your attention. If it makes you feel any better, I'll make it all better later." She winks while I rub the pain in my chest. Shit, that legit hurt.

I give her a puppy dog apology look. "I'm sorry, babe, what was it you were saying?"

She smiles at me before walking back to the stove to sir something in the big pan. "I said that I was making shrimp and veggie stir fry over rice."

At the sound of that, my stomach growls. This time she hears it and throws her head back in laughter while she continues stirring the pan, which I now know is full of veggies.

"Zach is in the shower, and Haylee is on her way from class. Why don't you go get changed and come back and you can help me finish."

I get up from my stool and take another drink of water. "What? You don't love me in my work clothes?" Dani turns around, and her eyes take in my appearance: black pants and a tight purple button-up shirt that is rolled at the sleeves, the top two buttons undone.

She saunters toward me, reaching up for my collar. "Why yes, I *do* enjoy the view of you like this, but I need a moment to finish my song, so I kind of need you to leave for a moment. *Also*, if you don't leave the kitchen, I may have to keep unbuttoning this shirt..." Her hands go from my collar to the buttons, and she plays with the first one that's not undone. "And then dinner is going to be ruined, which means you won't also get dessert...so there's that."

I'm not sure if she is referring to real dessert that she baked or *her*—either way, I want my dessert. I quickly kiss the top of her head and run out of the kitchen toward my bedroom. I hear her laughing in the distance, and the music turns back up; this time I recognize the song to be "Baby, Baby" by Amy Grant. I only know this because she has been singing this song a lot in the shower. I hurry up and get changed into gym shorts and a T-shirt so that I can get back to the show in the kitchen.

I apparently wasn't fast enough. By the time I get back there, Zach has taken a seat at the table and Haylee is in the kitchen with another spoon, dancing with Dani. Well, so much for getting a chance to sneak a peek at dessert. I take a seat next to my best friend while we enjoy the view of our girls laughing and having fun. They seem to be dancing to some Katy Perry remix. From what I have heard, these two used to be extremely obsessed with her.

Zach looks almost as if he is in pain, rubbing his hands over his face, but I see him smiling as his hands come down. He looks back at the girls and shakes his head. I hit his arm, getting his attention. "What's with the face?"

He blows out a breath, trying to hide his laugh. "You've created a monster. You do realize that since my sister is happy all the time and singing around the house, these two"—he points to the girls—"are back to their crazy Katy Perry ways. You think it was bad listening to Haylee listen to her songs. Oh no, buddy, you ain't seen nothing yet. They'll start putting on two shows a night pretty soon." He rolls his eyes so hard I think they're going to roll into the back of his head and stay there. I know that he is enjoying this though. His sister is happy and smiling, and it makes me feel fucking awesome knowing that I put that smile on her face.

I realize this is what it's all about. I know that I need to tell her soon how I feel, but maybe it can wait another day. Right now, I want to soak in the view in front of me and hope that when the time does come for me to tell her, she feels the same way I do or is at least open to the idea and this can be what our days/nights feel like from now on.

CHAPTER 35
Danielle

Kyler and I come rushing out of the bedroom and into the living room when we hear Haylee's shriek. I start to panic, rushing down the hallway. Is she okay? Is Zach okay? I can't lose either of them, and my chest starts to tighten. I hate that my mind first goes to that, but after Emmett, I guess I just fear losing anyone else I love. We come to an abrupt stop when we see Zach down on one knee in front of Haylee holding a black velvet box in front of him. The box is open, and I can see a diamond ring in it.

"Haylee Grace Hanks, I have had the honor of knowing your love and friendship for twenty-two years. Throughout those years I have watched you go from the silly nerdy girl next door to this incredibly beautiful and charismatic woman. We had to go through an earth-shattering tragedy to find ourselves." I look down and catch my breath since I know he is talking about Emmett. "Your love and comfort put me back together. You make me laugh, smile, and feel complete. I look at you and not only see my past and present but also my future. I am so head over heels in love with you. Please let me spend the rest of my life making you as happy as you make me. Hails, will you marry me?"

"Yes! Yes! God, yes!" Haylee shouts as he slides the ring on her finger and pulls her into an embrace. I realize that I am crying as Kyler rubs my back. He must think I am crying tears of joy for them, but it's the complete opposite. Kyler walks toward the newly engaged couple, cheering and hugging them both, but I haven't moved from my spot. Zach pulls Haylee into his arms and looks to me to say something, anything, but I say nothing. I can tell he is unhappy about my response or lack of.

"Dani, say something."

"Are you fucking kidding me?" I can't hold my tears back—tears of sadness, heartbreak, and pain all rushing back. Tears knowing that should've been me getting engaged. This Jacobs getting engaged to a different Hanks. Tears of jealousy that my brother gets his happily ever after, and anger of them moving on. That was supposed to be us, damn it.

In my rage, I don't even notice Kyler walks back up to me and places his hand on my arm. "Aren't you excited for your brother and your best friend?"

I pull back from him. "Are you seriously going to lecture me right now?"

Haylee has begun to cry. I've clearly upset her, and Zach places his arm in front of her as if to protect her from me. "Fuck, Dani! Why can't you just be happy for me and Haylee? Huh? It's always just about you still, isn't it?"

Shaking my head, I run back to the bedroom and grab my purse, phone, and keys and head to walk out the door. "Oh please, love is for assholes. All it brings is pain, and anyone would be a fool to believe in that shit...that happily ever afters can actually happen."

Kyler grabs my hand to try to stop me from walking out, but I turn and snap at him, "Don't touch me. What, you think you can fix me? That we can just play house and live out our happily ever after bullshit? You're nothing but a replacement.

You may have replaced Emmett in my brother's world, but you won't in mine. This is... This is..."

I can see the hurt in his eyes; it's written all over his face. "What, baby... It's love? It's real? It's raw? Because it's all of those things, Dani! Why can't you just let me in?" I've never heard him this angry before.

My eyes are overflowing with tears. "It was a mistake, Kyler. You can't make me happy, and you're a fool to believe you can. I'm incapable of loving or being loved. I'm just broken." I shrug him off before slamming the door. I run to my car, knowing that I probably shouldn't drive, but if I don't get out of here, they might come looking for me. I hurry out of the driveway and try to plan an escape. There is only one place I want to be, so I hop on the highway and head to the one person who can make this all better.

CHAPTER 36

Danielle

*I*t's been almost five years since I have been here. I refused to come here because then I would be accepting the fact that he was really gone. The two-hour drive goes by pretty fast. At first, I drove in silence, but I could hear the catches in my breath as I continued to cry, so I decided to drown out my thoughts by turning on the radio and getting lost in the music.

The air is sucked right out of my lungs as I pull into the gates at Glen Ridge Cemetery. I'm headed to talk to Emmett, and oh how I wish he could respond. I park my car on the hill by the pond, knowing he is just about a hundred feet away. I somehow find the strength to open the door. I know that my eyes and face are swollen from all the crying. Haven't I cried enough over the years?! I wrap my arms around my stomach and force my feet to move. There are fresh flowers in the vase, showing someone was here recently— maybe his mom or mine —next to the gravestone that reads:

I can't breathe. This isn't real. I close my eyes and remember the last time I was here.

Sitting in those uncomfortable green chairs, I couldn't stop fidgeting with my hands. My mom sat on my right, and Haylee was to my left with her parents seated next to her. Zach stood behind me with his hands on my shoulders, and my father stood behind my mother. I looked up at Father John as he was speaking, but it was as if I was deaf. I saw that his mouth was moving, but I refused to process what he was saying, so my body chose to not listen. I had zoned out completely that I missed when Father John called me up to read the poem I had reluctantly agreed to read. Ms. Natalie had asked if I would read or say something graveside since Zach read at the service and Haylee gave the eulogy.

At first, I had declined. How was I supposed to get up there and speak? But my parents had convinced me that this was what Em would want. What he would want... What he would want was to still be alive. I felt Zach's hand squeeze my shoulder, and as I looked up, my mom whispered, "They're waiting for you." I took a deep breath and stood up on shaky legs.

I took five steps to the front of the crowd, standing next to the spot that Emmett would call his final resting place. I looked over at the casket where he was laid and asked—no, begged—for strength to be able to not only get through this reading but to be able to get through tomorrow. How appropriate it was that the poem selected was "If Tomorrow Starts Without Me."

I looked around at the crowd and then down at my paper. I began to speak:

"When tomorrow starts without me,
And I'm not there to see,
If the sun should rise and find your eyes
All filled with tears for me.
I wish so much you wouldn't cry
The way you did today,
While thinking of the many things,
We didn't get to say..."

I was forced to take a few deep breaths to try to fight back my tears. I still had so much left to read, but I could hear the sounds of sobbing around me. I looked up and my eyes were met with Ms. Natalie's—a mother burying her son today. I tried to find the strength for her, for Em.

"I know how much you love me,
As much as I love you,
And each time you think of me,
I know you'll miss me too."

I heard the sobbing begin again, loud painful wails, crying uncontrollably, and then felt strong arms around me. I turned to see my brother holding me up, and it was then that I realized that the loud sobbing was coming from me. This was really happening. I really wasn't just having a nightmare that he was gone.

My mother had gotten up from her seat and had her arms around Ms. Natalie. Zach escorted me to my seat and pulled me into his lap, rubbing my back while I released a fountain of tears, fisting his shirt in pain. I just wanted the ache in my chest to stop. My dad had taken the paper with the poem and continued to read it to the end.

I drop to my knees in front of the headstone and lose it.

"Why! Why, did you leave me? I'm broken without you. I'm so lost without you. I've tried so hard to move on with my life, but I can't without you. Was my love not enough to keep you here? Am I being punished for us being too happy too young? Why can't you answer me? We had plans and promises, and they're gone."

Pausing, I try to find the words that I have kept in for years. "I just can't be happy for them...I can't. That was supposed to be us. We were supposed to be getting engaged, married, having kids, living a long life together to die in our old age after we spent so much time together. Not one wintery night at eighteen, ripping you from our lives.

"I hate you for leaving me. I hate you for loving me so fucking much that without you I can't breathe. I don't want to be sad all the time anymore—I just don't know how to do that without you. Please help me, baby. I miss your laugh, your touch, your kisses, your voice, your love, your everything. I miss who I was with you. How do I move on when I spent my whole life loving you? I didn't get to say goodbye to you. Our last conversation was about boners in the library. Why did you leave me behind? We were supposed to be together forever—that's what you promised. That was the plan!"

I pull my knees from underneath me and wrap my arms around them. I let the tears fall. I cry for Emmett, for the life we would've had. I cry for his parents, his sister, my brother, our friends. I cry until I feel like I've cried every last tear there is.

Taking a deep breath, I rest my chin on my knees. I replay this morning's events: my brother's engagement, my fight with Kyler, my one-sided argument with Emmett and God. I'm not sure how long I've sat here, possibly hours. I had turned my phone off on the drive. Kyler and Zach wouldn't stop calling or texting, but I'm not surprised I hadn't heard from Haylee. I had ruined what was supposed to be one of the best days of her life.

I hear a car door close in the distance and a female voice approach. I don't turn around, but I know that voice that says, "Yeah, I found her, she's okay. We'll be home soon...love you too." Putting her phone away, Haylee sits down next to me.

"I figured this is where I'd find you. I come here when I need a moment too." Turning to the headstone, she places her hand to Emmett's name. "Hey, big bro. About time she visited, huh?"

We sit there in silence. I'm not even sure where to begin with her—apologizing for this morning, ask how Kyler is doing, does he hate me, does Zach hate me, should I move out? Haylee can sense my hesitation and thoughts, I guess, so she opens her mouth and closes it a few times before speaking,

"It's okay, Dani," she says as she places her hand on my wrist.

I shake my head. "No. It's really not. I'm not sure how to do this. I'm a mess. I ruined this morning, and then I said some very hurtful things to Kyler. Then I come here for the first time since the funeral and I scream. Like seriously at the top of my lungs, wake-the-dead-style scream. I'm surprised no one called the cops to haul my ass out of here. I'm just still so angry. Where do you find the strength to move on?"

Haylee ponders my question, and her grip on my wrist tightens a bit. "It's not easy. It's honestly a lot of work, but I take it one day at a time. Some days I am so angry that he's not here, and others I use the anger I have that he's not to power me through the day. I'm angry for all the big events he has missed and will continue to miss."

She takes a deep breath. I know this is hard for her too. This was something we didn't talk much about after the fact—all my fault, I know.

"I'm upset that he isn't here to celebrate my big news. I hurt for my parents, for you, for Zach. I use it to make something of my life—a life he didn't get. I was in a bad place after he died...I not only lost my brother, but I lost my best friend. I felt like I had lost everything. I mean, I did. So did Zach. He had lost his best friend and his only sister.

"Zach and I started hanging out and were just friends, but then it turned into something more—we drew strength from each other. Moving on doesn't mean I'm any less sad or miss my brother any less. It just means I'm living."

She continues. "Please don't think that I'm not dying on the inside, all because I appear to have my shit together on the outside. There have been plenty of nights that I have cried myself to sleep and Zach will just hold me and let me fall apart. I cry if I see something that reminds me of him or when I see something that I think he would've liked. But I also know that he wouldn't want me to be sad and not live my life. I know that I get to spend the rest of my life living for my brother and have a man next to me who I love so much.

"Through Em's death, I found Zach. Yes, I've known him my whole life, but it wasn't till we were both so broken and lost in the darkness and consumed by our grief that we found light in each other. We healed each other. It's still a process, but we are facing it together. He would be so happy for us...well, after he thoroughly kicked your brother's ass, of course."

We both laugh at that thought, especially since Emmett could totally have kicked Zach's ass. "He would want you to live too, Danielle. He would hate you like this; you and I both know it."

Ugh, I am so tired of being tired. Haylee is clearly not giving up, so I respond with "But I feel guilty..." but she quickly interrupts me before I can finish what I feel guilty about.

She raises her hand, making sure I stop speaking. "I know how madly in love my brother was with you and vice versa. I know the dreams you guys planned and the life you both wanted together. I was there for both of you. I saw both sides of your love as his sister and your best friend. And then life stepped up to the plate and gave a big fuck-you and destroyed them, all of them—your dreams, mine, my parents', and anyone who ever did or would have known Emmett. I know that Em wouldn't want this for you. He told me once that all he wanted was for you to be happy—it was why he did stupid shit like the singing and dancing in public or verbally proclaiming his love for you as if he just discovered new land. He said his sole purpose in life was to make you smile. Yeah, he actually said that—big bad Emmett was pretty whipped. I never understood any of that until Zach."

I notice that her cheeks redden, and she smiles while looking down at her new bling on her finger. Now I feel like an even bigger asshole for blowing up at them.

"Ya know, I don't know exactly where my brother is right now, but I hope that he is at peace. And of course, if he chooses to haunt me, I hope he at least doesn't do it while Zach and I are, well..." She waggles her eyebrows and giggles as I put my hand up, inferring that she should not finish that sentence. She continues. "But what I do know is that he would hate you not being happy. He would hate knowing that the smile that he made sure he saw every day was gone. He would understand and want someone to be able to put that smile back on your face if he can't. We know that if he were here that you both would be together and hopefully by now I'd be spoiling the shit out of my nieces or nephews," she says, smiling, but that smile quickly turns to a frown and the unshed tears start to spill over. "But he's not. He's never coming back. So, Dani, I need you to live, for you, for Emmett, for the dreams, and for the memories. You can't live your life carrying the weight of my brother's death, you just can't. I won't allow it. We let you walk away once before, and fuck if we are going to let you do it again. Prove that my brother's death wasn't for nothing but his dreams dying with him and yours as well. We can't change your dreams together falling apart, but you can still do something about yours—make new ones."

Fuck not being able to hide my tears and my shoulders trembling. "But I just feel so guilty that I get to live and he doesn't."

Haylee pulls me into an embrace, and we are both crying uncontrollably. She cups my cheeks, forcing me to look at her. "I know, I know, but I need you to fucking stop. Don't let your guilt get in the way of being happy. You did not cause that accident. That's what it was—an accident. A wrong place at the wrong time. I need you to make the decision to stop feeling guilty. To make the decision of living your life. You only get one, and how amazing is it that in that one life you get two great men who love you when most people don't even get one."

In a bit of shock, I pull back from her. "Kyler doesn't love me."

She tries to hide her laugh. "Oh yes he does. I've known him

273

for a few years now, and I've never seen him look at someone the way he looks at you."

Hmmm.... How does he look at me? Is she about to go full-blown Shakespeare up in here with me?

"And how is that?" I respond.

She puts her forehead against mine, and I'm brought back to being kids when we would try to make a point. It was our version of trying to get into the other's head—kind of alien vs magic shit that we believed.

"Honey." Haylee pauses. "Ky looks at you the same way Emmett used to." She gives me a brief smile as she grabs my hand and squeezes it. "It's also the same way you look at him."

There is no use in hiding my feelings no matter how much they scare me. I nod in silence, I do love him, but hopefully I didn't fuck this all up for us by our fight. I need to fix this, to fix us. It has felt good to smile again, to feel loved. Wiping the tears away, I'm sure smearing my already day-old makeup even more, and running my fingers down my hair to help calm the mess, I find myself giggling. "Shit, Hails, when did you become the smart and wise one out of the two of us?."

Haylee gets one of those shit-eating up-to-no-good grins that I see often on my brother's face, and I instantly know I will regret hearing whatever her answer is.

"Probably around the same time I started sleeping with your brother."

Even through my laughter I make a playful gagging sound as if I just threw up a little in my mouth. Haylee lets out a loud, cackling laugh that I haven't heard in forever. It's like a sound of coming home, of memories that made us laugh so hard we snorted, cried, and sometimes peed our pants. Okay, so the last one only happened once, and I was ten.

"If that's not the pot calling the kettle black, missy. Remember every time we talked about boys growing up and all your firsts? I had to hear about my brother, so bleh," she says, sticking her tongue out at me. And just like that we are both rolling over laughing. How we went from tears of sorrow to joy, I'm not sure, but I'd like to think Em had something to do with it.

Taking a deep breath to regain some composure, I ask my best friend, "So you're really going to marry my brother, huh?" I grab her hand to properly inspect that gorgeous rock he gave her this morning. The ring is simple yet beautiful, just like her. It feels as though so much has happened today that I can't believe it was just a few hours ago that Zach was on one knee in front of her giving her this.

"Yeah, I am," she says, wearing a grin from ear to ear. She turns to face Emmett's gravestone, holding up her left hand. "Did you hear that, big bro? I'm getting married, can you believe it?" Haylee looks up to the sky and squeezes her eyes shut before turning back to me. "But you know what's better than him becoming my husband?"

I put my thinking face on and move my head around as if I'm giving it serious thought. I playfully respond, "A root canal? Maybe natural childbirth? Falling out of the tree house and breaking your arm?" A smile comes to my face when I say the last one, remembering when we were kids and Haylee did exactly that.

Shoving me playfully, she is all full of smiles when she says, "Bitch! No, I was going to say, I still get you as my sister. See? That plan didn't change."

I'm forever thankful that my relationship with Haylee isn't ruined. I know I made lots of mistakes over the years including leaving my family and friends behind. I was worried that Hails wouldn't want anything to do with me, but that's not her. And she's right, after all these years, the one thing that never changed was that Haylee and I were meant to be sisters. It's just a different Hanks and Jacobs marrying this time.

I pull her in to what is possibly our millionth hug of the afternoon. "I love you, Hails."

"I love you too, D. Now, what do you say we get back to the apartment because I'm pretty sure Kyler has officially driven Zach insane and possibly paced the floor away."

I nod as we stand up and brush the grass off our clothes. Haylee steps forward and kisses the headstone. "I'll see you later, big bro. I promise I'll take care of her. I miss you. Love you, E."

"Can you give me a minute?" I ask Haylee as she steps back. She nods and turns to head toward the cars. I bend down, kiss my hand, and place it on the dash between Emmett's birth and death date. I am reminded of the poem Zach spoke at Em's funeral, "The Dash" by Linda Ellis.

Emmett was only on this earth for eighteen years, and he spent most of those years loving me. He loved me with everything he had and will always be in my heart. I've wasted years of my dash angry, sad, and hurt, thinking my dash was over when his ended. It's time to rearrange my life and start living. There will never be a day that I forget Emmett. He lives with me, and I hope that he will be with me every day till the end when I hope one day we will be reunited.

"I love you, Emmett Adam Hanks."

I close my eyes and take a deep breath, imagining him standing there in front of me. *"I love you, Cupcake."*

Blowing out that breath, I respond, "Forever and always." I

smile as I turn and walk toward my car where Haylee is standing next to my brother's Jeep. We silently nod at each other before hopping in the cars and heading back to Pennsylvania.

CHAPTER 37
KYLER

"If you don't stop pacing and sit the fuck down, I'm going to punch you. You're gonna wear a hole in the floor, and then we'll never get back our security deposit," Zach chuckles before taking a sip of his beer.

I stop pacing and take a seat on the chair next to the couch. I'm so anxious, I adjust myself in the seat four or five times before Zach puts his hand on my arm and looks me in the eye. "Ky, you need to calm down. Hails said they're on their way back. She's okay."

"I know. I just really love her, man, and I'm afraid it's all fucked up," I tell him honestly.

He smiles. "Nah, my sister is stubborn as fuck, but she's got a good head on her shoulders." He pauses and looks to his hands before looking back at me with unshed tears. "It's been a really long time since I've seen a true honest smile on my sister's face. And you did that, Ky, not me, not Haylee, but *you*." I'm startled at first when he pulls me to my feet, slapping my back in true man-hug fashion. "Thank you for bringing my sister's smile back."

Shit, now I'm on the verge of crying. What the fuck is wrong with us men... *Love*, that's what.

"I'd make her smile for the rest of my life if she'll let me one day."

Still wrapped up in our embrace, we completely miss the sound of the key turning and the door opening, until we hear a throat clearing. It brings us to the present, and we see Dani and Haylee standing in the doorway. We quickly separate, making all sorts of macho noises and grunts that I'm sure do nothing to help our case except make us look stupid. I look up and see her. God, she's beautiful.

Haylee giggles. "Ummm, we can always come back, but Kyler, maybe you should remember that this Jacobs is already taken, and I don't like to share." She walks toward her fiancé and wraps her arms around his waist. Zach leans down to her and gives her a deep kiss that clearly makes them forget that Dani and I are still standing here in the same room.

I look over at Dani, who is nervously playing with her hair and looking down at the ground. There must be something interesting on her shoes because she hasn't lifted her beautiful blue eyes in a few minutes. As if she can feel my stare, she looks up at me and mouths, "Can we talk?" and looks toward the hall-way. Nodding, I follow her to the guest room, leaving the future Mr. and Mrs. Jacobs standing in the living room still making out. Oh, young love!

I take a seat on the edge of the bed as she closes the door. Danielle begins to pace back and forth. To break the awkward silence, I joke, "You may want to stop pacing because we may end up in the crawlspace below after all of my pacing may have weakened the floorboards. And for some reason, your brother still thinks there's a chance we're getting our security deposit back and doesn't think we need to remodel the floors."

Her head jerks up, and her eyes narrow at me before they soften. I am almost expecting her to bitch me out, but instead she smiles at me and I'm not talking about a half-assed fake smile—I'm talking a real Danielle Jacobs smile. It warms my heart as I remember a time when I would have given anything to see that smile on her face.

Dani takes a deep breath and begins to speak. "Okay, so I'm going to say something, and I need you to let me get this all out without interrupting, which you love to do..."

"I don't love to interrupt you," I say, doing exactly what she said for me not to do.

Tilting her head at me, she gives me a *seriously, yes you do* look. I smirk, putting my hands up in surrender. She continues. "So I need you not to interrupt so that I can get all of this out because if I don't, I'm worried I won't have the strength to say all I need to." She takes another deep breath, and her eyes land on something in the corner. I follow her gaze to the nightstand where I know the photo of Emmett sat, but it's no longer there. Did she move it? How am I just noticing? Then again, we don't spend much time in this room. Dani sleeps in my room every night but still keeps all of her stuff in here.

Dani takes a few deep breaths; her eyes give the impression that she is giving herself an internal pep talk before she starts to speak again. "First, let me say I'm sorry for lashing out at you this morning. I was diverting the shock of my brother getting engaged and displacing it on you. It was wrong and unfair. You're not just a stand-in or replacement. Please don't think that's how I see you."

I know she didn't mean it. Her eyes fill up with unshed tears, and her voice trembles.

"To be honest, it freaked me out but not in the way you think. See, when I saw my brother down on one knee, I envisioned my happily ever after. For the longest time I thought I didn't deserve one, but actually it was that I wasn't allowing myself to have one.

"There is not a memory in my mind for eighteen years that didn't have Emmett in it, and then all of a sudden he was ripped from this world, and I didn't know how to face the new reality of it. Or well, more that I didn't *want* to face it. I felt guilty at the thought that I get to live, and he didn't, so I pushed all possibilities of a future away."

Dani begins a slow pace around the room. She just can't keep still. I want to reach out and touch her to let her know it's okay, but I refrain to let her finish.

"When you answered the door all those months ago, something inside me woke up. It was something that I had convinced myself had died along with Emmett. But you brought me out of the darkness and into the light, and well, that scared and still does scare the shit out of me. I only ever loved one man, and I have been broken and empty for a long time, so I might not be very good at this, but I want to try...with you."

Is she saying what I think she's saying?

"I loved Emmett with all my heart, and when he died, my heart was crushed into a million pieces, pieces that I never thought could be put back together...until *you* put me back together. God, the first time you kissed me..."

She begins to blush, so I think it's safe to assume her mind has taken her back to that memory as has mine, and I adjust myself in my pants to hide what that memory does to me. Thankfully, she doesn't notice.

"That first time you kissed me, I knew you would knock my barriers down. The first time I looked into those beautiful brown eyes, I knew I was in trouble. But if I thought of you and fell in love with you, then it meant that I loved him less and was betraying his memory. But I was wrong—yes, I'm admitting I was wrong."

My eyes go wide in shock, and she points at me. "But don't

get used to it."

Her expression goes serious again. The lighthearted moment, though, eased the tension in the room. "I was betraying his memory by letting life pass me by and not living. I love you for your patience, your kindness, your willingness to learn, your bad jokes, and horrible taste in movies. I love that you make me feel complete and whole again. Maybe I came home from being lost for you to find me. I guess what I'm saying is..." She pauses and bites the inside of her lip, her eyes locked on mine, desperately trying to finish that sentence for her. "Kyler, I'm yours if you'll still have me."

I see my girl is nervous as fuck since I haven't said anything yet. I mean, what do you say to the girl of your dreams when she just gave a speech like that? That's some serious Jerry Maguire "you complete me/had me at hello" shit.

After a few moments, I realize I can't wait any longer, I need to touch her. I stand and stalk toward her in two strides. I place my hands on her hips and look her directly in those beautiful baby blues. "You really don't like my jokes?" How I'm keeping a straight face right now I have no clue. It's not until she smacks my chest, smiling, and says, "Seriously? Out of that entire speech, *that's* what you remember?" that I smile back at her and push a strand of hair behind her ears.

"No, apparently you also think my taste in movies is shit." That earns me an eye roll just before Dani tries to slip from my grasp. *Oh no she doesn't.* I quickly pull her back into me and take a seat on the bed with Dani straddling me, her thighs on the outside of mine. One hand is placed on her hip and the other firmly under her chin so she sees me loud and clear, and I say what I need to say. "And that you love me." I bring my mouth to hers, knowing she can feel my smile on her lips, then break our kiss. "Which is good because I love you too."

I stare at her for a moment, not saying anything, letting ourselves get lost in the moment before I crash my lips against hers again. This time I kiss with such passion, as if she were the air I breathed, which let's face it, she is. I pull on her bottom lip, earning a very sexy moan from her mouth. I'm lost in her kiss, the way her lips mold to mine, her fingers playing with the hair along my neckline as she grinds her hips against my growing erection. I release her lips only long enough to pull her shirt over her head. I can't get my hands on her fast enough. I kiss her jaw and down her neck as I reach around and unhook her bra, releasing her perfect breasts. They were made for my hands. As my fingers brush across her taut nipples, Dani releases a small moan, and I know I am going to make love to my girl all night long, but if I don't get inside her now, I might blow my load right here.

Before I can move my hands to unbutton her jeans, the bedroom door flies open. "You guys wanna go out or order piz...*fuck*! Not again," Zach yells before slamming the door shut. He then yells from the other side of the door, "Seriously, Dani, haven't you ever heard of a fucking door lock?"

Looking at Dani, I see she has tears filling her eyes, but this time they're tears of joy and laughter.

In between her fit of giggles, she yells back, "Haven't you ever heard of knocking first?"

"I told you to knock first. Maybe you should listen to me more often," Haylee adds from the other side of the door in between her laughter.

We continue to hear him groan and curse as he stomps away. Our laughter is out of control now, and I end up falling back on the bed, taking Dani back with me, still wrapped in my arms. I push the hair off her face.

"Wait, if you envisioned your happily ever after, why did you freak out? What am I missing here?"

"Don't you see, Kyler, when I thought of my happily ever after, it wasn't Emmett I saw down on one knee. It was you."

I roll her over onto her back and settle between her legs.

"I love you, baby."

"I love you too. Now how 'bout you show me how much."

"Well, that has to be a record."

Naked, sweaty and absolutely beautiful with her hair strewn across the pillow, Dani pinches my side and I flinch. "You are so full of yourself."

I snicker. "Actually, babe, you are full of me."

She groans and buries her face into the pillow.

"Come on. My jokes aren't that bad."

Lifting her head, she raises her eyebrows at me. I smirk holding my hands up in innocence. "Okay, okay, maybe they are."

I reach for her and pull her into my arms, right where I want her to be always. A few minutes of silence passes before I speak. "Move in with me."

"You do realize I live here, right?"

My palm grazes her cheek. "No, I mean move in to my room. You already spend every night in there. We can move all your stuff officially in there tomorrow."

"We're really doing this?"

I roll over to my side, and Dani matches my position opposite of me. "Dani, I want this, all of this, with you. I love you. What do you say?"

"Yes."

CHAPTER 38

Danielle

Kyler spent the whole night showing me how much he loved me. We passed out somewhere around 3:00 a.m. How it is I am awake this early, I'm not sure—guess my body doesn't care what my night entailed, just that it needs caffeine. Encased in Kyler's arms, I have to be quiet as to not wake him. I quietly slide out from under his arm, causing him to make a tiny groaning noise. I lean back on the bed and press a kiss to his cheek. "Stay asleep, baby."

He groans back before rolling over onto his other side. I grab his T-shirt off the floor and slip into a pair of shorts from my dresser. I slowly open the bedroom door, turning around and smiling at a sleeping Kyler before quietly closing the door. I'm not sure if anyone else is awake in the house, so I creep toward the kitchen but am quickly hit with the smell of coffee as I approach the living room, so someone must be awake.

"Good morning," I hear my brother say before I see him. His voice startles me, causing me to jump.

"I'm sorry, was I not loud enough for you?" He raises his eyebrows at me, clearly a dig at the volume of Kyler's and my lovemaking last night. Oops. I give that sly Jacobs smile, pleading the fifth. I walk over to the cabinet reaching for my favorite mug before pouring the delicious liquid into my cup. I reach into the refrigerator and grab the container of almond milk to pour into the coffee. Bringing the mug up to my nose, I inhale the yummy smell and can feel it already seeping into my veins.

My brother laughs from where he is sitting, diverting my attention back to him.

"What?"

He shakes his head. "Did Kyler fuck your brains out to the point that you forgot you drink coffee and not sniff it?"

Rolling my eyes at him and holding back a laugh, I take a seat next to him. "Oh, dear brother, maybe I should tell Haylee to reconsider the thought of marrying you." I can't help but laugh before I finish my statement. "And you're gross," I say, sticking my tongue out at him. He pushes my arm. Thankful for my quick reflexes, I catch the mug before any coffee spills.

"Hey, don't waste perfectly good coffee, asshole."

We both sit in silence, enjoying the morning caffeine. It has been a long few days. "So, Zach, I'm really sorry about yesterday. I haven't even told you congratulations, big brother."

I get up and wrap my arms around his shoulders from behind and give him a big bear hug before sitting back down on my stool.

"I can't believe you're getting married. Holy shit, both of you! I don't think I can apologize enough for ruining your moment yesterday."

Shaking my head in embarrassment, I avoid his gaze. How was that only yesterday? Less than twenty-four hours ago, I witnessed my brother get on one knee in front of my best friend and confess his undying love for her and promise her forever. Damn, who knew he was such a romantic?

Zach nods. "I spoke with Haylee last night and she explained. I'm sorry, too, that you felt that way, but I need you to always be open and honest about things before they blow up. I need you to talk to us—that is the only way we're going to get through this and move forward," he pleads with me, and I agree. "Speaking of moving forward, so you and Kyler said the *L* word, huh?"

I smile, recalling how good it actually felt to tell him that I loved him. I didn't think there was a better feeling, that is until he said it back. I gather the strength to ask the question I had never thought to ask him before. "Are you okay with this?"

Zach looks at me almost as if he's looking through me, but I speak again before he can answer. "I mean, I feel like it's happening all over again, me falling in love with your best friend. I don't want to take anyone from you."

My eyes begin to fill, but I don't allow them to spill over. Zach puts his coffee mug down on the island and pulls me into his arms. Thankfully he is wearing gym shorts and a T-shirt instead of boxers which is what I sometimes find him in when I come into the kitchen early in the morning.

"Dani...I just want you to be happy. You deserve the world, a man worthy of your greatness, and nothing but happiness. The fact that you chose that in not just one of my best friends but both, as weird as that sounds, means I kick ass at picking best friends because only the best will do for my little sister."

He kisses my forehead and grins at me. "You have been dealt a super shitty hand these past few years, and I finally see my sister. Kyler brought you back to me, to all of us, and if you want to be with him, I will support you 100 percent, but Jesus Christ, Dani, please use the door locks—they were invented for a reason."

And there it is, the heartfelt moment gone. Typical Zach ruining a good moment. I push off him and take a seat back on my stool.

CHAPTER 39

KYLER

The last year and a half has been amazing. Time with Dani is something I never take for granted, or plan to. Her love is a gift that I am forever grateful for. Dani and I ended up moving out of the house and had gotten a place of our own just down the street.

I know what I want to do next, but I need to talk to three people. Last week I took her dad to dinner and Zach out for drinks, leaving our women at home, and the third person is what brought me here. There is one last person I need to ask permission. I turn the key, shutting the ignition off to my truck. My phone buzzes in my pocket. Pulling it out, I see her name on the screen with a photo I took of her one night while she was in the kitchen baking. I felt bad lying to her earlier, saying that I was going to be in meetings all day, but I didn't want her to know that I had taken the day off and traveled down here to have this conversation.

"Hey, baby!"

"Hey, how's your day been? Are you still in meetings? I didn't think you were gonna answer."

"No, I'm just leaving one, headed to another. Should be home in about three hours."

"Oh okay, well, I just wanted to see if you wanted to go out tonight to eat or stay in?"

"Can we stay in and...I eat you out?" I know she is on the other end of the line blushing and possibly squirming around in her chair thinking about that. Man, how fucked-up am I having this type of conversation here of all places? I think I'm definitely going to hell. "Baby, you still there?"

"Oh yeah, sorry... I was..."

I interrupt her. "Thinking about me and all the things I'm gonna do to you tonight?"

"Maybe." Yep, I totally called it.

I smile knowing this girl has me wrapped around her finger.

"Well, babe, I gotta go. I'll see you later tonight."

"Okay, I'll make veggie lasagna. Haylee said all this wedding stress was making her crave carbs."

"Can't wait, that's my favorite. I love you."

"Love you too!"

Once Dani and I hang up the phone, I place my phone on the dashboard and get out of my truck. Here goes nothing. I approach the headstone and stoop down to remove the wilted flowers from the vase.

"Hey, Emmett. I'm Kyler."

I had come with Danielle, Zach, Haylee, and their families here on the five-year anniversary of his death, but I stood to the side to give them space. Dani had said some words and then stood next to me, never letting go of my hand. I felt it was important, though, to have a man-to-man talk and introduce myself. He was just as important in her life as her father and brother.

Running my hand over the stubble on my jaw, I try to remember the speech I had planned on the two-hour drive here from the city, but all words seem to have left my mind, so I guess I'm winging it.

"Well, seems like we have the same taste in best friends but also women." Realizing this is a little awkward standing here talking, I decide to take a seat on the ground. "I'll cut to the point, I guess. I want to marry her. I mean, I don't *guess* I want to marry her, I *know* I want to marry her. I know that if you were still here, you would have married her. I hope that I meet your standards; our girl deserves the best. Your sister helped me picked out a gorgeous ring for Dani." I pull the small box out of my pocket and open it and stare at its beauty. Every morning I grab it out of the nightstand drawer and take it with me to work where I usually lock it up in my desk. I've been worried that Dani would find it if I hid it anywhere around the house, so I just always keep it with me.

"I really hope she loves it. I love her, man. I want to make her happy. I hope I do. She's amazing...not sure why I'm telling you that since you know that. I can't thank you enough for loving her and turning her into the woman she is."

I pause and compose the rest of my thoughts. "I just want you to know that I'm going to take care of her, be there for her, love her, make her laugh and smile for the rest of my life. I don't know how she went so long without showing the world that smile because it's the most beautiful thing I've ever seen as I'm sure you know." I go to get up and wipe the grass from my pants. "I'm gonna do right by her, and I hope you continue looking out for all of them."

I look up to the sky, not really sure how to end this conversation. "Well, I'll see ya round, man." I press my hands against the gravestone as if I were squeezing Emmett's shoulder and head back to my car.

As I climb in the truck, I feel good and ready to take this next step with Dani. I wasn't sure I'd ever get to this point with anyone, but honestly, since the day I met her, that all changed.

Now all I have to do is ask her. My mother's favorite phrase of "All you gotta do is" rings through my mind.

I start the ignition and turn the radio on. I go to change the station as a familiar tune rings through the speakers, and I instantly focus on the radio when I hear Heartland's "I Loved Her First" playing. Not exactly what I was expecting on this station. Dani once said that she believed that Emmett would talk to her through music. She would turn her iPod on shuffle and wait for him to talk to her through the music or would sit in her car and talk to him, and when she would turn the radio on, it would be a song that she swore was him reaching out to her. I don't know if it's some sign from somewhere else or just a coincidence, but it makes me smile, and I'd like to think that's Emmett's way of approving. While I know this song is about a father and daughter, I sit and listen to the lyrics, and it's true, Emmett did love her first and loved her for all his life. The lyrics are so powerful and the message I want to believe was behind it, I can't help but let the tears welling up in my eyes spill over. I sit there listening to the entire song, and as it ends, I wipe my eyes and know it's time to go get our forever.

I make my way out of the cemetery and head back home to my girl.

CHAPTER 40
Danielle

I shake my coat off and place it on the back of the chair. "How come we aren't at our regular table tonight and stuck up front by the stage?"

Looking at Haylee, Zach takes a sip of his drink. "Oh, well, we were running late, and the table was already occupied."

"Oh." I take a seat. Looking around, I ask, "Where's Kyler? I thought he was meeting us here?" I pull out my phone and reread his text from earlier.

KY: *Running behind at work, I'll meet you at the bar. Love you!*

The spotlight on the stage appears as the waitress approaches the table with my margarita. Scott takes the microphone, and everyone cheers, myself included.

He waves his hands in the air to quiet the crowd down. "All right, all right, everyone. Tonight we are doing something a little different—our favorite dynamic duo is flying solo. Let's everyone give Kyler a warm welcome and see if he is actually any good without his partner in crime. Thank God this is just one night and one night only."

He steps aside and claps his hands together. Kyler appears on the stage. He looks so handsome with his dark jeans and fitted black button-up shirt rolled up on his forearms. He must have changed at the office because he didn't stop at home to change his clothes, and after our fun morning together, I watched him dress in a navy suit and white dress shirt. He looked so hot that I wanted to just rip it right off him and throw him back on the bed for round two. I can feel my cheeks heating up just thinking about this morning's wake-up call.

"Tonight, I'd like to dedicate this song to my girl, Dani. I love you. Here it goes."

Kyler doesn't have his usual confident face on right now. As the music begins, he actually looks a little nervous. Once he spots me, though, that confident smile begins to appear. The song name appears on the screen, "Danny's Song" by Loggins and Messina. The irony is not lost on the play of the name— that's cute, but I am not too familiar with this one. He begins singing as if I'm the only girl in the entire room. I can feel my eyes start to fill up as I listen to him sing the lyrics. He is putting his heart out for all to see right now, and I'm still trying to figure out what I did to deserve this man's love.

These lyrics are so sweet, although the more I listen, I'm pretty sure it's really a song about a man soon becoming a father. So just to make sure no one gets the wrong idea, I keep taking sips of my delicious margarita that is *full* of tequila. The more he sings, the more I see the confidence start to wane and the nerves kick back in. I don't know why he's so nervous since his song is almost over. Is it just nerves because he had to be on stage without Zach? When the song ends, everyone applauds, including Haylee, who gives one of those ear-numbing whistles. Rubbing my ear, feeling as though I can't hear now, I can't help but give a "Woo!"

Instead of leaving the stage, he stands there for a moment. He then takes the microphone off the stand and heads toward our table, right in front of me specifically. He takes both of my hands in his, a smile across his face and his eyes full of love.

"Dani, I have possibly been in love with you from the moment I met you—or at least since the first time I tasted your cupcakes."

I chuckle, remembering he confessed his undying love to it.

"When you walked into my life, I didn't realize that something was actually missing. Even though you claim that I saved you and put you back together, I know that it was really you. You saved me by showing me what it meant to really love someone and to be loved by someone. Maybe in a way we saved each other. You bring out the best in me and I in you. You are the light in my darkness. Life is never going to be easy as we both know that from the journeys that brought us here, but with you, I feel as though I can face anything and everything that is thrown at me. I love you so much. I know you hate my jokes and my apparent bad taste in movies, but I want to spend the rest of my life proving to you that *Office Space* is, in fact, a funny movie."

I laugh through the tears and gasp as he gets down on one knee. Oh my God, this is really happening.

"Danielle Kathryn Jacobs, I love you with all my heart. Will you marry me?"

Looking around, I see Zach and Haylee beaming at us. I look a little farther and see my mom and Haylee's parents sitting in the corner booth, and in the booth next to that is Kyler's sisters, Lauren and Kate, and his mom. How did I not notice them when I came in? I turn my attention back to Kyler, who is waiting for an answer. I wipe my tears and smile at him. First, I respond by nodding, another moment in my life when I can't even manage a simple yes. Both moments forever changed my life.

"Yes, baby, a million times yes!"

He slides the ring on my finger, and it is absolutely stunning —a white-gold trio princess cut pavé diamond ring. Kyler rises to his feet, and I wrap my hands around his neck, pulling him close to me. He wraps his hands around my waist and leans me back in one of the most passionate kisses of my life.

By the time he brings me back upright, my head is spinning and my heart is full. After another brief kiss, I put my forehead against his and laugh.

"What's so funny, babe?"

Our family has now left their seats and joined us over at our table, waiting to congratulate us.

"You do realize that that song is about having a baby and we —" I turn to our family, throwing my hands up in innocence. "— are *not* expecting, just to clear that up."

Everyone laughs, but just then the last thing I expect happens—Zach and Haylee look at each other before Haylee shouts, "No, but we are!"

Zach yells, "Surprise!" with his hands in the air as if he just did a magic trick.

There is an awkward silence for just a moment before everyone erupts in cheers. "Holy shit, you're gonna be a dad!" Kyler shouts as he gives Zach one of those man hugs with the half hug, half back slap. Haylee and I jump up and down in excitement. Everyone hugs and the moms all check out my new bling as Mr. Brian, Dad, and Zach pull some tables that were next to us together, forming one giant table.

As Mom takes a seat, she places her hands together with excitement, looking at both Ms. Natalie and Mrs. Lawson (I guess I should get used to calling her Ms. Liz, or Mom, since she is going to be my mother-in-law). "Well, ladies, looks like we have now *two* weddings *and* a baby shower to plan." All the moms look excited, and I can already see the wheels turning in their minds. Lord help us.

I can't stop smiling, and neither can my now fiancé. I look down at the ring, and it seriously is beautiful. My man did good.

Kyler leans over and kisses my cheek. "Are you happy, future Mrs. Lawson?"

I place a kiss on his lips. "Why yes, Mr. Lawson, I am very happy." And I am. It's in that moment I realize that I get my happily ever after, after all.

We're lying in bed, and I'm stroking Dani's hair down her back while our breathing evens out after a serious lovemaking session. Our clothes started flying off the moment the front door closed. Dani and I scooted out early from Lucky's. I couldn't wait to get my fiancée home and to officially celebrate with her, which we did twice already. Not that I don't love spending time with our families—I loved that they were all able to be there with us. How I *actually* pulled off this surprise I am still trying to wrap my head around. This beautiful woman next to me actually said yes. Also, holy shit, my best friend is going to be a dad—the same man I watched eat a five-pound container of cheese balls on a dare, do keg stands at 7:00 a.m., and run naked across the quad after finals senior year. Oh, the stories I will tell that kid one day, I chuckle to myself.

I can tell Danielle is off in her own world, so I push her hair to the side and rub her shoulder to bring her out of her thoughts. "Where's that pretty little head of yours at, baby girl?"

She looks up at me and smiles. I will never tire of seeing her smile at me.

"Well, for one, I can't believe I'm going to be an auntie. I'm so excited, but wow, Zach and Haylee are going to be parents," she laughs, clearly thinking the same thoughts of ridiculous moments with those two.

She lays her head back down on my chest and raises her left hand to admire that gorgeous rock on her finger. "I am also over-the-moon happy. I still can't believe I'm engaged and that this is real."

I wrap my arms around her tighter. "You better believe it's real, babe. You're stuck with me forever now. *Foooor-rrrreeeeevvvverrrrr!*"

I can feel her smile on my chest. "How did you pull all this off?" she asks as she traces my chest with the tips of her fingers.

I kiss the top of her head. "Well, I had some help—Haylee helped me pick out the ring, I asked your dad and brother for permission." I pause. "I even asked Emmett for his permission."

Dani jolts, pushing up on my chest. "What?"

"I drove the other week to the cemetery and sat there to chat with Emmett, man to man." I am watching Dani's eyes fill up with tears. "The day I told you I was in meetings all day I had really gone and talked to him. I had asked all the men in your life for permission, and he was no different." I pull myself to an upright position and cup her face, my thumb catching a stray tear.

"I can't believe you did that, Ky," she says in between tears, leaning into my palm. "You are unbelievably amazing, you know that?" She then leans in, placing a deep, passionate kiss on my lips. "And I can't wait to spend the rest of my life with you," she says, hovering over my lips before taking them again. I can feel the desire pouring out of her, and I pull her on my lap to straddle me. She is ready for me.

Looking into her eyes as I line myself up to her entrance, I say, "I love you, Danielle Jacobs."

"I love you too, Kyler Lawson," she breathes as I enter her. The past two times tonight were frantic; this time I'm going to take my time savoring every bit of her, the woman I love.

EPILOGUE
KYLER

Fourteen months later...

The day has finally arrived. I am standing behind my best friend as he is about to marry the woman of his dreams in front of his family, friends, and most importantly, his daughter. Emme Danielle Jacobs, named after her uncle and aunt, was born five months ago. She is the spitting image of her mother, thank God, but I can already tell she has that Jacobs personality that I love that my best friend and fiancée both have. Zach and Haylee had asked me and Dani to be her godparents prior to her birth, and of course we accepted. There was no other option for us.

The first time I held my goddaughter in my arms, I instantly fell in love and knew there would be no greater feeling in the world like this until the moment I would hold my own child for the first time. Dani and I try to watch Emme twice a month at least, but really whenever we can so that Zach and Haylee can have date night, catch up on sleep, or maybe work on making a sibling for Emme. It gives us practice with a baby—now, I know what you're thinking, and no, Dani is not pregnant...*yet*. But every time I see her interact with our niece, my heart swells.

When she rocks her to sleep in her arms, I imagine our future son or daughter in her arms, and I can't wait to start our family.

My girl is everything, and I fall in love with her more and more each day. When I saw her walking down the aisle moments ago in her dark purple dress that accentuates every curve on her beautiful body, I almost fell over. Zach elbowed me in the stomach jokingly when he saw my smile mimic hers as she got closer.

"Hey, remember this is my day—you get your day in six months, so knock that eye banging my sister shit out."

I laugh, leaning over to him. "I'm pretty sure you aren't supposed to say 'shit' in church...or talk about banging."

Now it's his turn to laugh. As Dani approaches us and takes her place across from me, she gives us a "what the fuck and cut that shit out" look. Zach and I both straighten up, and I wink at her while mouthing *I love you.* She mouths it back as the music switches to "Heartbeats" by José González. We all turn our attention back to the entrance where Haylee and her dad stand, ready to make the journey to the altar. As they make their way down to us, I watch both Dani and Zach wipe tears from their eyes. My best friend is man enough for me to not make fun of him for shedding tears as his bride approaches because I know if I made fun of him, he is bound to do the same when it's my turn.

I can't wait till Zach and I swap places and it's Dani making her way to me dressed in white. Only six more months—183 days to be exact, not that I'm counting till Danielle Kathryn Jacobs becomes Danielle Kathryn Lawson, my wife. I look around the congregation and see my future in-laws on one side of the church and Zach's future in-laws on the other side. It's crazy to think Dani gets to be related to her best friend and I will get to be related to mine. Emme is in Natalie's arms in a beautiful lilac dress. When Zach said that Hails chose dark purple, lilac, and gray as the wedding colors, I joked saying that everything would look as if doused in grape soda. But now seeing it all come together, it looks amazing.

I know today is tough for all of them with one very special person missing. There is an empty chair next to Brian for Emmett even though if he had been here today, I know he would've been standing where I am. Here's the thing though: we can't guarantee that had Em not have died, Zach and Haylee would have found each other the way they did. With his passing and Dani's abrupt departure, they found a love through healing each other. Being the romantic that I am, and after all the chick flicks I have been forced to watch over time with Dani, I'd like to believe that they were always meant to be; it just took a little longer to figure it out.

I bring my attention back to the bride and groom as they begin to recite their vows. They really are two peas in a pod: Zach vowed to only ever compliment her cooking—I am so glad Dani actually cooks and cooks well at that—and Haylee vowed to never go near his gym bag. That causes Zach to scowl and Dani to snort. I'll be sure to ask her what that's about later. Our eyes meet once again, and my mind goes back to the first time we met at my front door upon her return home.

We don't lose eye contact until the minister says, "You may now kiss the bride," and then our eyes are on our newly married best friends as they share their first kiss as man and wife. As they turn to walk down the aisle, I slap Zach on the back before stepping forward to meet Dani. Zach and Haylee first walk over to where their daughter rests in her grandmother's arms and each place a kiss on her head. It is a super-sweet moment, and the photographer better have captured it so we can put it on our mantle—yep, we are those type of people.

I extend my elbow to Dani. "Future wifey."

With a smile, she loops her arm in mine. "Thank you, future hubby."

I lean over and whisper in her ear, "You are the sexiest woman I have ever seen, especially in that dress. I can't wait to make you my wife...but until then, I can't wait to get you out of that dress."

Judging by the ear-to-ear smile she is wearing as we make our way to meeting her brother and his new bride in the back of the church, I think she is thinking the same thing.

Danielle

I can't believe my brother and Haylee are finally married and have the most absolutely amazing little girl ever. I have no shame saying my niece has me wrapped around her finger, and Kyler even more so. Uncle Kyler has been in love with her since he first held her. He will be the most amazing dad ever. There is nothing sexier than watching the love of your life being an amazing father, or uncle/godfather in our case.

The reception has been so much fun thus far, and I am about to present one of my gifts to the bride and groom. I am standing here on the stage by the DJ, microphone in hand ready to perform the song for their first dance. Yep, that's right—they are getting "Can't Help Falling in Love" in the style of Hayley Reinhart but performed by the one and only Danielle Jacobs. I look around the room and realize how far we have all come.

Some days are still a bit of a struggle, but my wonderful fiancé helps me through it.

In the far corner of the reception hall, there is an In Memory Table with photos of Emmett with both Haylee and Zach. There are some that include me as well. There is a sign that sits on the table reading, "We know you would be here today, if heaven wasn't so far away." Planning this wedding knowing Emmett would not be here has been difficult on all of us; Haylee especially has broken down many times in both Zach's and my presence over time, even worse when her pregnancy and postpartum hormones were out of control. But she is not the only one who feels his absence. Emmett Hanks will always be a part of me, and I will love him forever, but in time and my own healing I know that his memory will never go away. My past is his, and it always will be.

While the DJ announces for Mr. and Mrs. Zachary Jacobs to take the dance floor for their first dance, I find Kyler in the crowd holding Emme in his arms. She is passed out with her head on his chest. Her dress, which matches the color of her daddy's tie, looks wonderful against his dark purple tie that matches my dress. I see him standing there swaying as I begin to sing. I watch Zach and Haylee twirl around the dance floor, and I am truly happy for them. The journey bringing us all here to this moment in a way took forever to get here even though it has only been a few years.

My attention is brought back to Kyler as Emme begins to fidget in his arms, but he rubs circles on her back and she calms. He leans down and kisses the top of her head. I know he also snuck in a sniff of her sweet baby scent. He says over and over that he wishes he could bottle her sweet baby-fresh smell so that when she has nasty poopy diapers, he can remember she doesn't always smell like that. I don't think I can love him any more. He has the key to my heart; he is my present and my future. Kyler brought me back to life when I felt my happy ending would never happen and healed me. I will be forever grateful for our love.

Of course, I will always wish that Emmett hadn't passed, but I cannot go back in time to change it. Instead I look at the positive that it has brought us—Zach and Haylee, although I feel as though if they were meant to be, they always would have found a way for their love to happen, and it brought me and Kyler together. We have only six more months until our wedding, and I cannot wait to say "I do" and become Mrs. Kyler Lawson. Ky has teased often that we should just hop on a plane to Vegas and elope so we can be married as soon as possible, but I keep telling him no, even though, truthfully, I would have done it the day after he proposed. I learned in *When Harry Met Sally* and through losing Emmett that when you find someone to spend the rest of your life with, you want the rest of your lives to start right away. I don't think he or I want to handle the wrath of our moms, though, if we elope after they have spent all this time planning all these beautiful events.

The song comes to an end, and as I watch my brother and new sister-in-law share a kiss as he dips her back and everyone cheers, I am overwhelmed with love. Walking off the platform, I am swept into my brother's arms. "That was amazing. I can't believe you did that. Thank you for everything, sis. I love you."

I wrap my arms around him and squeeze. "Love you too, Zachy. You're a dad *and* now a married man. I can't believe you went and grew up on me."

"Hey, Mr. Jacobs, get your ass away from my sister-in-law. Go find your own best friend to hug."

My brother releases me from his arms so that I can wrap my arms around Haylee's waist. Zach turns around and kisses his wife's temple. "You're lucky I love you, Mrs. Jacobs," he says, emphasizing the *Mrs.* part.

Haylee places her forehead against mine and crosses her eyes while I make a silly face, sticking my tongue out to the side. "You guys are weird," my brother says. Turning toward him with our heads still together, I reply, "You know you love us though."

Haylee interjects, "And you're now stuck with both of us *forever!*"

He smiles back at her. "Sounds perfect to me."

Her smile mimics his, before she turns her attention back to me. "I can't thank you enough for today and all of this. Thank you for coming home and being okay with this. Thank you for being my best friend today and always."

I can feel the tears coming, but I refuse to let them ruin my makeup any more. I had to fix it all enough after the ceremony before photos. "I love you, Haylee Grace," is all I can get out without releasing those tears from my eyes.

"All right, all right, enough proclamations of love over here. What is this, a wedding or something? How about I trade you a precious little princess for my beautiful queen," I hear behind me.

Haylee pushes me to the side in a dramatic way and strides over to my fiancé to swoop up baby Emme in her arms. I know both Zach and Haylee are nervous about being away from her for an entire week while they are on their honeymoon in Punta Cana, but I have promised them over and over that Kyler and I will be just fine with her and to enjoy their time together. Kyler wraps his arms around me, pulling me tightly to his chest, and lifts my chin with his forefinger, bringing my mouth to his. A soft kiss at first quickly turns passionate—possibly a little too hot for the middle of my brother's wedding reception—and it isn't until we hear my brother clear his throat that we pull apart. I rest my head against Kyler's chest and listen to his heart beating rather quickly. I smile bigger knowing that I did that.

Ky leans down close to my ear and says softly so that only I can hear, "Have I told you lately how sexy you look tonight?"

I lift my head off his chest. "Nope, not within the last hour, but you can tell me again."

"Well then, baby, you are sexy in that dress, but do you know what would make this dress look even better?"

"What?" I ask, already feeling my panties dampening with his breath against my skin.

"If it were on the floor and you were in my arms naked writhing underneath my touch." I know he can feel my heart racing and my breath catch. "But first, dance with me."

Right now, and always, I would follow Kyler anywhere, but for now, I follow him to the dance floor as a familiar tune of "Say You Won't Let Go" by James Arthur plays. I smile knowing that in a few short months, we will be sharing the dance floor together as husband and wife for the first time to this song. Kyler wraps his arms around me again, pulling me closer to him while we sway to the music and get lost in the movement. I can hear him softly singing the lyrics to me. Ky had actually picked this song to be our first dance because he thought the lyrics were appropriate.

I think about all we lost—a lover, a brother, a son, a friend— and my heart hurts, but as I look around the room at what we have gained—a fiancé, a spouse, a daughter, a friend, and in-laws —my heart feels whole and complete. I watch my parents and Haylee's sway on the dance floor, laughing, and my brother holding his daughter and his wife in his arms, smiling ear to ear.

When the song ends, I look into Kyler's chocolate-brown eyes and see my forever. "I love you, Kyler."

He leans down to kiss me, but just before our lips touch, he says, "I love you too, baby. Forever and always."

THE END

Fall in love with Zach and Haylee all over again as we watch their story unfold from the beginning.

I Never Expected You
Book 2 in the *I Never Series*

Coming 12.09.19

PLAYLIST

1. You Said You'd Grow Old With Me – Michael Schulte
2. Forever – The Beach Boys
3. I'll Never Break Your Heart – Backstreet Boys
4. Hold On – Chord Overstreet
5. Ob-La-Di, Ob-La-Da – The Beatles
6. Foolish Games – Ashley De La Rosa
7. Tommie Sunshine's Megasix Smash-Up – Katy Perry, Tommie Sunshine
8. Danny's Song – Loggins & Messina
9. If You Say So – Lea Michele
10. Don't Wanna Write This Song – Brett Young
11. Like a Prayer – Glee Cast
12. I Loved Her First – Heartland
13. Helium – Sia
14. Forever & Always – Dylan Matthew
15. You Get What You Give – New Radicals
16. Piano Man – Billy Joel
17. Dangerous Woman – Ariana Grande
18. Say You Won't Let Go – James Arthur
19. Run – Leona Lewis
20. Can't Help Falling in Love – Haley Reinhart

21. Nothing Left to Say / Rocks – Imagine Dragons
22. Hallelujah – Lisa Lois
23. Speechless – Dan + Shay
24. All I Want – Kodline
25. Naked – Brielle Von Hugel
26. Say Something – A Great Big World, Christina Aguilera
27. Shoeboxes – David Ramirez
28. All We Needed – Craig David
29. Hurts Like Hell – Fleurie
30. Believer – Imagine Dragons

ACKNOWLEDGEMENTS

First, I would like to thank YOU for taking a chance on me and picking up this book. This book started as an idea while driving on 95 headed to Maryland for the holidays with family, and here I am sharing this story with the world. There may be times when you read this story and want to throw tomatoes at me; I totally understand but always remember I did put your broken heart back together, so you're welcome.

Travis, thank you for your support of yet another crazy idea in my head and for listening to me talk about my characters as if they were my real friends.

Jameson & Tucker, you boys are the reason I do everything. I love you both so much for understanding the nights when mommy has to work. A special trip to Dunkin Donuts' is necessary to celebrate.

The Chaddettes, I'm happy to have found my tribe in the writing world and have the love and support of you guys along this journey. We're all doing this thing – YAY! You guys were the first to read this story, and you didn't run in the opposite direction screaming, so thank you. Ya'll may have thrown tomatoes but you didn't run. Amanda, BJ and Claudia, I need to give you three a special shout out. You guys have dealt with my crazy the most. You three have listened to my word vomiting talking through scenes, my silly videos, and HEYOs and still love me all the same. I am so lucky to have you ladies in my life.

TK, can you believe it? I did it! All of those messages of "so I did a thing" finally paid off. Thanks so much for being there every step of the way.

Sandra, Jeanette, Angel & Clara, you four ladies are the ones who helped bring my book baby to life behind the scenes.

Lastly, I need to give a big shout out to the Surf City Dunkin Donuts. Without your morning and usually afternoon coffees, I wouldn't be able to get through the days and nights while bringing these stories to life.

ABOUT THE AUTHOR

Stefanie Jenkins writes contemporary romance and lives in Surf City, North Carolina with her husband and two sons. Born and raised in Maryland, Stefanie brings her favorite parts of her hometown to life in her books. She is a coffee addict, wine connoisseur, hockey fan & lover of all romances - give her all the swoon & angst.

Follow Stefanie on Social Media:

Facebook Page: https://www. facebook.com/authorstefaniejenkins
Facebook Reader Group – Talk Wordy to Me: https:// www.facebook.com/groups/sjtalkwordytome/
Instagram: https://instagram.com/authorstefaniejenkins
Goodreads: http://bit.ly/grsjenkins
Website: https://authorstefaniejenk. wixsite.com/authorsjenkins
E-newsletter Sign up: http://bit.ly/sjenewssignup

27116497R00192

Printed in Great Britain
by Amazon